"And you ar[e] [in]to m[y] [arms.]

Miles's face was very close to hers and his warm breath fanned her face when he spoke.

"Can you doubt it?" Olivia managed to say between her laughter. "What interest can I possibly have in a creature like you?"

"Does this not interest you?" And he bent and kissed her full on the mouth.

"No, sir," replied Olivia, breathlessly.

"Then what are your arms doing about my neck, pray?"

"I simply put them there to keep them out of harm's way," she answered innocently.

"You're quite certain they don't denote the merest hint of interest on your part?"

"None whatsoever," she assured him.

"Bother! That means I must make greater efforts!"

Books by Irene Northan

HARLEQUIN REGENCY ROMANCE
42–THE MARRIAGE BROKER

LOVE'S PAROLE

IRENE NORTHAN

Harlequin Books

TORONTO • NEW YORK • LONDON
AMSTERDAM • PARIS • SYDNEY • HAMBURG
STOCKHOLM • ATHENS • TOKYO • MILAN

First published in Great Britain in 1990
by Mills & Boon Limited

Harlequin Regency Romance edition
published August 1991
ISBN 0-373-31155-9

LOVE'S PAROLE

CHAPTER ONE

1813

THE autumn gale blew down the river valley, cold and blustery. Olivia Kingston grasped at her cloak, exhilarated by the fierce gusts which threatened to tear the garment from about her slight figure. It had been a good day. Regularly each week she struggled to instil some musical knowledge into the Vicar's numerous brood, and now it seemed that at last she was making progress. The children's latest combined effort had been almost recognisable as 'Sir Roger de Coverley', a singular triumph that had sent her home in high spirits. She sped along the road, buffeted by the wind, and encouraged by the thought of the cosy fire that awaited her.

Cheerfully she opened the front door and stepped into the passage. Then she stopped. A valise stood in the middle of the floor. Perplexed, she stared at it until realisation dawned. The French prisoner of war must have arrived! She felt a stab of annoyance. She had intended to be at home to greet this Frenchman, to let him be in no doubt from the first instant that he was to keep to his own room at the top of the house, and not to expect to fraternise with the family. She had disapproved of the scheme from the start. It had not seemed right, having an enemy prisoner living comfortably on parole in their home, while her young brother, Charlie, was suffering all sorts of deprivation in a French prison. But her mother had been so enthusiastic.

'Think what a benefit it will be to your papa to have another man in the house,' Charlotte Kingston had said. 'He is so sadly deprived of male company now that he is incapacitated, poor dear. And you need have no qualms about having someone quite unsuitable living in the house. Admiral Ranscombe has assured me that the prisoner is a gentleman, and from a very good family. So you see, you cannot have any objections, really you cannot!'

It was typical of Charlotte that she had not considered how they would manage with an extra person in the household, and only one elderly servant. Nor had she mentioned the really overwhelming benefit of having a paroled prisoner in the house. His lodging allowance! Such a consideration would never have entered her impractical head, but, no doubt, that had been why their kind friend, the Admiral, had proposed the idea. It was the only reason why Olivia had reluctantly set aside her misgivings. They needed the money desperately!

Now, it seemed, the unknown Frenchman had arrived. She would go upstairs to meet him. It was still not too late to inform him of the strict conditions under which he was to lodge with them. First, though, she went to tidy herself. These days she rarely had time to spare on her toilette. On this occasion, however, she took time to repair the ravages wrought by the wind, pinning up her long dark hair into its customary, almost severe style, and brushing off the mud from the hem of her well-worn dress. Only when she was confident that she was once again respectably tidy did she approach the drawing-room.

Through the closed door she could hear animated voices. When she entered, the first thing she saw was a man in naval uniform, comfortably ensconced by the fire, chatting with her parents.

'Olivia, you are here at last,' her mother greeted her. 'Such a thing, my love! Our guest arrived this afternoon, is that not splendid? Come and welcome him ... Sir, may I present our daughter, Miss Kingston.'

Olivia was surprised. Surely the Frenchman should have been presented to her, not vice versa? It was most unlike her mother to make such a blunder in matters of etiquette. There was something odd about her mother's manner, too, as though she were holding back laughter. Puzzled, Olivia looked questioningly towards her father, but unexpectedly he refused to meet her eye. There was no time for her to deliberate upon her parents' strange behaviour, however, for the Frenchman had risen from his seat and was regarding her steadily.

'Miss Kingston! It is my pleasure to make your acquaintance, ma'am,' he said, bowing low.

He was about thirty years of age if she were any judge, and his light-coloured hair held more than a tinge of russet. He was tall, well over six feet, yet markedly lean for a man of his height. Although his shoulders were wide his frayed naval jacket hung from them loose and ill-fitting. Olivia stared at him, stunned not by his shabby appearance, nor the fact that he needed a shave—it was his voice which astonished her, and his command of English. He spoke with an accent right enough, but it was not the one she had been expecting.

'You are not French!' she cried accusingly.

'I fear you are right, Miss Kingston,' he said, and smiled.

If his voice had not already made her wary that smile would have put her on her guard. It was uncomfortably attractive, lighting up his face and almost driving away the pallor. His eyes, shadowed as they were in a way that suggested past suffering, sparkled with humour. This was a man very well aware of his own attractions, and if there was one thing in the world she distrusted it was such evident charm. In her bitter experience it brought only destruction and pain.

'Then what are you, sir?' she demanded.

'I confess to being an American, ma'am. Captain Miles Gilbert, of the United States Navy, at your service.' He bowed again.

Olivia responded automatically, sinking down into a curtsey, then she recollected herself and rose again abruptly.

By now her parents could no longer contain their amusement and were laughing openly.

'To see your face, Olivia, my dear! 'Tis above anything!' chuckled her mother. 'Forgive us, but we could not resist keeping silent. Is it not the most splendid thing in the world? There we were, concerned about having a Frenchman in our house, and who arrives? Dear Captain Gilbert!'

So he was 'dear Captain Gilbert' already was he? And he had been partaking of tea in the drawing-room, the tray of cups was still there as evidence. That was a state of affairs destined not to flourish for long if Olivia had any say in the matter. French or American, it made no difference; this man was an enemy, he had to be put in his place.

She looked to her father for support, but found none. Edward Kingston was mopping his eyes with a kerchief.

'A capital joke! Capital!' he declared.

'Do you not think I was most cunning?' smiled Mrs Kingston. 'I did not say the dear Captain's name, or anything which would give the game away, did I?'

'You were most clever, Mama,' Olivia replied, refusing to betray that she did not share the joke.

'An American! I would never have guessed it. I did not think there were any Americans in town.' Mr Kingston was shaking his head in disbelief.

'I understand I'm the sole specimen of my race here, sir,' smiled Captain Gilbert.

'Then we had best take great care of you, eh? What say you, wife?'

'I agree most heartily with you, husband. Oh, it will be so much nicer having an American than a Frenchman! Just think, we will be able to converse with ease. We will not have to attempt outlandish dishes. We will not have to contend with any nasty foreignness at all. I declare I am quite overcome with relief. Are not you, Olivia?'

'I think, perhaps, Miss Kingston is disappointed that I'm not a Frenchman,' grinned Captain Gilbert.

She looked straight into his eyes. They were easily the best feature in his decidedly unhandsome face, for they were shining now green, now blue. To Olivia, however, they were a little too beguiling, a little too eager to charm.

'I assure you, sir, we would offer the same welcome to French or American without distinction,' she said.

The Captain appreciated the ambiguity of her statement, and humour sparked once more in those extraordinary eyes.

Mrs Kingston however, misunderstood her daughter.

'How can you say that, Olivia?' she cried. 'Of course we do not consider them to be the same. The French are our enemies and have been ever since I can recall, while the Americans . . . I really cannot fathom why we should be fighting the Americans at all. I can only assume it is some foolish misunderstanding. Someone of importance got into a rage about something or another, I dare say. You know what men are when they consider themselves slighted. Yes, this whole conflict with

America will turn out to be a silly mistake—they are our own people, are they not? At least, many of them are. Captain Gilbert, dear, I assure you, you are more than welcome here; you are now to regard this as your home until this unfortunate matter is settled. I fear our house is not as well-appointed as it once was, but we will exert every effort to make you comfortable.'

'Well said, my dear,' declared Mr Kingston approvingly.

Olivia could not believe her ears. To hear him agreeing in such a way! Not so long ago her father had shared her misgivings about having a prisoner in the house. He had been equally determined that the fellow was to be kept at arms' length and not allowed within the family circle. Her mother's words had been bad enough, but then Charlotte Kingston's understanding had never been strong. Olivia was genuinely shocked by her father's amiability. Had he forgotten that this man was a prisoner of war? An enemy? Olivia searched for some way to disassociate herself from her parents' sentiments, but the words were never uttered, for Captain Gilbert spoke first.

'To say thank you for your welcome is most inadequate, ma'am,' he said, his voice suddenly very serious. 'There have been times during the last year when—when I thought never to be among such decent people again or—or in such convivial surroundings. I wish I could say more than just thank you...'

'Poor boy, you need not thank us.' Mrs Kingston was openly moved as she patted the American's arm. 'We know—we sympathise—our own darling boy is imprisoned in France.'

Olivia's determination to be cold and dispassionate dissolved into pity. This man had been imprisoned for a year, and he had suffered. One look at his face, pale and gaunt beneath its scattering of golden freckles, told her that. And she thought of her young brother enduring the same fate. It was some time before she could dispel the lump in her throat. An awkward silence charged with emotion had fallen on the drawing-room. In an effort to break it and relieve the American of his evident distress she said, 'Perhaps Captain Gilbert would like to see his room now. I will ring for Abbie.'

As she pulled at the bell-rope she realised that already her attitude had softened a little towards the American. And she had not been in his company half an hour! She was annoyed at

her lack of resolve. As she remonstrated with herself to be more
stern in the future the door burst open and their elderly maid
entered, carrying a can of hot water in one hand and the Captain's valise in the other. As Abbie eyed the Captain her face
bore a definite leer of approval.

'I reckon you'm going to be cheaper to keep a week than a
fortnight by the size of you, Cap'n,' she remarked, looking him
up and down. 'We'm going to 'ave to feed you up a bit, though,
you'm naught but skin and bone.' The leer became positively
lecherous as she continued, 'Mind, I idn't saying that you don't
make me wish I was twenty years younger!'

Olivia held her breath. Abbie's approval could sometimes be
more hard to bear than her disapproval; it was not everyone
who would tolerate the maid's familiarity. This might be the
point at which Captain Gilbert discovered a serious flaw in his
new accommodation. She waited for the aquamarine eyes to
turn frosty; she waited for the haughty remark that would in-
dicate a set down. She waited in vain.

A mischievous smile crossed the American's face, and he
bent down so that his lips were close to the maid's ear. 'Don't
wish that, I beg of you,' he uttered in a stage whisper. 'Else you
would be so irresistible I'd be obliged to request a change of
lodgings for decency's sake.'

Abbie's toothless mouth hung open as she considered his
words, then her face became one delighted, wrinkled grin. She
gave the American a hefty jab in the ribs with a sharp elbow,
her ultimate accolade of approval. 'You'm a proper caution,
Cap'n, and no mistake. We'm going to 'ave to keep an eye on
you.'

'Abbie, Captain Gilbert wishes to be shown to his room,'
said Olivia crisply.

'Course 'e do! Why else would I 'ave brought 'is shaving-
water? Come on then, Cap'n, me handsome. You'm to bide up
yer. I've lit a bit of fire in the grate to warm the place through,
and I'll put an 'ot brick in your bed presently.'

'No angel could speak words more welcome to my ear,' said
Captain Gilbert. 'And no angel should carry such heavy loads.
Let me have my valise, I insist.'

'Angel? Ooh! 'Ark at the man!' shrieked Abbie delightedly
as she led the way upstairs.

'What a charming man!' said Mrs Kingston when the door closed behind him.

'Yes, charming indeed!' said Olivia. 'He seems to have charmed everyone in this house with no effort. Even you, Papa, who was so determined to treat him with scant civility yesterday.'

'Ah, but that was when I thought we were having a Frenchman. Obviously my attitude has changed now we have Captain Gilbert. Anyone can see he is a gentleman and a regular fellow!'

Olivia sighed.

'I can see you are not too sure about him,' said Mrs Kingston. 'But I am convinced you will find him much more agreeable when you get to know him better at supper.'

'Surely Captain Gilbert is not eating with us? I thought we agreed he was to take his meals in his room!'

'In his room? Why should he do that? It will be so cold up there—' Mrs Kingston's protests were cut short by the return of Abbie.

'I left the Cap'n settling in,' she informed them. 'I told 'im to come down to supper in 'alf an hour.'

'He is having his meals in his room,' insisted Olivia with increased determination.

'Well, you'm going to be the one who 'as to take 'em up, then! I've been up and down they stairs like a flag on a pole all day and my knees won't stand no more!'

Abbie did not wait for a reply, but stamped her way down to the kitchen. Olivia was left fighting a rising tide of frustration. She knew she had no time to rush about waiting upon Captain Gilbert, even if she had had the inclination. The Captain would be dining with them! Feeling annoyed, she followed the maid downstairs to help with the dinner.

'How splendid to be four at table!' observed Mr Kingston later, as they sat down to eat. 'We so seldom are these days. It's quite like having Charlie at home.'

'Your son is held in France?' asked Captain Gilbert.

'In a place called Verdun, when last we heard,' said Mrs Kingston. 'Olivia, do give the dear Captain more meat than that . . . Yes, a terrible place, we understand from his letters.'

'So you *do* get letters from him?'

'Very few, Captain Gilbert. Now, you are entitled to write home to your wife, I believe?' Charlotte added a generous slice of ham to the Captain's plate.

'I'm not married, ma'am.'

'But you have parents living?'

'Indeed, yes, I am happy to say.'

'Then I beg of you—nay—I insist you promise me that first thing tomorrow you will write and tell them you are safe and with friends,' Mrs Kingston urged. 'You have no idea how important it is for them to be told as soon as possible. We know only too well what anguish they will be feeling on your behalf.'

'I give you my solemn word, ma'am. And I hope your son is able to be paroled in France. If he has half my luck in his accommodation and in the family who welcomes him then he will be fortunate indeed.'

Olivia looked sharply across the table at the Captain, expecting to find some hint of insincerity in his expression, but there was none.

'Could Charlie be paroled? Is such a thing possible?' Mrs Kingston had snatched at the one hopeful phrase.

'Indeed he could, ma'am. I believe the conditions for parole are similar on both sides.' Captain Gilbert was addressing Charlotte but his eyes rested on Olivia. She wished she was not seated opposite to him, it meant she was unable to avoid his gaze.

'Then he might even now be comfortable with some good, kind family... I am convinced there are good kind families in France... We get so little news, letters are so infrequent.' Mrs Kingston's hands were clasped to her bosom. 'And to think we never considered it before. There, you have done us good already, Captain Gilbert. We are so glad you came to us!'

'Hear, hear,' agreed her husband.

Olivia permitted herself an unladylike snort, and immediately the Captain's eyes were upon her again, looking at her curiously with more than a hint of mockery. She did not like that look; it made her feel as though he were assessing her character, and she had no wish to be assessed by any American prisoner.

Aloud she said, 'You eat sparingly, sir. Is the food not to your liking?'

'On the contrary, it is delicious. I'm forcing myself to be abstemious for the sake of my digestion.'

'I assure you there is nothing indigestible on this table, sir! Abbie may have her defects but she is an excellent cook. And I oversee everything most carefully!' Olivia protested.

'Your pardon, Miss Kingston, I expressed myself badly. It's my digestion that might be found wanting, not this excellent meal. In fact, it is requiring great self-control not to over-indulge myself but, in truth, I have existed on such inferior and meagre rations these last few months that to enjoy too much of your supper might have unpleasant consequences. I would hate to begin my stay in your house laid low by a disordered stomach.'

The man had been starved! Horrified, Olivia stared at him, pity welling up within her once more.

The American mistook her expression for doubt, for he continued, 'I promise you it is so, Miss Kingston. My tailor is a master of his craft; when he made this coat for me it fitted to perfection.' He grasped the front of his jacket and pulled it to demonstrate the considerable slack.

'You were badly treated?' said Olivia in a low voice. 'For a whole year?'

'Not all the time. The captain of the vessel who captured us was a true Christian gentleman. He could not have shown greater kindness to us, particularly our wounded. While we were on board his ship we fared very well.'

'But conditions in prison were bad?'

'Indeed they were, Miss Kingston. A corrupt governor made certain that we seldom got our full rations—and what we did get was often inedible.'

In the flickering candle-light Olivia could see that his mouth had set in a tight line at the recent memory.

Mrs Kingston gave a tearful sniff. And Mr Kingston muttered, half under his breath, 'Appalling! Disgraceful!'

Olivia could not express the shame she felt, that men should be treated so, and in England! Some of her feelings must have shown on her face, for Miles Gilbert said:

'Don't take it too much to heart, Miss Kingston. Prisons are prisons the world over. I don't suppose Plymouth is any worse or better than anywhere else.'

He spoke gently, and it was his very gentleness which roused her. There was a near-seductiveness in his voice which alerted her senses. What had she been thinking of, feeling sympathy for him again? And why should he evoke shame in her? He was a prisoner of war!

She said sharply, 'You were unfortunate to have been kept at Plymouth. I understand the officers are usually sent on to Dartmoor.'

'I fear I wasn't always a model prisoner. I took such a delight in tormenting my guards that I spent more than my fair share of time alone in a particularly noxious chamber known, without affection, as the Black Hole.'

'Then I wonder that you were considered for parole.' Olivia's surprise superseded her dislike of the man. 'I thought it was offered only to well-behaved prisoners.'

'Seemingly I managed to convince those in command of my intention to reform. You've nothing to fear, Miss Kingston. I've given my word to abide by the conditions of my parole and I will keep it.'

'Of course you will!' cried Mrs Kingston indignantly. 'I am convinced you would never ever think of breaking your word.' She frowned reprovingly at her daughter.

'You must miss the company of your fellow countrymen,' put in Mr Kingston. 'You say you are a rare species here in Dartmouth and I think you are right. I've heard of Americans being held in Dartmoor Prison, and of some paroled in the towns about the moor, but none in this neighbourhood.'

'Yes, what happened to the rest of your officers and crew?' asked Olivia, deciding to needle the American to make up for her inadvertent sympathy. 'Did they escape? If so it was extraordinarily careless of you to be the only one captured.'

'Do not be so curious, child,' hissed Mrs Kingston in a low voice. 'It may be painful to the Captain to discuss such things.'

'Not at all, ma'am. The fact is, I'm accustomed to being unique. I was the sole American on board a French ship when I was captured.'

'A French ship? Had the American Navy no vessel for you to command?' demanded Olivia, ignoring her mother's frantic signals to keep quiet.

'I travelled merely as a passenger, Miss Kingston,' Captain Gilbert informed her gravely. He knew she was trying to irritate him, she could tell. His eyes held hers unflinchingly as he continued, 'I was required to take command of an American vessel lying at Brest. The captain had fallen ill. The first ship out of Boston, where I was, happened to be French, so I travelled on her as a passenger.'

'There must be a shortage of competent American sea captains if there was none nearer to Brest than Boston,' observed Olivia with mock innocence. 'This captain who fell ill, did his entire crew fall ill too, that there was no one in the vicinity to take charge of the vessel?'

'Really, Olivia! You have cross-questioned Captain Gilbert quite enough,' her mother broke in. 'I think you and I should retire to the drawing-room and leave the gentlemen alone.'

'But Papa usually comes with us and joins us for tea,' declared Olivia. Their household was not going to be reorganised for the American, not if she could prevent it.

Her mother thought otherwise. 'Usually he does, I agree, but we have another gentleman in the house now, and he may wish to stay and partake of a glass of port or smoke a pipe.'

'By George, that's a splendid idea!' Mr Kingston's face brightened. 'I might even take a drop of port myself.'

'Papa, Doctor Puddicombe advised you against it!'

'One glass would do no harm, and maybe a small pipe of tobacco,' insisted her father.

'But would you keep to one glass? I fancy the whole bottle would be consumed without you noticing it, while you were talking.' Olivia did not normally sound so crotchety, but she could not stop herself. It was Captain Gilbert's fault; he was having an irritating effect upon her, ruffling her feathers. Even when he sat observing her silently, his eyes unfathomable in the candle-light, he annoyed her. She could feel her resentment against him increasing steadily.

'The prospect of a glass of port is very tempting, sir,' said the Captain. 'I wonder, though, if I might postpone it until I've grown more accustomed to the good things in life once again?'

'Of course, my boy. How thoughtless of me! Yes, we'll save our port for a time when you are more up to it. It will taste all the better for waiting. Shall we join the ladies and take tea?'

'That sounds very pleasant.' Captain Gilbert rose while the female members of the company left the table.

As she pushed back her chair Olivia felt certain she detected a look of triumph in his eyes. Just because he had persuaded her papa not to drink port when she had failed!

'Maybe the dear Captain would prefer coffee,' suggested Mrs Kingston.

'We always have tea!' said Olivia.

'Tea would be most acceptable,' said Miles Gilbert.

He bent his head, so that she was convinced he was mocking her with his over-elaborate courtesy. To her irritation she realised he was merely examining the mechanics of her father's wheelchair in order to propel him into the drawing-room. It took considerable control for her not to push him away from the handles and cry, That's my job! Go away! She did not, of course. It would have been too childish, and she was already aware that she had not behaved very well.

Not that she cared. She was not bothered by what he thought of her. She had had doubts about having him in the house in the first place, and now she considered those doubts to be justified. He was a disruptive influence! She wished he had never come.

The kettle was already singing on its spirit-stove when they entered the drawing-room. While Olivia poured the tea Miles Gilbert's eyes wandered appreciatively round the room. His gaze settled on the piano.

'A fine instrument, is it not?' said Mr Kingston, noting his interest. 'You like music?'

'It's one of my greatest passions, sir.'

'Then you'll fare very well in this house. Some days we have music from morn till night. Not all of it good, not when some of Olivia's pupils are going through their paces. When she plays it is a different matter, of course. She has mastered the instrument most wonderfully.'

Honesty forced Olivia to qualify her father's remarks.

'Don't expect too much, sir. There are many imperfections in my performance,' she said.

'You're too modest, daughter. Play something for the Captain, so that he may judge for himself,' said Mr Kingston.

Olivia had no intention of submitting her musical ability for the American's approbation. Before she could object, however, her mother interrupted.

'Olivia can play some other time,' she said. 'Can you not see Captain Gilbert is almost asleep where he sits?'

Three pairs of eyes regarded the American curiously. Any other man might have been discomforted by such scrutiny, but not the Captain. Nevertheless, his pallor had been increasing and the shadows beneath his eyes had intensified. His face bore all the marks of exhaustion.

'You must think me very discourteous.' Captain Gilbert managed to smile with some effort. 'To tell the truth, I am fatigued. We were a day and a half on our march from Plymouth, and our quarters last night in a barn were not exactly restful. I fear the warmth and comfort of your fireside are taking their toll.'

'Then you mustn't stand on ceremony with us, my boy. A proper night's sleep is what you need! Off you go as soon as you please!' Mr Kingston waved a hand in the direction of the door.

'You are very kind. If you will excuse me...' He smiled wearily. 'A good bed with fresh linen—and your maid said something about a hot brick to air the sheets, too. No man can know any greater luxury in this world. I bid you good night, with much gratitude.'

'You'll need a candle. I'll get you one.' Olivia rose, and lighting a taper at the fire, preceded him out onto the landing. In the near-darkness she was very conscious of his presence there beside her. By the glimmer of the taper flame she selected a holder from the closet, inserted a fresh candle and lit it.

'Here, take this and guard it well,' she said, handing him the candlestick. 'I would be obliged if you would make sure it is properly extinguished before you go to sleep.'

'I promise I'll be most cautious.' He regarded her steadily, half-amused, despite his fatigue. 'I can see you are a most prudent and careful housekeeper, Miss Kingston. You must be a great comfort to your parents.'

'I try to be a dutiful daughter to my mother and father, sir,' she answered. 'And if you'll excuse me I'll return to them.'

When she returned to the drawing-room it was to find her parents sitting close together, holding hands like two young lovers.

'...It does your tender heart much credit, my darling,' her father was saying. 'However, I am certain he doesn't hold us to blame.'

'But I feel so responsible,' her mother whispered, close to tears. 'The poor boy has suffered most terribly; I am sure he has not told us a half of what has happened to him. And it was while he was here, in England. I feel so ashamed.'

'I presume you are talking about Captain Gilbert,' Olivia said.

'Indeed we are,' said Mrs Kingston. 'We are trying to devise ways of recompensing him for everything that has happened to him. Ways of making his life a little more cheerful and comfortable. Have you any suggestions, dear?'

'No, I have not,' said Olivia. 'I refuse to tax my brain over the subject for one second. Certainly I regret that Captain Gilbert's imprisonment was so hard—but we are at war. He will be comfortable enough here as it is without us making any extra effort.'

'Oh, how can you be so callous!' cried Mrs Kingston.

Very easily, when I think of all poor Charlie is enduring at this minute, said Olivia. But she said it to herself, so that her mother did not hear her.

'The Cap'n gone up already?' remarked Abbie, when Olivia took the tea things to the kitchen. 'I must say 'e looked fair wore out when 'e got yer. Best let 'im lie on in the morning. 'E needs the sleep.'

'I don't know why everyone is so concerned,' Olivia protested. 'The fellow is one of our foes; with the exception of Mama we were in one accord to treat him coldly, yet now everyone seems to have fallen under his spell. He has charmed you all!'

'That 'e 'ave!' sighed Abbie with satisfaction. 'A proper man is the Cap'n. The sort as I'd like to get me teeth into.'

'You haven't got any teeth!' Olivia reminded her bluntly. 'And I don't see what the fuss is about. He isn't at all handsome.'

This was true, she reflected. Miles Gilbert's face was badly constructed, it lacked symmetry, the planes were wrong; his nose was too long and decidedly crooked, his cheek-bones too high, his eyes, for all their unusual colour, were too hooded. As for his mouth, his lower lip protruded slightly, denoting petulance . . . ? Passion . . . ? Olivia was rather startled to realise she had observed Captain Gilbert quite so closely.

'A man like the Cap'n don't need to be 'andsome,' said Abbie. 'A man of 'is sort can have a face like the back of the par-

son's mare and any warm-blooded woman'd still follow 'im to
the ends of the earth.'

'Then I must have ice-water in my veins, for I would not follow him anywhere!' declared Olivia.

Abbie chuckled. ''Tis early days, my lover. 'Tis early days.'

Irritated by the maid's attitude Olivia reached down and
picked up the cat. It had been an extraordinarily tiring and
trying day, and she held the sleek body closely, seeking comfort.

'Everyone in the house seems bewitched by that man, Tibby,'
she whispered into one twitching grey ear. 'Only you and I are
standing firm now. We won't succumb to any easy charmer, will
we? Especially not to one who is a prisoner.'

Standing there, with the cat in her arms, she found herself
wishing that their new guest had been any other sort of a man—
shy, morose, argumentative, she could have tolerated any of
those traits. It was unfortunate that fate, in the guise of Admiral Ranscombe, had sent them the one type of character that
disturbed her the most. She had good reason for her mistrust.
Already in her life there had been two charming men, both of
whom had caused her upheaval and pain.

The first was her father. For all she loved him dearly she was
only too well aware of his weaknesses. Edward Kingston was a
charming man, everyone said so. That was why people had
smiled fondly when he preferred enjoying himself to looking
after the prosperous wine business that had been built up by
generations of Kingstons. That was why people had continued
to give him credit long after it was obvious his finances were in
deep trouble. The crash, when it had come, had brought ruin
not only to his own family, but also to many small traders in the
town.

Olivia had been catapulted almost overnight from a life of
ease and comfort to one where she was obliged to give music
lessons to keep a roof over their heads. To her surprise she had
found that she enjoyed teaching almost as much as she enjoyed music. Then, soon after the collapse of the family business, her father had suffered a seizure, and so Olivia had taken
charge of the household. No one had suggested that her mother
should assume this responsibility. That had been too preposterous an idea even to be contemplated, least of all by Charlotte Kingston herself. Quite a burden had fallen on Olivia's
slim shoulders, yet she had coped. During the last eight years

she had come to take a great pride in balancing their tiny budget, and in gradually repaying some of their debts. She did not pretend that she liked poverty, or the insecurity it brought, but some aspects of her new existence had proved to be unexpectedly rewarding.

It had been one more loss, one that had nothing to do with money or position or fine clothes, that had caused her the greatest anguish. It had been the loss of the man she loved.

Richard Hayter had been a charmer too. He had always been able to make her smile, or bring a warm surge of happiness to her heart. It had been impossible not to love Richard, and when he had proposed marriage to her she had had no doubts about saying yes. Then news of her father's business difficulties had broken. She still found it difficult to understand how Richard could have deserted her quite so immediately, or so cruelly. What she had seen as love, in him had been superficial charm, nothing more.

Now a third charming man had entered her sphere! Was it any wonder that she should regard him with caution and suspicion?

'Yes, Tibby. You and I seem to be the only ones not blinded by this man's wiles,' she said softly. 'We are the only ones with any sense.'

Tibby purred a brief response, but instead of remaining contentedly in Olivia's arms, as she usually did, the cat struggled to be free. She made a dash for the open door and up the stairs towards forbidden territory. Olivia hurried after the animal to retrieve her, but she was not quick enough. In the dark stillness she could her the soft paws padding swiftly upwards towards the floor where Miles Gilbert slept.

Even Tibby had deserted her. Olivia was alone in her resolve not to make the American welcome!

CHAPTER TWO

'I'VE tidied the dining-room and laid the table for breakfast. With luck I'll have time to start on the drawing-room before anyone is astir.' Enveloped in a holland wrapper to protect her gown, Olivia had already begun her morning chores before it was light.

'That's right, get un done afore your Pa and Ma are on the move,' said Abbie, coaxing the kitchen fire into life.

'The master and mistress,' corrected Olivia automatically.

'We won't see they for a good hour yet,' said the maid ignoring her. 'And the Cap'n were that tired last night I don't expect 'e'll join us this side of noon, either.'

'Good! That should give us a chance to get some work done.'

For some time, as Abbie had grown older, Olivia had taken on more and more of the housework, learning through necessity until she could complete the tasks with swift efficiency. Her parents had never been early risers, not in the days when they had been affluent, and certainly not now. She suspected that some of their tardiness might have been their reluctance to see her cleaning the house. They hated to see her doing a servant's work, yet could think of no practical alternative, so they did not appear until the house was tidy and the holland wrapper removed.

Olivia collected a brush and duster from the cupboard.

'I've lit the drawing-room fire, but see if you can do aught with un,' Abbie called after her. ''Twas all smoke and precious little else when I left.'

The maid was right; the drawing-room fire was looking very miserable when Olivia entered. Propping the broom against a side-table she set about coaxing the reluctant flames into life. From the street below came the sound of tramping feet and the babble of French accents as a group of prisoners was marched in the direction of the castle to their day's work, building walls. In the house all was peaceful and quiet. When the fire was blazing to her satisfaction she bent down, her back to the door, to tidy the hearth. She was quite unaware she was not alone in the room.

The hand that suddenly caressed her behind was large, firm, and very practised. Startled, Olivia shot upright and turned to face her assailant.

'Captain Gilbert!' she cried.

'Miss Kingston!' The startled astonishment on the American's face would have been funny had she not felt so outraged.

'Captain Gilbert!' she repeated, too shocked to say more for the moment. As she took a deep breath fluency returned. 'Captain Gilbert! How dare you!'

'Your pardon, ma'am. I offer you my sincerest apologies. I am truly penitent.' Despite his regret he remained remarkably self-possessed for a man who had committed such a shocking transgression. In fact, the corners of his mouth were beginning to twitch. He actually thought the situation to be funny.

'Your sense of humour is sadly misplaced, sir,' she snapped. 'There was nothing amusing in your act. There is never anything amusing in an insult.'

'No insult was intended, I swear to you.' He was clearly trying hard to suppress his laughter. 'I fear my baser instincts overcame me for a moment, and I gave way to temptation. If I had realised it was you bending over in such a provocative way—'

'Whom did you think I was?' demanded Olivia, deliberately ignoring the word 'provocative'.

'Well, I didn't expect— I didn't recognise—' His eyes went from the broom to her dowdy holland wrapper and thence to the duster in her hand.

'You thought I was a servant?'

'I do truly beg your pardon, ma'am.' Now he did sound contrite.

Olivia pursed her lips. 'Sir, I don't know what is considered acceptable behaviour in your country, but in this household we will not tolerate such licentiousness. And lest your baser instincts should threaten to overcome you once more I warn you, we have only one servant, Abbie, and if you ever dare to treat her in such an overly familiar manner you will regret it.'

'Ah, now there I do agree with you, ma'am. And I thank you for the timely warning.' His lips were twitching again.

'Sir, you aren't taking this matter seriously!' she cried.

'On the contrary, Miss Kingston, I'm taking your warning most seriously. Though I fancy the situation is not likely to arise. If it had been Abbie's—er—form I had espied I don't think my baser instincts would have been tempted at all.'

'Oh, you are impossible! We shall consider the matter closed. I have no intention of prolonging this conversation.'

'As you wish, Miss Kingston, but first let me repeat my deepest regrets for my action. I'm truly sorry.'

At last Olivia believed him, and she calmed down.

'I accept your apology, sir,' she said more quietly. 'Now let us end the matter. I wouldn't have my father get to know of it—

'What is it you don't wish your father to get to know?' Edward Kingston's voice came from the doorway. He had devised a way of propelling himself in his wheelchair using his good leg. He could only manage short distances but enough to take himself along the landing from his bedroom to the drawing-room.

Olivia groaned inwardly. Too much excitement was bad for her father, and if he should get angry at Captain Gilbert there was no knowing the consequences.

'It was a misunderstanding, nothing more, Papa,' she said.

'It must have been quite a misunderstanding to bring such a bright colour to your cheeks, my love. What have you been up to, Captain Gilbert? Come, tell me, or I shall suspect all manner of dastardly things.' In spite of his words his tone was jovial.

'I can see there's no help for it but to confess, sir, and humbly beg your pardon as well as your daughter's.' Captain Gilbert was making a manful effort to sound contrite, but not succeeding very well. 'Please understand, sir, I didn't know how many females you have in your household, so when I saw a womanly form—a trim, womanly form, if I may say so—bending over the fire I—er—let my feelings get the better of me. From that angle I didn't recognise Miss Kingston, of course. I'm very sorry.'

'So, you pinched her behind? If that isn't priceless!' Far from flying into a temper her father was convulsed with laughter. 'No wonder your face is glowing, daughter! It's done you the power of good. I haven't seen you in such good looks for an age.'

'Really, Papa! You are as bad as Captain Gilbert!'

'Oh, don't be so prim, my love. No harm was done. The Captain was only behaving as any proper man would have done in the circumstances, especially one who has been deprived of female company for an age. And you can't complain that he mistook you for a servant, not when you wear that wretched garment.' His amusement subsided as he cast a censorious look at Olivia's wrapper. 'Do go and get rid of it, there's a dear child, and come to breakfast looking like my pretty girl once more.'

'Very well, Papa.' Olivia had no alternative but to obey him, even though the drawing-room was still covered in dust. Somehow she would have to find a few minutes between lessons to come up and finish her task.

'Captain Gilbert, will you oblige me by giving me a push towards the dining-room, sir?' Edward Kingston was chortling once more. 'I think it best that Mrs Kingston does not hear of your little misunderstanding this morning; women tend to view these matters in a much more serious light. But one last word of advice! Always identify the backside before you strike!'

'I certainly will, sir,' said the Captain.

And the two men went into the dining-room still laughing.

'There, did I not say that having another man in the house would be of benefit to your Papa?' said Mrs Kingston again after breakfast. 'He was in splendid spirits this morning, was he not? Quite like his old self.'

Olivia had to admit that this was so. To herself she acknowledged that if Captain Gilbert could keep her father so cheerful then it was worth putting up with the American's presence. Only her father's well-being would be worth such a price, though.

'Really, Abbie is getting so slack these days. This room is filthy!' Mrs Kingston ran a finger along the mantelpiece and examined it, frowning.

'Everyone was up much earlier than anticipated; I expect that was the cause,' said Olivia, unwilling and unable to give a fuller explanation.

'Yes, I quite intended to stay in bed longer, but your Papa was for getting up,' said Mrs Kingston, her attention successfully diverted from the dust. 'I expect it is all the excitement of having the dear Captain with us... Really, I had not appreciated how dull we had become.'

Privately Olivia thought that life had become considerably too eventful of late, but she kept her opinions to herself.

It was with some relief she heard Captain Gilbert leave the house soon after breakfast. She was due to give Maria Rowden a lesson and she had no wish for her pupil—and particularly her pupil's mother—to encounter the American one minute before it was necessary.

When the Rowdens arrived she took one look at Mrs Rowden's glowering countenance and feared the worst.

'Miss Kingston, what's this I hear? I couldn't believe my ears. I hope to learn from your lips that it isn't true!' The small woman bridled with agitation; the feathers on her bonnet seemed to rustle in keeping with her emotion.

'I can neither affirm or deny anything until I know what you have heard,' said Olivia calmly.

'Why, that you have a French prisoner of war staying in your house!'

'In that case, I'm happy to be able to deny the rumour absolutely,' said Olivia with some relief.

'I thought it couldn't be. I said so as soon as I heard it. I said "Miss Kingston wouldn't tolerate to have one of those foreign scoundrels under her roof for a minute, you may be satisfied!"' Mrs Rowden relaxed somewhat, looking pleased at her own perspicacity.

'However, I must admit that an American prisoner does now lodge with us,' Olivia went on.

'An American!' exclaimed Mrs Rowden, as if Olivia had confessed to housing someone from another planet.

'Yes, Captain Gilbert of the United States Navy.' Olivia wondered if Mrs Rowden had as much an aversion to Americans as she had to Frenchmen.

'An American, you say?' Mrs Rowden was doubtful. 'You can't mean one of those savages who go about naked and stick feathers in their hair?'

'No, certainly not!' Olivia strove to suppress the laughter that momentarily ousted her anxiety. 'No, Captain Gilbert is quite civilised, and his dress would cause no comment anywhere in England.'

'And what manner of man is he?'

'Oh, a perfect gentleman,' said Olivia, deciding to ignore Captain Gilbert's recent lapse from polite behaviour.

'I don't know what to think.' Mrs Rowden was hesitant now. 'There can be no guessing how Mr Rowden will take the news; he can't abide foreigners. He is quite likely to fly into one of his passions and forbid Maria to enter this house again.'

Olivia tried to imagine the shy, self-effacing shoemaker in a passion, but her imagination was not sufficiently robust. In a lifetime's acquaintance with the man she had never heard him utter anything more spirited than 'Good morning'. It was his brisk, efficient little wife who organised the home, the business, and the man himself.

'Upon consideration, Miss Kingston, I'll permit Maria to remain for her lesson today; and I'll broach the matter with Mr Rowden this evening. I can promise nothing of the outcome, though, for Mr Rowden is as fierce as a lion where the welfare of our child is concerned.'

'It does him great credit,' murmured Olivia, deciding not to overtax her imagination with this new vision of a leonine Mr Rowden. 'And I thank you for letting Maria remain this morning. Come along, Maria. Let us begin.'

Maria, a stout, plain little girl, beamed at Olivia with devoted adoration. She was a child with an abundance of affection which overflowed onto everyone she knew. Olivia was extremely fond of her and would have been sorry if she had ceased to come, for Maria's sake as well as for the additional income she represented. As well as affection, Maria exuded enthusiasm which she directed towards music. Sadly, she equated force with skill, and the piano in the downstairs music-room rocked and shuddered beneath the vigour of her playing.

At last the lesson was at an end and Olivia showed mother and daughter to the door.

'Don't look to see us again next week, Miss Kingston.' The ruffles on Mrs Rowden's bosom rose and fell energetically. 'There's no knowing what Mr Rowden will think of this news... No knowing at all. I fully expect him to forbid Maria to come.'

'Oh, Ma, but I want to come again,' wailed Maria, suddenly realising the threat to her music lessons.

'Then you must be a good girl and not aggravate your Pa,' her mother admonished her. 'Even then, there's no knowing...'

Olivia closed the door behind them and for a moment leaned against it deep in thought. Maria was only the first! She had more than a dozen pupils who came to the house. What if they all ceased to come? It did not bear thinking about.

'You look worried, Miss Kingston.' Miles Gilbert's voice startled her. She had not noticed him on the stairs.

'I thought you'd gone out, sir!' she said.

'So I had, bent upon exploring the town and making the necessary arrangements to send a letter home. I wrote it most punctiliously first thing this morning, then promptly found I had left it behind. I had to come back for it.'

'You take it to the prisoners' agent, Mr Brooking. He is an attorney. His rooms are close by St Saviour's Church; you'll find them easily enough.' Olivia spoke absently, her mind still on her problems.

'Your pardon, Miss Kingston, but you look distinctly distrait. If you will forgive my impertinence I would say do not concern yourself so. It's not your fault. The task is beyond anyone's powers.'

'What fault? Whose powers?' declared Olivia, surprised out of her reverie.

'The fact that you have failed to instil any musical ability into that child. After having been obliged to listen to her, mercifully briefly, I'm convinced no one could teach her to play. Even Orpheus would give up in tears and sell his lute.'

'Maria's lack of ability is not the problem. I only wish it were. I'm concerned because I'm likely to lose her as a pupil, not because I have to teach her. And I fear more will follow her.'

'Has something happened, that you are losing pupils suddenly?'

It was on the tip of Olivia's tongue to say that yes, he had happened, that he was the cause of the trouble; but she could not. He was so obviously delighted with his new surroundings after the strictures of Mill Prison, and her father was so revelling in his company that she could not bring herself to speak.

'The times are difficult for everyone!' she said, and stalked into the music-room.

To her annoyance he followed her. He looked about the small, dark room with interest, taking in everything.

'So this is where you toil so diligently,' he said, picking up the guitar which lay on a low table. 'You teach this instrument as well as the piano?'

'I do,' retorted Olivia. She was about to tell him to put it down before he did any damage, but the chords he strummed were skilful and accomplished. 'You play the guitar?' she asked instead.

'I trifle with it only. I confess that my belief in my ability as a guitarist waned sharply after I heard Paganini play. I knew I could never attain—'

'Whom did you hear?' demanded Olivia.

'Signor Paganini. Perhaps you haven't heard of him—'

'Of course I've heard of him!' retorted Olivia. 'The greatest living virtuoso of the violin in the world.'

'Ah, now I understand your look of astonishment. He is, as you say, a violinist of overwhelming brilliance. Few people realise that he's equally talented as a guitarist. He rarely gives concerts on the instrument these days, so I was particularly fortunate to be in Florence at the right time.'

'You've heard Paganini play? In Florence?' she said, her voice filled with awe.

'I heard him play the guitar in Florence. I had the privilege of listening to his performance on the violin in Brussels, I think it was... Yes, Brussels.' He had been idly playing a few random chords on the piano and now he looked up and saw her expression. 'Really, Miss Kingston, you look as if you don't believe me,' he said, laughing.

It was not disbelief that Olivia felt, but longing. Restricted to the confines of a small town she was sorely starved of good music, and she hungered for it with an intensity that was at times almost painful.

'You've heard Paganini...' she repeated, her voice almost reverential. 'You—you go to concerts frequently?'

'Not while I was a guest at Mill Prison, of course. Otherwise, I don't miss a concert or a musical performance if I can avoid it.'

'And Paganini ... is he as brilliant as everyone says he is?'

Captain Gilbert considered for a moment. 'I think his performance even exceeds his reputation,' he said. 'He plays with such an extraordinary amount of spirit and passion. People say he's sold his soul to the Devil in order to play so superbly. An absurdity, of course, yet as you listen to him you could almost believe it were true.'

Olivia let her breath out in a long slow sigh of longing.

'Do you go to concerts often, Miss Kingston?' he asked politely.

Olivia paused. How could she compare the amateur playing here in Dartmouth with the performances of genius he was accustomed to hearing?

'I used to, when I was at school in Exeter,' she said wistfully. 'There is, sadly, little opportunity here, even if I had the time. I confess I miss it sorely. My great hope is to go to Exeter again, or perhaps Bath, or London, and listen to music hour after hour until my head is full of it and I'm quite giddy.' She stopped, curtailing her mounting enthusiasm.

'Most young ladies would go to such places for the pleasures of the balls and assemblies and the routs,' he grinned.

'I'm not young!' she replied, fearing he might be mocking her. 'Nor am I as well travelled as you. You appear to have gone the length and breadth of Europe pretty thoroughly.'

'I *am* a sailor,' he reminded her.

'So you are! I keep forgetting.' It was strange how she could not register him in her mind as a man of the sea. Yet surely Vienna was a considerable distance from the coast? But geography had never been her strong suit; she decided she might be wrong. 'And I fancy, from the few notes you have played here, that you are a more accomplished musician than you pretend,' she continued.

The Captain smiled. 'I amuse myself with the piano and one or two other instruments; and I sing a little. I think I'm what is best described as a drawing-room baritone. I've not yet heard you play properly. Will you not oblige me now?'

'I can't, sir. I've to give a lesson in five minutes,' she said hurriedly. She had just recollected the time, and she was reluctant to risk losing a second pupil because of the Captain's presence. She was also disturbed to find that she and the American had anything in common so important as music.

'Perhaps this evening, then. Maybe we could try a duet or two? If it wouldn't disturb Mr Kingston, that is.'

'My father is passionately fond of music, he is never disturbed by it,' she said before she could stop herself.

'Except when it's trampled to death by the child who was your previous pupil, eh?' he grinned. 'I tell you, I feared for the fabric of the house at times. Now I must go and leave you in peace. I'll find the agent by the church, you say? *Adieu* for now, Miss Kingston. I look forward with great pleasure to our musical evening.'

'Goodbye, sir,' said Olivia. She hoped her voice sounded firm and dismissive.

When she met Miles Gilbert again at table for the midday meal he had the air of a man well satisfied with his morning.

'Did you find Dartmouth to your liking, Captain?' asked Mr Kingston as they sat down to eat.

'It seems to me to be a capital place, sir,' replied the American. 'I feared the restrictions of my parole might prove onerous in time, but I can see this won't be so here. Not only are the surroundings exceedingly beautiful, there's so much to watch on the river. There must never be a dull moment.'

'I agree absolutely, my boy!' cried Mr Kingston. 'Sometimes there is so much going on I can hardly bear to tear my eyes away.'

'Also, I can go walking. Provided I stay on the turnpike I can go a full mile beyond the town boundary, which should give me plenty of scope to stretch my legs.'

'Ah, but what of the curfew, sir? How will you like leaving the fleshpots of Dartmouth before the curfew bell rings for you at five o'clock?' demanded Mr Kingston jovially.

'Charming as it is, Dartmouth didn't strike me as being overendowed with fleshpots,' chuckled the Captain. 'Being enforced to spend my evening here in the company of you all will be a pleasure not a punishment, especially now that Miss Kingston has promised we shall make music together.'

'Miss Kingston doesn't remember promising any such thing,' said Olivia tartly, annoyed at seeing her parents beam at his last remark. Determined to change the subject she asked, 'Did you find Mr Brooking and get your letter sent?'

'I did, thank you.'

'Good, it is most important to let your poor parents know how you are faring now,' said Mrs Kingston busying herself with the dishes, though it was Olivia who did most of the serving.

'I agree, ma'am. And this one was doubly important for it included an appeal for funds.'

'Will your government not pay you an allowance?' asked Mr Kingston.

'In good time, no doubt, once they've decided who I am and where I've got to. I fear by then I might be toothless and white-haired. No, I prefer to put my faith in the paternal affection of my father. I know he'll do his best to send me money as promptly and as securely as possible.'

'Yet it will take a deal of time to arrive from... Where was it you said, Captain, dear?'' Mrs Kingston asked.

'From Providence, Rhode Island, ma'am. You speak truly. But my father is a man of great resourcefulness. He'll get money to me somehow.'

'I hope he does not resort to sending it in by smugglers, Captain Gilbert,' said Mrs Kingston. 'I have heard of that happening—and of all people I cannot abide those villains! They caused the ruin of Mr Kingston's business as a wine merchant, you know—their activities and this dreadful war combined!'

In Olivia's opinion the smugglers and the war had played only a minor part in her parents' financial downfall. She said, 'I don't think you need to fear on that score, Mama. I fancy Rhode Island must be well beyond the range of the most intrepid local smuggler.'

'Indeed so,' agreed the Captain, keeping his face grave with difficulty. 'You can rest assured that my father will be most prudent in his means of despatch.'

'But how will you fare until your money arrives?' asked Mrs Kingston, full of concern.

'I'm my father's son, ma'am, and extremely resourceful. I'll manage very well, you need not fear.'

'Many of the Frenchmen are skilled with their hands, and live quite well by selling their carvings or their straw-work,' observed Olivia. 'Others teach French or dancing.'

'I'm sorry for anyone who is forced to be taught dancing by me, Miss Kingston, and though I'm quite proud of my command of French, with such an abundance of native speakers I don't think I would have many pupils. No, I've other talents upon which to rely.'

Olivia was about to ask him what they were, but her father spoke up first.

'And have you found our Assembly Rooms, my boy?'

'I have, sir. I gravitated to them like a pigeon to its roost. I thought the coffee-rooms to be quite splendid. As for the card-rooms, they exceeded anything I expected to find in a town of this size.'

'Ah, the card-rooms . . .' Mr Kingston said wistfully. 'Many a pleasurable hour I've spent there in the past in the company of my friends. Not for many a long day, though; not since being inflicted and forced into this wretched chair. Those days are now gone, alas.'

'I thought I might put my head in there this afternoon for a while,' said the Captain. 'Just to look at the company and make myself known. When I come back I'll tell you how things have fared in your absence, eh, sir?'

'I'd enjoy that above all things,' chortled Mr Kingston. 'We might even share that glass of port, too. What say you?'

'I'm absolutely in favour, sir, and look forward to it.' The Captain raised his glass, which held only a very inferior wine, and toasted his host.

Olivia's resentment of the man swelled up. She might have known that he would be a gambler and an *habitué* of places like coffee-rooms. Nor was he reticent in putting himself forward. It might be the American way of behaving, but it was far from her taste. Then she looked at her father. He was enjoying his conversation with the Captain, it was plain on his face for all to see. She swallowed her annoyance with difficulty. Whatever her dislike of the American she would have to keep it under control for her father's sake.

After the meal Olivia hurried away to her room to get ready. She had more pupils that afternoon, the offspring of one of the more wealthy inhabitants of Dartmouth, and so she visited their home to give lessons. She had no wish to be escorted into town by Captain Gilbert, so she dawdled over her preparations until she heard the front door shut. Only then did she make her exit. In her haste to leave the house she did not look where she was going and almost cannoned into a man going in the same direction.

'*Bonjour,* Mademoiselle Kingston,' he said politely.

'Oh, Lieutenant La Fontaine! Your pardon—er—*bonjour!*'

Belatedly she recognised the French prisoner who was lodged on parole in the next house to them. He fell into step beside her, obviously searching for some way to open the conversation. He was a pleasant young man, quiet to the point of being diffident. For a while they walked in silence towards the town, their road following the river. The gale had slackened to a stiff breeze which flecked the grey waters with white lace caps, and sent the river craft scurrying before it.

'The winter, I think it soon approaches,' said the Lieutenant at last.

'Yes, the weather has turned much colder, has it not?'

'This morning I speak with Mr Brooking, the agent. He says that you also have a prisoner on parole in your house.'

'Yes, Captain Gilbert arrived yesterday.'

'Capitaine Gilbert, you say?' He pronounced the name in the French manner, with a soft G. 'But I think I know him. He is a Norman, from Le Havre, *non*? A short man, with black hair?'

'No, I am afraid Captain Gilbert is not your friend. He isn't even French, he is an American.'

'American? *Extraordinaire!* I did not know there were American prisoners here. But I hope I will make his acquaintance soon.'

'I'm sure you will. And now I must leave you, Lieutenant. This is where my pupils live.'

'We walk together a short way only, but I find it very pleasant. You listen to my poor English with much patience. I am very grateful.'

'You speak English well, I wish my French were half as good,' said Olivia.

'You are very kind, Mademoiselle Kingston.' The Lieutenant bowed his farewell. As he walked away she was surprised to find herself thinking how much more agreeable it would have been if the shy Frenchman had been lodged with them, instead of Captain Gilbert. If they had to have a prisoner in the house a man like the Lieutenant would have been less disruptive, one would have been barely aware that he was there.

Unfortunately she was all too well aware of the Captain's presence in the house. That evening, after their meal, he remained in the dining-room with her father to enjoy their long awaited glass of port. Their uproarious laughter could be heard quite clearly in the drawing-room.

'The dear Captain!' declared Mrs Kingston, listening to their merriment. 'When did you last hear your Papa so cheerful, Olivia, my love? I declare I cannot remember him laughing like that for an age.'

'I think it's just as well we don't know the cause of their laughter,' said Olivia darkly. 'I'm wondering if Captain Gilbert is going to be quite such a good influence.'

'Because he makes your Papa laugh? I do not know how you can think that, child. Gentlemen do like their jokes, and if those jokes are not suitable to be repeated in front of ladies I do not see that it matters—not if we are well out of earshot.'

'I only meant...' began Olivia.

At that moment the man himself appeared, pushing her father in his wheelchair.

'I hope we haven't kept you waiting, my loves,' beamed Edward Kingston, 'but Captain Gilbert here tells such a tale, not even a stone saint could resist laughing. The port, too, was capital... And you needn't look at us like that, Olivia, my girl. We were most abstemious, though I must admit that it was because of Captain Gilbert; if he poured out the rum ration on board ship in the meagre way he poured the port then I wonder he never had a mutiny on his hands.'

'Your pardon, sir. I felt I should become acclimatised slowly to such fortified wine,' said the Captain.

'Acclimatised fiddlesticks! I know what you were doing, my boy. You were being deliberately parsimonious for my sake, and I appreciate it. Now then, you young folk, what about this music I heard so much about earlier today? Are we to be in for a treat?'

'I'm hoping to hear Miss Kingston play at last,' said Captain Gilbert.

'Olivia, my love, off you go to your piano and show the Captain how it should be played,' said Edward Kingston.

Obediently, but reluctantly, Olivia went to the instrument. First she played a rondo by Mozart, then some country dances. When another encore was demanded she demurred.

'That's enough until I hear the standard of Captain Gilbert's performance,' she said. 'My musical education was not as thorough as I would have wished,' she explained. Then she was furious with herself for virtually apologising for her playing.

'Then that musical education must have been very well learned,' said Captain Gilbert politely. 'I enjoyed your playing enormously.'

Common courtesy required that he could not say less, decided Olivia.

'Now for you, Captain dear,' said Mrs Kingston. 'What will you do to entertain us?'

'If Miss Kingston will kindly accompany me I'll sing for you, if you are agreeable.' He began rummaging in the canterbury for some suitable music. It was quite remarkable how much at home he had made himself in an incredibly short time.

'A book of Italian songs! Just the thing!' he exclaimed triumphantly. 'I'm familiar with this one; if you please, Miss Kingston.'

Miss Kingston did not please, but she smoothed the music and adjusted the candles in their bracketed sconces on the instrument. Wishing that Captain Gilbert would stand further away from her, she played the opening few bars.

As soon as he began to sing Olivia felt the frisson of mingled pleasure, excitement, and nameless sensations she always experienced when listening to fine music. Captain Gilbert was

far more than the 'drawing-room baritone' he had claimed. He
sang in Italian. The song was about love; she did not need her
scant knowledge of the language to tell her that much; the way
he sang, bringing extraordinary warmth and expression into the
simple melody, was enough. Olivia found memories of other
times creeping unbidden into her mind. All the joys, the happy
anticipations, the poignant feelings she had thought securely
locked away in her past were now evoked by the power of this
man's voice. She struggled against this unwanted upsurge of
emotion, but it was no use. By the end of the song her eyes were
blinded with tears and her fingers were forced to find the keys
by instinct rather than intention. It had been a masterly performance.

For quite a while after the last notes had died away no one
spoke. It was Mr Kingston who broke the silence. He could
only manage to say, 'Superb! Superb!'

Mrs Kingston, who had long since resorted to dabbing her
eyes with a handkerchief, whispered tearfully, 'So beautiful,
dear Captain . . . So very beautiful . . .'

Olivia remained staring unseeing at the music, waiting for the
mistiness to clear from her vision and the tense knot which had
gathered in her throat to disperse before she dared to speak. She
was reluctant to give praise to the American, yet her honesty
acknowledged that his voice was far beyond the ordinary.

'You've had good masters, sir,' she said at last.

'Yes, I've been fortunate.'

'You have excellent teachers of singing in Providence?' she
asked, somewhat surprised.

'Certainly. We're quite civilised there, you know. I believe a
city ordinance will soon be in force, ordering us to remove our
wigwams and begin living in proper houses!' Captain Gilbert
grinned. Then seeing Olivia's look of contempt at this attempt
of humour he went on, 'In all seriousness, Miss Kingston, yes,
I did have a particularly good teacher at home in Providence.
Also, I had the good fortune to study in Paris and Milan.'

'Did this not hinder your naval career, sir?' she asked.

There was a moment's hesitation before he replied, 'We sailors learn to snatch our opportunities when we can, Miss
Kingston . . . Can we hope to hear you play once more?'

Olivia wondered at the determined way he was changing the subject, but her parents were now watching her expectantly. She was tempted to suggest that Captain Gilbert should sing again, only, she was not certain she could bear to listen to him without her emotions overwhelming her completely.

'Is that the time?' she cried. 'Goodness, we've sat half the night away! We'll none of us be fit for anything in the morning!'

Later, in her room, she reflected that now she had another reason to regret Miles Gilbert's presence in the house. With one song he had made her feel again; with one short song he had re-awoken emotions she would have preferred to keep dormant. If she had had no other cause to disapprove of him, that one reason alone, the power of his voice, was enough for her to wish him gone.

Captain Gilbert did not go, of course. He was there at breakfast, and at every other meal, day after day. She never failed to marvel at the way in which he managed to fill the house with his presence. It was more than just his size or his untidiness—for he was prone to leave books, music, and newspapers scattered about—it was the sound of his feet running up and downstairs, his singing to himself when he thought he was alone, his laughter as he and her father shared an anecdote together. Her parents were delighted to have the house resounding with life. Olivia, however, was not so pleased. It was as if he were gradually filling the spaces in their lives with his charm and the force of his character, and she did not like it. She felt she was being crowded by him in some way she could not explain. She fancied he was conscious of her dislike of him. Sometimes, if she spoke sharply to him, he would look at her with a half-quizzical, half-bemused look in his blue-green eyes, as though he could not understand her.

I don't suppose he can comprehend it, she said to herself more than once. I dare say that women fling themselves at his feet in their droves and have done so throughout his life. Well, here is one who is immune to the attractions of Captain Miles Gilbert, and who is determined to remain so!

In contrast, Abbie's adoration of the American had increased with each passing day.

"Ark at the Cap'n' she remarked softly one rainy morning as she and Olivia were busy in the kitchen. 'Singing like an angel, 'e be.'

Olivia duly listened. Sure enough the Captain was singing softly, accompanying himself on the music-room piano.

'I don't know who gave him leave to use my music-room so freely, simply because it is too wet for him to go into town,' she snapped.

"E don't 'urt none. You idn't using un!' said the maid. 'Push the door ajar, so's us can 'ear 'im proper.'

'You are besotted with the man!' Olivia said. Nevertheless, she pushed the kitchen door open, the better to hear him sing.

'Maybe I is and maybe I idn't. What's besotted mean, anyway?'

'It is what you feel for Captain Gilbert,' said Olivia unable to suppress a grin.

'In that case, 'tis a word your Ma wouldn't approve of you knowing!' Abbie chuckled wickedly then heaved a dramatic sigh. "E'm beautiful, there's no doubt about it... 'E's one body's work, mind. 'E needs someone following after to clear up behind 'im. I told 'im. "Cap'n, my 'andsome," I says to 'im as I was cleaning 'is room, "if you'm going to sling your drawers on the floor in such a way when you'm finished with 'em they'm going to 'ave to lie where they falls. My back idn't up to all that bending down".'

'Abbie! I don't think Captain Gilbert's undergarments are a fitting subject for conversation!'

'Why not? 'E wasn't in 'em at the time!' Abbie's leer became positively lecherous.

'You are incorrigible! And don't ask what that means, I pray, else we'll get nothing done!'

Abbie did have a point about the Captain's untidiness, Olivia decided. Most naval men she knew were neatness personified. Even her scapegrace of a young brother had gone into the Royal Navy a mischievous schoolboy and returned a year later honed by discipline and experience into a neat, precise young man. The transformation had been staggering enough to prompt Abbie into giving him the singular honour of referring to him as Master Charlie, instead of her usual expletives of 'You young varmint!' or 'You little Turk!'. Olivia wondered at the difference between her brother and Captain Gilbert. She could not imagine that conditions in the two navies would be so dissimilar.

She had not time to dwell upon the Captain's shortcomings; the time had come round yet again for Maria Rowden's weekly lesson. The thud of the front door betrayed that, in spite of the rain, the Captain had left the house. Olivia was relieved. It meant that yet again an encounter between him and Mrs Rowden had been avoided.

Maria's mother, though she still insisted on shifting the onus onto Mr Rowden, had not made up her mind about Maria's lessons. The hour passed without the subject being resolved.

'Mr Rowden is pondering on the matter very carefully,' Mrs Rowden announced. 'He has his doubts! Serious doubts! If you knew the persuading I had to do, to get him to let Maria have her lesson today, well you wouldn't believe it, Miss Kingston, you really would not!'

'I got him round though, didn't I, Ma?' Maria beamed proudly. 'I showed him how good I can play. I played until Ma's china dog was shook right off the mantelpiece, didn't I, Ma?'

'That you did, my pet!' agreed her mother proudly. 'And now we must hope your Pa will let you go on with your lessons, so's you can learn to play even better.'

Olivia tried not to smile at Maria's method of proving her musical ability. Nor did she allow herself to hope that the child would stay with her as a pupil; she knew from past experience that the Rowdens were not given to hasty decisions.

Any day which began with Maria's music lesson was bound to be more than usually fatiguing, and by bedtime Olivia felt worn out. As was her custom, after they had bidden Captain Gilbert good night, she saw to it that her father took his medicine before he retired. Then she helped her mother to get him into bed. Afterwards she set about checking the doors and windows, and damping down the fires. She was doing a final tidying of the drawing-room hearth when she heard a footstep behind her. Swiftly she turned round and found herself confronting the Captain.

'Don't worry, Miss Kingston, I won't make the same mistake again,' he said with a grin. 'You can lower your weapon.'

She realised she was wielding the hearth-brush in a threatening manner. Feeling rather foolish, she put it down.

'Is there something you need, sir?' she asked coldly. 'I thought you'd gone to bed.'

'Have you seen the book I was reading? I put it somewhere and now I can't find it.'

'Is this it?' She handed him a leather-bound volume she had already retrieved from under a chair. 'You should take greater care of your things, sir,' she reproved him.

'It is not mine. A fellow I met in town loaned it to me. And let me save you the bother of saying the words that I'm sure are hovering on your lips—I should take even greater care of someone else's possessions than I do my own. There, is that not right?'

'If you know the lesson so well I wonder you don't practise it, sir.'

'I do try... But inanimate objects seem to develop a life of their own once they are in my care.'

'So I've noticed. If you are intending to read in your room can I repeat my warning: please make sure you extinguish your candle before you retire. A candle-flame is one object I would prefer to remain inanimate, if possible.'

'I won't forget, you have my word on it.' He began to make for the door then changed his mind. 'You do not like having me in your house, do you, Miss Kingston?' he said, turning to face her once more.

'It isn't my house,' she replied, startled by the abruptness of his question. 'I have no control here.'

'Yet it is Miss Kingston who attends to everything, I notice. Miss Kingston who orders the food, sees to the house, pays the bills. From first thing in the morning until last thing at night, any crisis, from the cat being sick to a fall of soot from the kitchen chimney, it is you who copes, yet you say you are not in control.'

'Abbie is getting too old; we are not in a position to employ another servant; and my mother... my mother wasn't brought up to such tasks.'

'Nor, I fancy, were you. It doesn't prevent you from performing them most efficiently.'

'I had no alternative but to learn, sir. Now, if you please, I've had a most wearying day. Can we end this conversation?'

'You haven't answered my question. Ah, I see you looking at me most disapprovingly. I dare say that an Englishman wouldn't have approached the subject in such a forthright manner. I'm not an Englishman; in my country we are much more direct. I ask again. You don't like having me live here, do you?'

'In that case, I'll give you a direct answer. No.'

'Why not?'

'You can ask that? You have affirmed yourself that you are American—as if I could forget! You are an enemy and a prisoner of war.'

'Those are not your only reasons, are they?'

'Dear heaven, sir! How many more reasons do you need?'

'I recognise that my nationality and situation are against me in your eyes, yet I fancy that if I were suddenly to become English you would dislike me just as much. I would like to know why.'

They were standing close together now, facing one another in the darkened room. Only one candle was still lit. Its solitary gleam fell upon the Captain's face, illuminating the irregular lines, emphasising the shadows, and turning his red-gold hair to amber. Olivia did not want to remain there with him. She knew a confrontation would be foolish. It could only lead to friction in the household.

Then her dislike of him took the upper hand. 'You are right, sir. Other considerations apart, I don't like you as a man.'

'May I know why? I've tried my utmost to be agreeable.'

'Precisely. You are too agreeable!'

'Surely such a thing is not possible?' He seemed taken aback.

'I beg to differ! It is possible. You men who are charming know not the harm you do. All you are interested in is getting your own way, and you care not who gets hurt in the process. I know your type; you are dangerous and destructive as well as totally untrustworthy. I don't like you for what you are and who you are. I don't like the way you've insinuated yourself into our lives, and would have us at your beck and call. There! Now you know how you stand! I don't approve at all of hav-

ing you here, but as I have no say in the matter I must tolerate
you. And a hard task it is too!'

He took a step back, clearly startled by the vehemence of her
opinion.

In truth, Olivia was a little shaken herself. She had not meant
to be so stinging in her remarks, but once she had started she
had found it impossible to stop.

'I deeply regret that you feel this way,' he said quietly. 'Of
course, first thing tomorrow I'll apply to the agent to find me
somewhere else to lodge.'

'No,' she said wearily. 'That won't be necessary. My father
enjoys your company so much, as does my mother... My feelings are unimportant.' She did not add that they needed his
rent.

'If you are sure...? Your concern for your parents does you
credit. I think I can guess the reasons for your emotions. Obviously I won't speak of it for delicacy's sake, but pray be assured that I understand. If, at some time, you've been
disappointed by someone of my sex it is only natural—'

'Oh, how typical!' snapped Olivia. 'A woman can't dislike
a man without the blame being laid at the door of a failed love-
affair. I dare say you find it hard to understand that I just don't
like you! Probably you have been able to charm every woman
who has come your way, from the midwife at your birth on-
wards. Now you must accept that there are exceptions; and I
am one. You can charm away to your heart's content and you'll
find I won't shift.'

'Miss Kingston, I promise you—'

'Don't begin by vowing you have no evil designs on my vir-
tue, sir,' said Olivia ominously. 'Never for one moment did I
think you had. That is another misconception prevalent among
your sex. Now, if you will take your book and return to your
room I would be grateful. I wish to extinguish this last candle
myself,' she placed careful emphasis on the last word, 'Then go
to bed.'

'As you wish, of course, Miss Kingston' He spoke softly. 'I
bid you good night.'

Despite his words he did not move. He remained looking at
her, his expression suddenly grim. 'You'll change your opinion of me, I'm determined you will! Before I'm through you'll

like me, no matter what you say!' He spoke with the low urgency of someone throwing down a challenge.

It was a challenge Olivia was more than willing to take up.

'You can try,' she said contemptuously. 'Much good will it do you.'

'We will see. The outcome should prove interesting.' His eyes glinted in the light of the solitary candle, whether with anger or excitement she could not tell.

'Oh, go to bed!' she exclaimed, too tired to cope with this man who had so suddenly invaded her life.

When he had gone, Olivia took one slow look about the place, extinguished the candle, after lighting a taper, and went to her room. Once there she sank onto a chair in front of the mirror, suddenly wide awake. Thoughts of sleep had been banished by the confrontation with the Captain. Slowly she removed the combs from her hair, letting it tumble onto her shoulders as she had done when she was a girl. In the soft candle-light she did not look so different from that happy, carefree creature. For the first time in an age she let herself dwell upon all she had lost, until she found herself on the very brink of weeping. The first tear that trickled down her cheek was rubbed brusquely away, along with her self-pity. This was all Miles Gilbert's fault, this reawakening of her past misery, and she refused to tolerate it! Let him do what he pleased! She would never like him! No, not in a million years!

CHAPTER THREE

AFTER her outburst Olivia was wary of the Captain. She was constantly on her guard against ways in which he might try to erode her dislike of him. To her relief he did not bombard her with compliments, or constantly pay her attention, or any of the other obvious ploys she had feared. Instead he treated her with cool civility, paying more attention to her parents than he did to her. Only in the evenings did she have any real contact with him, as she accompanied him on the piano when he sang or when they played duets together. If she could she would have avoided even this association with him.

Outside the house Captain Gilbert's sphere of acquaintances seemed to grow at a prodigious rate. This made itself apparent when he escorted Olivia and her mother to church at St Saviour's on Sundays. The first time he went with them he was an object of curiosity, the second time he seemed at least on nodding acquaintance with a fair number of people, and on the third he was hailed amicably by name on all sides.

'I declare he appeared to know half the congregation!' Olivia complained to Abbie later. 'So many folk wished a word with him afterwards I thought we'd never get away.'

'And most of they was women, I bet,' said Abbie.

'They were, certainly. With my own ears I heard Mrs Giles invite him to tea.'

'The widow as lives up Slippery Causeway? He'll get more'n tea and muffins there.'

'Abbie, don't be coarse!'

'You shouldn't know as I *is* being coarse! The Widow Giles, you say? Mebbe that's why he bought a new shirt.'

'A new shirt? Surely not. I don't think he has any money. He can't have received any from home yet.'

''E bought a new shirt, all the same, along with two neck-cloths, two pairs of drawers, and four pairs of stockings. The parcel was delivered from Sheppard's yesterday.'

'And how do you know what was in it?'

''Cos I was the one as put the things away. Can you see the Captain putting things tidy in 'is closet? If 'e did it'd be the fust time since 'e set foot in this 'ouse.'

'Then, how did he pay for them? Sheppard's won't give credit to any of the prisoners.'

'Mebbe 'e took tea with Miss Sheppard an' all.' The maid grinned wickedly.

'Abbie!'

In spite of her protest Olivia could not help wondering if Abbie might not be near the truth. Now she thought of it Captain Gilbert's social life did not seem curtailed by poverty, and it was not unknown for a personable man to be able to extract money from infatuated women. The whole idea made her stomach turn with disgust and she refused to dwell on it any longer.

She observed the Captain carefully during the next few days. In that time she never heard him once complain he was impecunious or show by any means that lack of money was inconveniencing him.

Captain Gilbert's financial affairs were destined to be swept from her mind most dramatically. It happened one morning as she was helping her father settle in his favourite place at the window. She removed the cover from the telescope and, as usual, manoeuvred the spyglass to be within convenient reach. As she was placing the other things he needed by his side—his spectacles, his book, a carafe of cordial—he exclaimed suddenly, 'By George, that's odd!'

'What is, Papa?'

'There's a deuced lot of smoke coming from somewhere up-river. Here, take a turn and see what you think.'

Olivia looked through the telescope and, true enough, a thick column of smoke was rising from just beyond the town.

'Someone burning rubbish?' she suggested. 'Probably one of the yards on Coombe Mud. Or it could be a little further up-river than that.'

'That's a deal of fire for rubbish, in my opinion.' Her father took up his position at the telescope again. 'Oh, hullo! I can see flames! It's Newman's Shipyard, you mark my word!'

As she looked Olivia was conscious of running feet in the streets below; and on the river, before her gaze, a flotilla of small boats began to head upstream towards the scene of the conflagration.

'Whatever is going on, husband?' demanded Mrs Kingston, coming into the room. 'There is such a bustle going on outside. What can be the matter?'

Before either Edward Kingston or Olivia could reply Captain Gilbert came up the stairs.

'You are back early, Captain. You haven't been gone more than twenty minutes,' remarked Mr Kingston.

'I'm confined to barracks, sir, by order of Admiral Ranscombe himself—not that this house is like any barracks I have ever heard of.'

'But why, Captain, dear? Did you say something to offend him?' asked Mrs Kingston.

''No, ma'am.' The American smiled. 'I'm not the only one to be ordered off the streets of Dartmouth. All prisoners of war have been commanded to return to their billets and remain there until further orders. Even the working parties building the walls have had to return.'

'But why?' Olivia asked.

'There are so many rumours flying about it is difficult to choose the most probable. But since a new frigate has been destroyed by fire, my guess is that the authorities suspect sabotage.'

'Sabotage? You mean one of Bonaparte's agents has been at work in Dartmouth?' cried Mrs Kingston.

'There is no need to alarm yourself, ma'am. These are only rumours, I'm sure they will come to naught, and everything will be back to normal in no time.'

The Captain was right. By the afternoon the curfew on him and his fellow prisoners had been lifted, and life in Dartmouth resumed its ordinary leisurely pace. Just the same, the burning of the frigate had been a fact, and though there was no definite proof, rumours of sabotage continued to circulate round the town for a long time.

The one morning in the week when Olivia never accepted pupils was Friday, market-day. She quite enjoyed wandering through the stalls set up by the countrywomen who came in from the outlying villages such as Dittisham and Blackawton. The displays of fresh eggs, butter, cheese, and thick clotted cream were tempting. Some of the items threatened to stretch her slender purse, but she had grown adept at finding the best bargains. She regarded it as a challenge to buy as much and as well as possible for the few coins at her disposal.

On this particular Friday Dartmouth still hummed with excitement. Sightings of French spies were reported from locations as varied as the top of St Saviour's tower and the bar parlour of the Ship In Dock.

In spite of this Olivia went about her marketing with determination. The basket soon began to weigh heavy with purchases and she was forced to put it down to flex her weary arms for a moment. As she lifted it again its sudden lightness startled her, until she realised that someone else was grasping the handle.

'Allow me,' said a familiar voice.

'There is no need, Captain Gilbert. I'm quite capable of carrying it, thank you,' she said.

'I'm the more capable of the two of us.' He did not let go. 'You can't carry this weight back to South Town. It's far too much.'

'It's no more than I carry every week.' Olivia maintained her grasp.

'Then be thankful that such toil is unnecessary on this occasion.'

'I haven't finished my shopping.'

'In that case, I will accompany you. I've no objection to following behind as your beast of burden.'

'Sir, you can't be seen in uniform carrying fruit and vegetables. It is too undignified.' She looked pointedly at the bundle of early rhubarb which protruded from the top of the basket.

'A very dignified plant is rhubarb. And necessary!' If anything his grip tightened.

Olivia was conscious that they were attracting attention, each refusing to let go like a pair of overgrown children. Nevertheless, she was determined not to give in.

'Are we playing a game, Miss Kingston?' asked Captain
Gilbert hopefully. 'I like games. On this occasion, however, I
fear tug-of-war would prove a very unequal contest. The advantages are on my side. And as for the outcome—now that
would prove undignified!'

Knowing that she was defeated Olivia scowled ungratefully.
'Have it your own way, sir!' she snapped, letting go.

'I always do get my own way. You told me so not long since.
I only wanted to prove the truth of your words.'

'Oh!' Olivia ground her teeth with annoyance. She almost
turned on him to give him a scolding. Then she remembered
they were in a public place, and restrained herself. She had to
be content with setting off at a hurried pace through the crowd,
hoping he would have difficulty in following her. Her luck was
out. When she stopped before a display of poultry he was still
behind her. While she picked out a plump capon he chatted
amicably with the farmwife behind the stall, so amicably that
when Olivia made her choice the countrywoman threw in half
a dozen fresh brown eggs free of charge.

'You should bring me more often, I'm a good influence,' said
the Captain, as they walked away, the woman's parting cry 'See
you next week, zur' still ringing in their ears.

'I wasn't aware I had brought you here in the first place,' she
retorted. 'And as for being a good influence... I doubt that very
much.'

'You are too hard on me, ma'am,' he said cheerfully. 'Now,
where do we go next?'

Olivia longed to torment him. She toyed with the idea of
embarrassing him by trailing him through the ladies' drapers.
Upon consideration she abandoned the idea. She decided it was
way beyond her capabilities to make Captain Gilbert blush at
anything.

'Home!' she said.

The crush was beginning to thin. Other people were making
their way homewards and the country folk were packing up and
heading for the inns and the eating-houses before making the
journey home. It was, therefore, impossible for Olivia to avoid
being seen by Mrs Rowden as the latter emerged from the pas-
trycook's; it was impossible for the Captain also to avoid being seen by that lady. The meeting Olivia had been dreading was

about to happen. She steeled herself to confront the rustling indignation that was Mrs Rowden in an ill humour.

There was no indignation, no ill humour, no chilling words. To her astonishment Mrs Rowden coloured, looked pleasantly agitated, and positively simpered.

'Captain Gilbert, this is a delight to see you,' she said, adding almost as an afterthought, 'And you too, of course, Miss Kingston.'

'You two have met?' asked Olivia, bewildered.

'Indeed we have met. I had the pleasure of making the acquaintance of Mrs Rowden some days ago, and her delightful little girl. How is dear Maria, ma'am?' the Captain asked solicitously.

'Extremely well, thanks to you Captain.'

Olivia could not believe it. Mrs Rowden's eyelashes were fluttering seductively.

'Thanks to the Captain?' she repeated, thunderstruck.

'Certainly, and it's no use trying to deny it, Captain Gilbert! It was last week . . . or was it the week before? The day of Maria's lesson, when it came on to rain in torrents. I was most concerned for my girl, you know how delicate she is. Any cold on her chest would be with her till midsummer; I was dreading her getting soaked. Then just as we were leaving your house we met the Captain on the doorstep. He insisted on escorting us home with his umbrella. Every step of the way he came in all that wet and wouldn't so much as take a glass of elderberry wine as a reward.'

'The pleasure of your company was reward enough, ma'am,' said the American.

'Oh Captain! Mrs Rowden's eyelashes resumed their fluttering. 'Now, I fear, I must tear myself away and see to Mr Rowden's meal. It must be served up on the dot of noon, he's quite the tyrant about it. Maria will, of course, be along for her lesson as usual next week.'

'Goodbye, Mrs Rowden, and thank you,' Olivia said weakly. She did not know which she believed the least, a delicate Maria, a tyrannical Mr Rowden, or a simpering Mrs Rowden. Then she knew! It was Captain Gilbert putting himself out to be agreeable to her pupils. That beggared belief!

'Why did you do it?' she demanded.

'Do what?'

'Fawn on the Rowdens.'

'Ah, you accuse me of licking their boots, eh? Most appropriate since I understand Mr Rowden is a bootmaker.'

'Captain Gilbert, stop your tomfoolery and give me a straight answer.'

'As you honoured me the other night by giving me a straight answer I can do no less than be honest with you. I have become conscious that my presence in your house might have repercussions which would affect you. It occurred to me that if I had children I would be doubtful about letting them take lessons in a house where an enemy prisoner was lodged. I appreciate the hospitality and the kindness shown to me by the Kingston family far too much to wish to injure them how ever inadvertently. Being charming to the Rowdens is a small price to pay. As you say yourself, being charming is something at which I excel.'

Olivia did not know what to say. She wished he had not thrown her words back at her in such a way. There had been no spite in his remark, but it made her feel guilty. Never for one moment had she suspected he appreciated her circumstances quite so clearly. His often frivolous manner gave no hint that he was capable of such perception. Nor that he would be willing to redress any harm his presence might cause. 'I can only thank you, sir,' she said. 'I confess that to lose Maria—to lose any of my pupils—would be a hardship.'

'I thought so.' The Captain nodded his head with satisfaction.

They walked along in silence for a while, the Captain casually swinging the basket, to the detriment of the eggs. It had been a long time since Olivia had had a personable man walking with her for any distance. She had forgotten the sense of security a tall, reassuring figure by her side could provoke. As he escorted her along Higher Street, steering her through the hazards of the narrow road, she felt almost cherished. She could not remember the last time anyone had been so protective towards her. It was a most pleasurable sensation. Too pleasurable! This was Miles Gilbert towering above her. She came to her senses sharply.

Oh, how careful she would have to be! In a moment of weakness she had almost let his insidious charm weaken her resolve—and that would never do. Annoyance put a fresh spring in her step.

'I didn't know you had an umbrella,' she said accusingly, for the sake of saying something.

'Umbrella? Oh no, nor had I until that very day.'

'You bought it in Dartmouth?' A foolish question. Where else could he have bought it?

'I didn't buy it at all. I won it.'

'Won it? You are a gambler? You played cards for an umbrella!'

'Certainly not . . . ! Billiards!'

'Billiards?'

'It is quite charming the way you keep repeating everything I say, Miss Kingston. But I must deny that I'm a gambler. I prefer to consider I won the umbrella by skill. My opponent happened to be a little short of the ready. He had an umbrella—it was raining hard—we came to an amicable arrangement.'

'Then you are a gambler!'

'Because a wager was involved? Oh no! I'm a good enough billiards player to be certain of the outcome most times.'

'Then you do play for money?' She could not keep the disapproval out of her voice.

'Of course. I have no other source of income at the moment. What would you have me do? Sing at street corners, my collecting-cup in my hand?'

'It might be more honest.'

'What could be more honourable than two opponents facing each other across a billiard-table? There are many worse ways of making a living.'

So there were. Extracting money from gullible women, for one . . . All the same, it was satisfying to discover that he was a gambler and a profligate. It was what she would have expected of him.

'And where do you practise this honourable occupation of yours?' she asked. 'I didn't know there was a public billiard-room in town.'

'I don't think there is. At least, I've not found one. So far I
have played only in gentlemen's houses; at Mr Holdsworth's,
Mr Seale's, Mr Hunt's. Very respectable people.'

Respectable! Olivia was speechless. He had just named the
three wealthiest, most powerful men in the town. So, his mysterious income was accounted for and his occupation, when
away from the house, explained.

In the following days his engagement calendar must have
grown increasingly full, he seemed forever dashing to some
appointment or other. However, on one of Olivia's rare free
afternoons he happened to be at home too.

The pupils Olivia usually taught at that time had developed
measles, and so she decided to spend her free time reading. Her
mother was sewing, and at the other side of the cosy hearth the
Captain and her father were enjoying a game of chess. It was
an extraordinarily intimate scene. Captain Gilbert seemed to fit
into the family with consummate ease. She tried to resent him
for it, but it was so enjoyable there by the fire, and a brief hour
of leisure such a rare luxury she could not bring herself to
summon up the energy.

A knocking at the street door interrupted the peaceful crackle
of the logs and the clatter of chess pieces, then came the sound
of a familiar female voice. Peg Jenkins, Charlotte Kingston's
closest friend, had arrived. They heard her declare, 'Do not
bother, Abbie. We will announce ourselves.'

There followed the thud of feet coming up the stairs and a
brief rap at the drawing-room door. Mrs Jenkins entered, a
fashionably dressed dark-haired man in her wake.

'How delightfully domestic you all look,' declared Mrs Jenkins. 'It seems a shame to spoil your tranquillity.'

'When has your presence ever spoiled anything, ma'am?'
replied Edward Kingston.

'Oh, Mr Kingston, you are ever the courtier.' Peg Jenkins's
plump face beamed a porcelain smile far whiter than nature had
ever intended, and her bonnet bobbed appreciatively.

The wealthy widow of a prosperous linen draper, her air of
cheerful vulgarity excluded her from the higher levels of society. In their household, though, she was always welcome, for
she was good-hearted and generous to a fault. It had been Mrs
Jenkins who had bought Olivia's precious piano when the

Kingstons' home was sold up, only to return it to Olivia on permanent loan. After Mr Kingston's illness, she had sought out another piano for the downstairs music-room, her excuse being 'You can't have your pupils up in the drawing-room disturbing your poor Papa, now can you, dear?' There had been innumerable other kindnesses, always done with genuine goodness of heart and a plausible excuse.

Now, Peg Jenkins's bonnet was bobbing with top-heavy enthusiasm.

'See, I have brought you another visitor. A proper one, for I am of no account. I met Mr Dunsford in town and he kindly escorted me here. He was all for turning away at the door but I insisted. "No, Mr Dunsford," I said, "I am sure my dear friends will be pleased to meet you, for you and Mr Kingston will have so much in common, you being in shipping."'

Olivia knew Joseph Dunsford by sight and reputation. He had come to Dartmouth about two years previously—some said from London, others from Portsmouth—to set up a shipping business. He seemed to be flourishing too, for his vessels sailed in and out of the Dart frequently. She had often seen the stocky figure of the man himself walking about the town. They had never met, though, because the Kingstons were no longer part of Dartmouth society.

'The *Morning Star* is yours, I believe, sir?' said Edward Kingston after the introductions had been made and the tea-tray brought. 'A splendid vessel, she takes the tide like a bird.'

'Yes, she is one of my ships, along with the *Mary* and the *Sea Vixen*.' Mr Dunsford spoke in a loud, decisive voice, as though accustomed to giving orders. Olivia wondered if he ever commanded any of his own vessels. His next words confirmed her suspicions. 'In fact, I am taking the *Sea Vixen* out myself tomorrow.'

'Then you will have a fairly uncomfortable trip. She rolls a bit when the wind is easterly, does she not?' said Mr Kingston.

'She does indeed. I see you know your ships, sir.' Joseph Dunsford turned to Miles Gilbert. 'And what vessels did you command, Captain?'

Olivia sensed a brief hesitation before the American spoke.

'I've been on several vessels in my time, Mr Dunsford. In fact, I was on my way to a new command when we had our little encounter with the Royal Navy and—'

'Yes, this wretched war!' broke in Mrs Kingston. Olivia had a distinct feeling the Captain heaved a brief sigh of relief at the interruption. 'If it is not the fighting then it is the smuggling, spoiling plans, taking away honest trade from people. I hope that you are not troubled by either the war or the smugglers, Mr Dunsford?'

'I've been fortunate not to have encountered the French, ma'am. My skippers have explicit instructions to sail as close inshore as safety will allow. As for smugglers, my chief cargo is coal, and I don't think they have an interest in that commodity.' He spoke slowly as if he were considering each word carefully.

'And what of you, Captain Gilbert?' Peg Jenkins had been regarding the American with interest ever since she had come in. 'I have long been eager to meet you. Where are you from?'

'From Providence, Rhode Island, ma'am.' The Captain's eyes sparkled with mischief. And Olivia knew he had been well aware of the lady's interested gaze.

'And is it a large place, Providence?'

'Sizeable, ma'am, and prosperous.'

'And your family what do they do in this sizeable, prosperous place?'

'My father controls his estates and my mother controls my father.'

'You are not married, I believe, Captain?' said Mrs Jenkins blithely going beyond the bounds of polite curiosity. 'Does that mean you haven't found a young lady who pleases you?'

'No, on the contrary, Mrs Jenkins, ma'am. I have found so many! I can't bear to choose one and know the rest are denied me.' His gaze was bold and teasing as he smiled at her.

Olivia saw Mrs Jenkins flush, dimple, and fall completely beneath the American's spell. Really, no woman was safe from him!

'Do you find Dartmouth to your liking?' Olivia asked Mr Dunsford, who had seated himself next to her.

'I do indeed. An excellent harbour, though tricky at times. I have hopes of increasing the extent of my wharves soon, so I will have every facility I require.'

'You trade in coal, you say?'

'Mainly. I also handle general cargo. That is why I am going to Plymouth. It should be a good voyage. I look forward to it.'

'You find it irksome being in your counting-house?'

He regarded her with surprise. 'The counting-house is a vital part of my business, Miss Kingston. How can I find it irksome?'

'You were anticipating your trip to Plymouth so much I thought, perhaps, you preferred to be on the open sea.'

'Oh!' A look of understanding crossed his face. 'No, it is no pleasure cruise I embark upon. I go because I gain more trade that way. It pays to get out and about. You would be surprised how much business I have picked up by frequenting the right coffee-houses, or by dining with acquaintances in chop-houses and such.'

'You sound most industrious. I wonder you find any time to go into society.'

'I confess I'm not much of a one for doing the social round in the ordinary way, Miss Kingston. Routs and balls and such are not for me.' He paused. 'Now that I find how much society here in Dartmouth has improved, however, I think I may reconsider my views.'

Olivia was surprised by the heavy-handed compliment. He did not strike her as a man to whom flattery came naturally. He had been much more at ease when discussing his business. Before she could think of a reply he spoke again.

'I understand you are very accomplished, Miss Kingston. You are proficient in many instruments?'

'I play only two, the pianoforte and the guitar.'

'That is most interesting. I am very fond of music.'

'You are?' Olivia brightened. 'Do you have a piece of music which is your particular favourite?'

He seemed nonplussed by the question. '"The Mallow Fling" is a jolly tune,' he said at length.

So, Mr Dunsford was not as musical as he had indicated!

The hilarity of the others drew her attention. They were laughing uproariously at something Captain Gilbert had just said. Olivia stifled a yawn. Mr Dunsford seemed a very worthy man, but no one could accuse him of being amusing.

'You get your coal mainly from South Wales, I presume, sir,' Edward Kingston addressed his guest.

'I do, yes.'

Mr Kingston shook his head gravely. 'That's a long, hazardous journey round the Lizard. It's a pity there is not a canal from the north to the south of the county. The distance between the two channels, the Bristol and the English, is nothing compared with sailing right around the Peninsula.'

'My thoughts exactly, sir! I have been spending much energy of late on that very subject.' For the first time Joseph Dunsford looked really animated, and his rather solid features brightened. 'A canal should be dug right across Devon . . . ! I fancy that would be the answer.'

'Surely it would be an exceedingly expensive venture?' pointed out Captain Gilbert. 'You would have the hills of Exmoor to contend with, and the great granite mass of Dartmoor.'

Joseph Dunsford looked across at the American. 'You seem well informed about the county of Devon, sir.'

'Not really,' confessed the Captain. 'The printseller in the Butterwalk has an excellently engraved map of the county in his window. I happened to scrutinise it the other day, to pass the time. I do have a fleeting acquaintance with Dartmoor, however, round its southern fringes on my way from Plymouth to here. Also, I have acquaintances whose knowledge of the moor is uncomfortably extensive.'

This joking reference to the American's imprisonment failed to raise even the glimmer of a smile on Dunsford's face. He merely said, 'Ah, yes. Quite so.' There was an odd note of satisfaction in his voice, and Olivia wondered what had so pleased him.

'I fear we must depart.' Mrs Jenkins replaced her teacup on the table. 'We have interrupted you quite long enough. Besides, my *coiffeur* is due to call on me within the hour, and if I am late it throws him into a fit of the sulks.'

'This has been a delightful interlude.' Joseph Dunsford rose too. 'I thank you for your hospitality.'

'Yes, it has been delightful, has it not?' cried Mrs Kingston. 'We do enjoy company, and we get so little these days.'

'Why do I not give a supper for us all?' exclaimed Mrs Jenkins. 'Perhaps one or two others, but not a great crush. We could have a delightful time and— Oh, I forgot. You wouldn't be able to come, would you, dear Mr Kingston? Nor you, Captain?'

'I fear I have to be indoors by five of the clock, like a good boy,' said the Captain. 'But please don't let consideration for me spoil your plans. Mr Kingston and I can keep each other company and amuse ourselves tolerably.'

'But it wouldn't be any fun without you both!' Peg Jenkins protested.

'I know! Why do *we* not give the supper here?' cried Mrs Kingston. 'We have not entertained properly since I do not know when, and it would solve our problem. We could all be together. Maybe Admiral and Mrs Ranscombe would join us. Is it not a capital idea?'

Everyone else exclaimed with approval. But Olivia tempered her enthusiasm with misgivings. Anxiously she considered what fruits would be in season, what meats would be available—and if the Kingston purse would stretch to feed eight. She need not have worried; beneath Mrs Jenkins's ostentatious exterior there lurked a practical soul.

'The perfect solution!' Peg declared. 'You provide the venue and I will provide the food. No, do not argue! I insist, as I put the idea into everyone's heads. My cook can come here and take charge of everything. You will have no worries.'

'We had best give Abbie the night off,' smiled Olivia. 'If she has to share the kitchen with your Sukie I can see the result resembling one of the Duke of Wellington's smaller but more vigorous battles.'

'How true, my dear!' chuckled Mrs Jenkins. 'Then, it is agreed?'

'It is, with many thanks.'

'Only if we can supply the wine,' said Edward Kingston. 'I still have a few decent bottles down in the cellar saved from the wreck. I dare say Captain Gilbert will oblige and go down and fetch them.'

'If that is my only contribution to the evening then I am faring very well,' smiled Miles Gilbert.

'No, it is not. You shall be required to sing and Olivia must play. Is that not so, Peg? A supper-party! I declare that I am quite excited already.' Charlotte Kingston clasped her hands in happy anticipation.

'Then we'll arrange the date as soon as Mr Dunsford gets back from Plymouth. You will accept our invitation, I hope, Mr Dunsford?' Peg Jenkins sounded as though she would brook no refusal.

'Indeed I will. Most gratefully. How could I miss the opportunity of hearing Miss Kingston play?' Joseph Dunsford bowed over Olivia's hand.

A little embarrassed, she escorted the guests downstairs.

'My many thanks for your suggestion, Mrs Jenkins,' she said at the door. 'Did you see the expression on my parents' faces? This supper-party will give them so much enjoyment.'

'It's to be hoped you will gain enjoyment from it also, Olivia. You work too hard. It is time you had some amusement.'

'Meeting you has been a great pleasure, Miss Kingston,' said Joseph Dunsford as he followed Mrs Jenkins into the street. 'I look forward very much to our next meeting. I hope it is soon.'

Olivia closed the door behind them and went upstairs thoughtfully. She was not certain she enjoyed Mr Dunsford's style of compliment. He lacked the casual ease with which Miles Gilbert would have delivered the same words. But then, she observed, Captain Gilbert had undoubtedly had considerable practice. When she returned to the drawing-room she was somewhat disconcerted when everyone looked at her speculatively.

'Well, Olivia, my love, I think you have made a conquest,' said her father.

'Whatever can you mean?' she asked.

'Why, Mr Dunsford. He paid most particular attention to you, do you not think?'

'No, I do not, Papa,' she laughed. 'Since we were sitting side by side the poor man could not, in all conscience, ignore me. He does not deserve to be labelled my suitor just for that.'

'How can you say that?' protested Mrs Kingston. 'Mr Dunsford was attentive quite above the ordinary. Do you not agree, Captain?'

Olivia was indignant that Miles Gilbert should be asked to give an opinion on something which was none of his business. She waited for him to demur, on the grounds that the subject was too personal a matter for his comment. To her annoyance he leaned back comfortably in his chair, stretched out his long legs and said, 'I can see I must be exceedingly impolite to disagree with one lady in order to agree with the other. I am bound to side with you, Mr and Mrs Kingston. I think Mr Dunsford showed a particular interest in Miss Kingston. I wouldn't be surprised if he found some excuse to call again before the supper-party. In fact, I would put good money on it...' Here he caught Olivia's furious glance and added hastily, 'If I were a gambling man, of course.'

'I suppose he is very eligible,' said Mrs Kingston cautiously. 'He is a bachelor with a good income. And I am sure he is respectable, though I know nothing of his family.'

'Certainly he is respectable! Peg Jenkins would never have him in tow if he were not!' insisted Mr Kingston. 'And as for his income, I hear that those wharves he is extending are going to be large indeed. Admiral Ranscombe reckons he must be thinking of increasing his fleet to need so many extra berths.'

'I wonder how old he is?' Charlotte Kingston mused.

'About thirty, I would say.'

'The perfect age for a man. A time when his faculties and powers are at their peak. The prime of life!' Captain Gilbert said complacently.

'I gather from the self-satisfaction with which you speak that you and Mr Dunsford must be of an age, sir,' said Olivia.

'My age is a most delicate subject, Miss Kingston. I must beg of you to speak of something else or you will embarrass me quite beyond bearing.'

Olivia gave a derisory smile. 'I doubt that such a thing is possible, sir,' she said. 'And before you play the modest violet with too much conviction I must beg you to remember you have just been discussing Mr Dunsford's eligibility as my suitor. If that isn't a delicate subject then I do not know what is.'

'You are quite right. I do beg your pardon. I was totally out of order. I swear that in future I'll never express an opinion on the subject no matter how I'm pressed.'

'We did ask the Captain's views on the matter. It is not nice of you to be so hard on him, my love,' Mrs Kingston reprimanded her.

Olivia decided it was silly to spoil an otherwise excellent day by standing on her dignity.

'Very well, we agree a truce,' she said. 'I'll make no further references to Captain Gilbert's age if he will desist from commenting upon my possible—or impossible—suitors.'

'It's a bargain. You are most generous, Miss Kingston.'

Miles Gilbert grinned lazily at her from the comfort of his chair. Every line of him was relaxed, his long limbs sprawled with easy grace in front of the fire; he looked perfectly at home and contented reclining thus. She half expected him to purr like a drowsy lion she had once seen in a travelling menagerie.

She could understand how other women found him so attractive, women who had not her perception of his true character. With some alarm, she found that her recollections of the time before he had arrived in their household were dim. He had merged with her family so easily and so completely he seemed always to have lived with them. Yet, when she mentally calculated the actual time since he had arrived, she was shaken to find that it was no more than five or six weeks. She wondered what havoc he would have wreaked among the female population by the time he had lived in Dartmouth for a year or two. Then she allowed herself a complacent smile. No matter what tricks and wiles he tried on her she would never succumb to the charms of Captain Miles Gilbert.

CHAPTER FOUR

THE air was crisp with frost when Olivia set out from the house next morning. She sniffed with pleasure at the salt-laden breeze which carried with it also the tang of tar and freshly-cut timber from the small boatyards at the water's edge. Trading wherries and fishing boats jostled to take the wind, as they tacked back and forth across the river, their coloured sails bright in the sunlight. Olivia wished she could stop and enjoy this animated scene. If only she did not have pupils waiting...

She had barely gone a few yards before she became aware of a heavy tread echoing her own light brisk step.

'Miss Kingston, I hadn't looked for such a pleasure so early in the morning.' Joseph Dunsford raised his high-crowned beaver hat to her, and kept pace by her side.

'I hadn't expected to see you today, Mr Dunsford,' she greeted him with a polite smile. 'I thought you were embarking for Plymouth.'

'We sail this afternoon, Miss Kingston. How fortunate I decided to go on the late tide, else I would have foregone the enjoyment of your company.'

'You've a delightful day for your voyage, sir,' she said.

'Indeed I have. And all the more delightful for this encounter. I hope you will grant me the privilege of escorting you on your way.'

This cumbersome attempt at pleasantry was so stilted that Olivia was hard put to it not to smile. Her suspicions had been right. Joseph Dunsford was not a man accustomed to delivering pretty speeches. Nevertheless, he was trying his best, and she was touched.

'Thank you, sir. You are most kind,' she said.

'And are you taking the air, on this beautiful morning?' he asked.

'Not really. I'm on my way to give a music lesson to the Mayor's daughters.'

'What fortunate young ladies, to have the benefit of you as their instructress. They can't help but become most accomplished, having so charming and superior a teacher.'

Olivia was finding it more and more difficult to keep a straight face. His compliments were not becoming any easier. Then she decided she was being too critical. She should bask in the rare pleasure of receiving any compliments at all!

'Do you intend to remain in Plymouth long, sir?' she asked.

'Only about a week. I've no intention of staying there any longer than necessary now that I've so excellent a reason for returning to Dartmouth.'

'And what reason is that, sir?'

'Why, the supper-party, and the prospect of hearing you play. I am much looking forward to it.'

Olivia was annoyed with herself. She had asked the question in genuine curiosity, not in an attempt to sound arch.

It shows how long it has been since any man paid you attention, she told herself. Aloud she said, 'I hope both the party and the performance come up to your expectations.'

'They will! I am sure they will.'

They seemed to have exhausted all topics of mutual interest, so an awkward silence settled on them as they walked. Olivia decided that, just as her companion was unused to paying compliments, so was he also unused to escorting a lady. It was impossible not to compare Captain Gilbert's performance of the service with Joseph Dunsford's clumsy attempt. The American had been quite unobtrusive in guiding her round the obstacles that lay in her path. The manner in which he had shielded her from being jostled had been equally natural and easy. Her present companion, however, had her elbow in a grip of iron, and was hauling her back and forth out of the way of hazards much as if he were in control of a recalcitrant puppy.

'We don't seem to have heard any more of the fire on the frigate,' she said, at last finding a possible subject of conversation. 'What is your opinion? Do you think it was the work of Bonaparte's agents?'

'Bonaparte's agents? No hireling of that scoundrel would dare show his face here, you may be sure of that. I'm convinced the blaze was caused by a forgotten candle, a carelessly discarded pipe or something of that nature. Dear Miss Kingston, you needn't be in fear. You are in no danger from those French villains.'

'It is comforting to hear you say so, sir,' said Olivia drily. Fortunately they were now outside the Mayor's residence, and she was conscious of relief at being spared any more of Mr Dunsford's company.

'We must part here, sir,' she said.

'Sadly our journey was all too short, ma'am. Happily I hope to be in your company for rather longer before too many days have passed, so now I must bid you *adieu.*'

Not able to think of a suitable reply Olivia bobbed a quick curtsey in farewell and turned to knock at the door. As she watched Joseph Dunsford stride away she wondered at this strange turn of events. It seemed she did have a suitor after all. She found it hard to believe, but her predominant emotion was one of bewilderment. Out of the many younger, prettier and wealthier women available to him, why had Joseph Dunsford's attentions lighted upon her?

'WHAT, no Captain Gilbert today?' commented her mother, as they sat down at table.

'I understand he has an engagement,' Olivia supplied.

'How dull it seems without the dear man.' Charlotte Kingston gave a sigh.

Olivia could not agree with her.

'It's pleasant to be by ourselves for once,' she said.

Her pleasure changed to perplexity when five o'clock came, and there was no sign of the American.

'He'll have to come home stealthily if he is to avoid being caught for breaking the curfew,' she observed. 'I think we had better go ahead and have dinner. I warrant Captain Gilbert will come creeping in at the back door before we are done.'

She was proved wrong. They finished their meal, the dishes were cleared, and still there was no sign of the American.

'I am sure something serious has befallen him. I can feel it here!' Charlotte Kingston clasped her hands to her bosom. 'Someone should go and look for him.'

'You are surely not suggesting that Olivia should wander round the streets calling his name? He's not a lost dog, you know, my love,' said Edward Kingston. 'You'll see, he'll be back as soon as curfew is lifted in the morning, full of apologies, and with some amusing tale to tell. My guess is that he is with some of his friends and hasn't noticed the time—you know what young men are like when the wine starts flowing! Doubtless he thinks it more prudent to stay where he is rather than risk being arrested in the street.'

'And have these friends of his no servants who could deliver a message to let us know he is safe?' cried his wife.

'Lottie, my love, Captain Gilbert is a grown man. He is quite entitled to visit whomsoever he pleases, even people who might not be exactly respectable. As a gentleman, naturally he wouldn't wish to broadcast the fact, not even to us. Especially not to us!' amended Mr Kingston.

'I am sure you are wrong, husband. Why should the Captain wish to keep his whereabouts from us? We do not mind if some of his friends are a little wild. It is only natural for young men to be a little wild, there is no need to be ashamed of the fact.'

'Papa is right, the Captain is a grown man. He can take care of himself,' Olivia said. 'Now let us stop worrying about him. Shall I play something for you?'

'That is a good idea. We would enjoy that, would we not, my love?' Mr Kingston tried to instil some enthusiasm in his wife.

Olivia took a piece from the canterbury at random and began to play.

'No, not that piece. It is one of the dear Captain's favourites!' interrupted her mother.

'Mama, the man is simply late, he hasn't left us,' protested Olivia.

She said the words without thinking, but they set her wondering. What if the Captain had gone? If he had broken his parole, and was even now being smuggled across the Channel to France in a fishing boat?

She could not prevent herself from feeling a little disappointed at the idea. Somehow he had not seemed the sort of man who would break his promise. Yet was not escape the most likely explanation for his absence?

'Something has happened to him!' wailed Mrs Kingston. 'He is normally so punctilious about being home on time. I fear he is lying injured somewhere, or else he is dead.'

'Don't take on so, my love. Olivia, fetch your Mama's smelling-salts, there's a good girl!' But Mrs Kingston would not be comforted. She continued to fret until she was beyond restoring with smelling-bottles or hartshorn. She began sobbing hysterically, and Olivia had to summon Abbie to help her get her mother to bed.

'It is a rum do,' remarked her father, when she returned to the drawing-room. 'The Captain's absence, I mean. I didn't like to say so in front of your poor mother, she is distressed enough as it is, but I can't help thinking something grave has indeed happened to him.'

'Would you like me to go and seek the advice of Admiral Ranscombe? He would know what to do,' suggested Olivia.

Her father considered the matter, then a wry grin spread lopsidedly across his face.

'Best not, my dear,' he said. 'The Captain might not thank us for sending out a search-party if he has simply found himself an agreeable female companion.'

Olivia smiled. Such a reason would not be at all out of character for the American. 'Perhaps you are right, Papa,' she said.

As the night wore on an increasing anxiety began to gnaw at her. A picture of Miles Gilbert lying somewhere in the darkness with a broken limb or with his head battered and bleeding kept creeping into her mind. He had spoken often of going fishing, he could have slipped on rocks easily enough. The more she thought of it the more the idea of an accident ousted her suspicions that he had broken his parole. Not that there was anything personal in her concern, of course. She would have felt the same about any beggar who was injured and whose cries for help could not be heard.

'Shall we have a game of chess, Papa?' she asked suddenly.

'Thank you, daughter, but I think not. The Captain and I are in the middle of one, and I prefer to finish it when he returns.'

There was a hint of hesitancy as he spoke the word 'when', and Olivia knew that he was worried.

The noise of the clock's ticking seemed abnormally loud. Outside, from the river below, came the lone cry of a sea-gull. To Olivia it sounded oddly dismal.

'It's getting late. Shall I help you to bed?' she suggested. 'Mama should be asleep by now.'

'I find I am not very tired. I think I'd like to stay up a little longer, if it doesn't inconvenience you?'

'No, Papa. I'm not sleepy either. I'm quite happy to sit here with you.'

But as they sat she knew that both of them were straining their ears for the sound of familiar footsteps in the road outside. None came! At last, fatigue finally drove Mr Kingston to go to bed.

After her father had retired and she went about her final rounds of the house Olivia was careful to leave the back door unlocked. An unheard of occurrence, but there was no telling, Captain Gilbert just might return during the night.

Such sleep as came to Olivia was restless and troubled by dreams. She kept waking then drowsing again, all the time her ears straining to catch the sound of the back door opening. The creaking of its iron hinges never came.

She greeted the dawn with relief. Now she could be active. She washed and dressed, trying to decide if she should go up to the Captain's room, just in case he had managed to creep in undetected. She was still debating the problem when there was a thump on the bedroom door and Abbie burst in.

'The Cap'n's in gaol!' the maid announced, panting hard from hurrying up the stairs.

'Gaol?' echoed Olivia aghast. 'Why is he there?'

'I dunno, now do I? All I knows is 'e's down the lock-up! You'd best get along there, quick.'

'If Captain Gilbert is in prison I dare say there's a very good reason. I don't see that I have any cause to rush to his aid.'

Olivia regarded herself in the mirror, securing her hair with pins as she spoke. Not for anything would she betray how much her calm exterior belied her true feelings of relief. Unpleasant as it would undoubtedly be in gaol, at least he was safe.

'Oh, so you'm idn't bothered, then?' asked the maid evenly. 'It idn't nothing to you the poor man 'as 'ad to lie there all night, in that stinking 'ole as is so filthy no decent pig'd call it 'ome?'

'I'm sure Captain Gilbert will be released in good time.'

'In oo's good time, though?' Abbie gave a derisive sniff. 'Well, if that's the way you feels there idn't no more to be said. The poor Cap'n'll 'ave to bide where 'e be. I didn't think you'd be so 'ard-'earted, seeing as you was the one as left the back door unlocked all night!' And she shot Olivia a mischievous glance.

'Very well, I'll go and see what I can do,' said Olivia, trying to put resignation into her voice.

'You was going all the time, wasn't you? I idn't fooled that easy.'

'Are you absolutely sure the Captain is in gaol? Who told you?' asked Olivia, ignoring Abbie's triumphant grin.

'The maid as brings the milk.'

'I might have known he would find a female to run his errands!'

''E only asked 'er to bring a message 'ere, saying where 'e wus, that's all. 'E didn't try to sedoos the maid!'

'Only because he lacked the opportunity, at a guess!'

'You'm proper vinegary this morning. Been awake 'alf the night worrying 'bout 'im, 'ave you? Thought so! You can't fool me.' Abbie gave a chuckle. 'There, while you'm finishing getting dressed I'll go and pack up a few things for you to take. There idn't nothing in that lock-up save vermin.'

Olivia tied on her bonnet, wishing that Abbie could not read her character quite so easily. Of course she had intended to go to the Captain's aid, because there was no one else. She paused as she passed the drawing-room, then went in and filled a small flask with some of her father's precious brandy.

'For medicinal purposes,' she said in answer to Abbie's raised eyebrows. She slipped it into the basket of food the maid had prepared, and set off.

She knew when she was approaching the old town lock-up long before it was in sight. The stench from the ancient building was a constant cause for complaint from those unfortunate enough to live close by. Olivia pushed open the heavy wooden door and blenched at the foul smell which assailed her. Putting a handkerchief to her nose, she entered. She found

herself in a small dark room so dismal and so abominably filthy
she thought she was in the gaol. Then she recognised the man
seated in the midst of the squalor as the turnkey and realised
that this was the fellow's living-quarters.

'Well, yer's a treat, for sure,' he leered. 'I don't often gets
lady visitors, specially not this early in the morning. What can
I do for you, my lover?'

'I believe you have a Captain Gilbert here,' Olivia said, ignoring the familiarity. 'I would like to see him, please.'

'The Cap'n, eh? Us've been and gone and locked up a
sweetheart of yourn, 'ave us, my pretty? Now that's a gurt pity.'
He moved closer to her and leered again, the pungency of his
breath causing her to reel backwards.

'I wish to see the Captain,' she said firmly.

'Please! You'm to say please. 'Tis only proper, since you'm
wanting a favour.'

'I will pay,' she said, handing him a shilling.

'That idn't much. 'E'm a gurt big chap, worth more'n a
shilling to a pretty maid.'

'Half a crown, then, but that's all. I've no more money.'

'Then let's 'ope 'e'm worth it.' The man chuckled coarsely.

'Let me see him at once,' snapped Olivia, her patience at an
end.

'Oh, playing the grand lady, are we?' The turnkey had noticed the basket on her arm, and went to rummage in it with
dirt-ingrained fingers.

Olivia slapped his hand away.

'You have had half a crown as a bribe, that is enough. Either let me see Captain Gilbert this instant or I will go immediately to the town constable and issue a complaint against
you.'

Much to her relief the threat seemed to work, and, mutter-
ing and swearing to himself, the gaoler selected a key from a
large bunch hanging at his waist, and opened the inner door.

It took Olivia's eyes a moment or two to grow accustomed to
the gloom of this inner room. When she did, she saw with horror that it was more squalid than anything she had ever imagined, and the foetid smell took her breath away.

'Well, Cap'n, be you in to company, today?' demanded the
turnkey. 'Or do I tell the lady you idn't at 'ome?'

Miles Gilbert was standing looking through the iron bars of the small window, his back to the room. At the turnkey's words he turned round.

'What are you doing here?' he snapped at her.

She almost recoiled. It was the first time she had ever heard him be irascible.

'I've paid a half-crown to see the peep-show, I intend to get my money's worth,' she retorted. Her harsh words were born entirely from her distress at seeing him in such a plight. She regretted them at once. 'I came to see if I could be of help,' she said more gently.

'I don't want your help. This is no place for you!' The Captain moved towards her swiftly, and angrily seizing her by the shoulders would have pushed her forcibly from the cell if she had not resisted him.

'This is no place for any human being,' declared Olivia, fending him off by placing her hands against his chest. 'I've no idea what all this is about, but it seems clear that you need help from someone, if not from me. Why are you here? What have you done?'

'I've been a fool, that is my crime.' He loosed his grip from her arms. 'Miss Kingston, I apologise for speaking to you so rudely, but I beg of you, please go away. I can't bear to be the cause of you being in a place like this.'

'But I am already in this place,' Olivia pointed out. 'And I hope I haven't endured this unpleasant experience to no good purpose. Captain Gilbert, accept that someone must help you. I am here, so I seem to be the most likely candidate.'

'I don't need any help, I tell you! Go away!'

'And I tell you it is blatantly obvious that you do!' she retorted, equally adamant. 'I don't know in what way you've been a fool, there's no need to tell me if it would embarrass you, but no one should be locked away in this awful place simply for foolishness. Tell me how I can help you to be released.'

'Miss Kingston, you are the most obstinate woman I have ever met!' He glared at her fiercely, but as she met his gaze without flinching, and still made no attempt to leave, his face relaxed. 'Since my rudeness won't drive you away, and you seem determined to help me, I must confess I'm finding being locked up a sore trial, and it is affecting my temper. Also, I'm ashamed that my plight has brought you to this hell-hole. Feeble excuses for my discourtesy to you, but I fear they are the only explanations I can give.'

'Neither explanation nor excuse is needed,' said Olivia. Unconsciously she held out her hands to him, and he grasped them tightly.

'You are right, of course, Miss Kingston. I am in need of help, and if you hadn't come I don't know what I would have done. At least now I have some hope of getting out of this awful place. I'm very grateful to you, though I may not sound it. However, when it comes to the reason for my imprisonment I must swear my innocence.'

'Of what crime are you accused?'

'I am accused of breaking my parole by straying off the road.'

'They would put you in prison for something so trifling?'

'They would indeed, though I protested that I wasn't guilty.'

'What happened?'

'I must blame my suffering on the weather. It was such a delightful day yesterday—was it only yesterday this happened? I feel I have been here for weeks! It was such a delightful day that after my appointment to dine I decided to go for a stroll. I was walking along the Totnes turnpike when I heard the most pitiful cries for help. They were coming from behind a hedge at the far side of the field bordering the road. I didn't think twice! I jumped over the gate and ran across the meadow . . .'

'Failing to remember that, as a condition of your parole, you aren't allowed to step off the road?'

'Exactly. But if you'd heard those cries, Miss Kingston. They seemed to be from a person in great distress.'

'I presume this unseen person in distress was female?'

'Well . . . yes.'

'I might have guessed it,' said Olivia, before she could stop herself.

'Don't be too hard on me, I pray, Miss Kingston.' His grip on her hands tightened. 'I fancy you are ahead of my tale of woe, but those cries might have been genuine, in which case I'd have been quite justified in breaking my parole.'

'They weren't genuine, of course.'

'No. I didn't get the chance to see my assailants. They jumped on me from behind the hedge. I did what I could to defend myself, though I think there were three of them, then a crack on the head sent me to oblivion. When I came to I was in here, a prisoner.'

For the first time Olivia noticed the livid bruises on his face. The Captain had given a good account of himself, that was certain.

'It was all a ploy,' she said. 'I have heard of similar cases before. The trouble is that the authorities pay a bounty for any prisoner recaptured or found breaking his parole. I fear your assailants laid a trap for you. And all for ten shillings.'

'Is that all I am worth?' Something of his normal good humour was returning to his voice.

'I'm afraid so.'

'Then I'm serously undervalued. I fancy myself worth a guinea at the very least.'

'Don't even suggest such a thing, sir. If you were worth a whole guinea then you'd never be safe for a minute.' She was relieved to see a genuine smile light his face, and she found herself smiling back in reply. 'I intend to leave you now and go straight to Mr Brooking,' she said. 'He should be at his desk by this hour. If he won't do anything to get you released, then I'll apply to Admiral Ranscombe. As the senior naval officer in the port he must surely have some influence!'

At that moment a bundle of rags in the corner stirred and groaned.

'My bedfellow,' explained the Captain ruefully. 'He overestimated his capacity for the local cider.'

'In that case make sure he doesn't get a glimpse of the contents of my basket,' said Olivia, suddenly remembering the brandy. 'I doubt if the food would interest him as much as my father's brandy flask.'

'It certainly interests me at the moment. Something to get the chill out of my bones will be most welcome. It is good of Mr Kingston to spare me some of his store.'

'He doesn't know he has contributed it yet. Rest assured, he won't begrudge it when he finds out it has gone to a good cause.'

'So you consider me to be a good cause, Miss Kingston? I did not think you would.'

Olivia became aware that he was still grasping her hands. With a certain reluctance she pulled them away.

'My father would consider you a good cause, sir, and that's what counts,' she said.

She turned and rapped at the door to be let out.

'*Au revoir,* Miss Kingston, and again my thanks,' said the Captain as she was departing.

'I'll be as quick as I can,' she said, over her shoulder.

As she stepped out into the brilliant sunshine Olivia could not hold back a gasp of relief. The fresh pure air filled her lungs, driving away the stench of that awful place. Thoughts of the Captain—of anyone—confined there hastened her footsteps towards her destination. This was not easy for there seemed to be a remarkable number of people abroad for the time of day. She noted that most of them seemed to be Frenchmen, and indeed, before long she found the narrow street where Mr Brooking had his chambers was entirely packed with prisoners of war. They were good-humoured enough, but so numerous she was brought to a halt. Jammed in by the tightly packed bodies her cries of 'Let me through, if you please' went unheeded, leaving her to fume impotently.

'Mademoiselle Kingston, I find you here?' said a surprised voice.

Turning her head, which was just about the only part of her anatomy that she could move, she saw Lieutenant La Fontaine beside her.

'Lieutenant! What on earth is happening? Why are all these people here?' she asked.

'There is a rumour that letters have come from France. We are all here in the hope of news from home,' the Frenchman explained in his heavily-accented English. 'I think perhaps I have a letter from my wife. It would make me very happy.'

'I am sure it would,' said Olivia absently. 'I am only sorry this should have happened just at this moment.'

'You wish to get through, Mademoiselle Kingston? You go to the church?' Lieutenant La Fontaine manoeuvred himself closer to protect her from the crush.

'No, I wish to see Mr Brooking most urgently. Captain Gilbert has been falsely accused of breaking his parole. He is in the town gaol, and I must do what I can to get him released. It is an awful place, no man should be obliged to stay there.'

'The American captain, he is in gaol? *Très bien,* I will help you. Hold to my belt, if you please.'

Acting with surprising speed the Frenchman wormed his way in front of her. He then proceeded to push his way through the crowd like a battering ram, showing remarkable strength and determination for so self-effacing a man. Olivia grasped his belt, as she had been bidden, and followed him thankfully through the mass of bodies.

'There, I deliver you sound and safe,' he puffed triumphantly if none too accurately, when eventually they reached the door of the agent's chambers.

'I thank you very much, sir,' said Olivia breathlessly, clutching at her bonnet, which had been knocked sadly awry in the struggle. 'I would never have managed without your help. I do hope there is a letter from your wife.'

'You are very kind, mademoiselle.' The Lieutenant gave his shy smile.

Olivia bade him farewell and entered the agent's chambers.

'Miss Kingston, is it not?' Mr Brooking rose to greet her. 'How can I help you? It must be a matter of some urgency for you to have made your way through the crowd outside. I fear it is ever thus when letters come from France. It is understandable I suppose—'

'You are correct, sir, when you say my business is urgent.' Olivia cut short the lawyer's speech. 'It concerns Captain Gilbert, the American prisoner of war who is on parole, and who lodges with us. He is in gaol. He has been falsely accused of breaking his parole by straying off the turnpike. It is nonsense, of course. He was tricked into it by people determined to collect the bounty. He must be released immediately. Can you do something about his plight, if you please? And promptly!'

'Releasing any prisoner is never an easy matter, young lady. Formalities, formalities ... There are always formalities to be observed. And for a prisoner of war, why that is worse, for then the Transport Office at Westminster must be informed and it takes time.'

'But there is no time. Captain Gilbert needs to be released as soon as possible. His health will deteriorate if he is left in that awful gaol. And he is innocent, I tell you, sir!'

'The young man has a fine champion in you, Miss Kingston.' The agent beamed at her over the top of his spectacles in a way that made her seethe inwardly. It was his help she wanted, not his approval, yet there seemed no way of persuading Mr Brooking to hurry.

'Yes, he is a charming fellow, the American captain,' went on the agent maddeningly. 'I had the pleasure of playing billiards with him at Mr Seale's house one day. An excellent player, very skilful.'

All the time he had been talking he had been rummaging among the documents piled high on his desk. Olivia had never seen so many papers or such disorder, so she was not surprised when he exclaimed, 'Oh dear, I don't seem able to put my hand on what I want, yet I had it this very morning, I know I did.'

'Sir, about Captain Gilbert . . .' she persisted.

'But the document I seek does concern Captain Gilbert!' Mr Brooking's aggrieved tone turned to one of triumph as he exclaimed, 'Ah, here it is! I knew I had it somewhere!' He held aloft a piece of paper. 'It is the order for the Captain's release, signed by Admiral Ranscombe himself. It was delivered very early, I had still not finished my breakfast. All the same, I passed the copy on most promptly. Your Captain is free, my dear. He will be home before you.'

Olivia had to restrain herself from crying out, Then why did you not tell me sooner? With masterly self-control she said instead, 'In that case, sir, I'll take up no more of your valuable time. I bid you good day.'

When she reached home she went into the kitchen in search of Abbie. At that moment Miles Gilbert entered through the back door, tucking his shirt into his breeches. His skin, flushed as if from an energetic scrubbing, glowed through the thin white cambric and his hair was wet, plastered against his skull in a dull gold mass.

'Miss Kingston!' His face lit up when he saw her. 'What miracle did you perform? I was released immediately after your departure!'

'The miracle wasn't mine, I am afraid,' said Olivia. 'Admiral Ranscombe had already signed the order for your release.'

'He had? But I hadn't made any formal statement of my innocence, or anything.'

'Perhaps the reputations of the scoundrels who laid the trap for you were known to him and he guessed the truth of the matter?'

'Perhaps. Whatever the reason, I'm eternally grateful to the Admiral, and to you.'

'To me? I've told you, I did nothing.'

'You came!' he said simply.

She felt she should make it clear she had acted out of common humanity, nothing more. She did not want him to get the idea that she had rushed to his aid because she had any particular interest in his welfare. She should tell him so, so that there could be no possible doubt. Somehow, though, the words would not come. It was something to do with the way he was standing close to her, and the manner in which his blue-green eyes held hers. It was the Captain who broke the odd tension of the moment.

'I must get out in the air! Come with me!' he exclaimed suddenly.

'With you? But where?' She was bewildered.

'Anywhere where there is good fresh air. I've already been in the wash-house and scrubbed the stench of gaol from my skin, now I must get it out of my lungs. Keep me company!'

'I can't. I have a lesson to give in less than an hour. I have not time—'

'Please,' he broke in, seizing her hand with the same intensity with which he had held it in the gaol.

She understood then that he needed human contact. There were private devils left from his imprisonment that he had yet to dispel.

'Very well,' she said. 'I will come.'

'Ah, I've a problem!' Miles held up his uniform jacket. It was ripped beyond repair. He gave the garment a regretful shake. 'Never mind, if I must go in my waistcoat, like a chop-house waiter, then so be it!'

'There is no need. I am sure my father will loan you one,'
suggested Olivia. 'It might be a little small but not much.'

Edward Kingston's jacket was a tolerable fit on the younger
man. A trifle tight, it was true, for Miles Gilbert had filled out,
thanks to the benefit of Abbie's cooking. He was too restless
and desperate to be in the open air to let such a small matter
hold him back.

'It will serve splendidly until I can make other arrangements, I thank you,' he said. 'Let's take our walk, before your
pupil arrives.'

'You still haven't said where we are going,' said Olivia.

'Anywhere!' was the reply.

She had been right about his need to dispel private devils. He
strode out at a pace that had her trotting to keep up with him,
nor did he speak. Olivia kept silent, sensing that he had to work
out his recovery in his own way. They took one of the roads out
of the town, and only when they reached the summit of the hill,
way beyond the houses, did he stop. All about them were woods
and fields. He took a deep, deep breath of air, much as Olivia
had done when she had left the gaol.

'Well done, Miss Kingston,' he said eventually. 'I used you
hard, but you kept up. Not many would have done so.'

'You refer to me as though I were a donkey,' she protested
indignantly.

'I have a great respect for donkeys, though be assured, my
respect for you is greater.'

'I thank you for the compliment, if it was a compliment,' she
said.

'I shall never forget how you have helped me today,' he said,
suddenly serious. 'Not only for coming to the gaol, but also for
your understanding, then and now. I appreciate it all the more
because I know you don't hold a high opinion of me. That
shows true compassion.'

Olivia was not sure how to answer.

'Most people would have done the same in similar circumstances,' she said.

'I think not, and you are not most people. I've come to understand that during my stay at your home. When I sent that
message with the milk girl I only wished you to know my
whereabouts. It never occurred to me that my plight would add
to your responsibilities. You have enough to bear without
shouldering my problems too.'

'I only do what I consider to be necessary,' said Olivia. 'I have no wish for your gratitude. Please understand, I would have done the same for anyone in such a predicament.'

'Of course you would,' he said, his tone all at once conciliatory. Olivia regarded him cautiously.

'What are you about now, sir?' she demanded. 'I mistrust you when you speak in such a way.'

'You have no cause to mistrust me,' he protested. 'I was simply wondering why you chose to come to my aid, and not that of my companion in sorrow, the town drunkard.'

'Because—,' began Olivia, then stopped, unable to think of a reply.

The Captain was grinning at her, waiting for her answer, mischief in his face.

'Because I'm not acquainted with that gentleman,' she said with asperity. 'We have never been introduced.'

Miles Gilbert hooted with laughter.

'My dear Miss Kingston, you are unique,' he cried.

'No matter how unique I may be, I am certainly not your dear Miss Kingston,' retorted Olivia.

Her annoyance only served to make him laugh more. 'Since you were kind enough to give me the pleasure of your company I had best see you get home again in good time for your lesson,' he said, when his mirth had abated.

Olivia hoped her relief was not too obvious. The turnpike road was unexpectedly deserted, and she had just realised how secluded they were, with the high Devon banks on either side. Coming out into the quiet countryside with a man as personable as Miles Gilbert was not a prudent thing to have done. If anyone observed them her reputation would be in tatters. This was not the only reason why she would be thankful to return home. Being so alone with Captain Gilbert was proving to be strangely disturbing. She was beginning to feel awkward in a manner she had not experienced since she was a young girl, and she did not like it.

'We should go back,' she agreed, trying to sound lighthearted. 'We've come almost to the boundary stone. If you went any further I could report you and claim the ten shillings bounty.'

'Shall we go into business together? I'll keep breaking my parole, you keep reporting me, and we share the ten shillings equally. I do believe I've hit on a way to make us both rich!'

'You don't think people would become suspicious?'

'Not if we use guile and cunning.' He tucked her arm through his, and they set off back to the town.

Miles Gilbert's stay in prison, brief though it had been, had its after-effects. Because of it Olivia found she could no longer regard him with the harsh animosity that had coloured her early opinion of him. She still did not approve of him, nor had she any intention of succumbing to his charm, but having seen him locked up had shocked her. No one should have to endure such conditions. The fact that her own countrymen had been the cause prompted guilt to mingle with her sympathy. Her resentment at having the American in the house began to diminish until she found herself able to accept his presence with equanimity.

'It is so good to hear you singing about the house these days, my dear,' said her father. 'It is a long time since I've known you in such good spirits.'

'It is a long time since I enjoyed such good spirits,' she replied, after a moment's consideration. 'It is this wonderful weather. I can't remember a milder winter.'

'Nor can I,' agreed Mr Kingston. 'And I think that now you've got used to having Captain Gilbert about the place, too, have you not?'

Again Olivia considered the matter.

'You could be right, Papa. It is agreeable having someone who shares my love of music. I still have my reservations about the man, but I admit I could forgive him much when he sings.'

'I wonder if, perhaps . . . well, if your heart isn't just a little bit engaged? He is a most agreeable man, you know.'

'I do know, Papa,' chuckled Olivia. 'And so do most of the females of Dartmouth, and so, most definitely, does the Captain himself. I am sorry to disappoint you, but I fear he'll have to exist without me sighing my undying love for him.'

'If you say so, my dear,' said her father, and she thought he sounded quite disappointed.

When Olivia set out once more to give yet another music lesson she was still smiling to herself at her father's fanciful notion. The idea of her falling in love with the Captain was ridiculous. Apart from her opinion of his character she had made up her mind that such affairs of the heart were beyond her now. Another birthday was looming large, and she was seriously considering whether it was time she went into lace caps. True, it did seem as though she might have a possible suitor in Joseph Dunsford, but she could not imagine herself feeling even the mildest affection for him. No, the idea of a love-affair was as grotesque as it was impossible.

Thoughts of lace caps turned her mind to matters of dress, or, more accurately, of stockings. Her old ones had been mended so often there was scarcely anything left to hold the darning thread. On her way, she crossed the road to see what Miss Sheppard had in stock. When she reached the shop she had to pause for a moment to avoid colliding with a couple who were just leaving.

'Why, Miss Kingston, this is an unexpected encounter.' Miles Gilbert smiled at her. 'Do you know Miss Hunt? Miss Hunt, this is my kind hostess, Miss Kingston.'

'We are acquainted, sir.' The pretty young girl spoke with a hint of coldness in her voice. 'Miss Kingston teaches my sisters the pianoforte. She taught me, too, when I was younger, but that was long ago. How are you, Miss Kingston?'

'Very well, I thank you,' replied Olivia, aware that the girl was not at all interested in her health. 'And I must disclaim that it was quite so long ago I taught you. It is no more than two years since.'

'No doubt two years seems a great time to someone as young as Miss Hunt,' said the Captain.

Olivia would have preferred it if he had not stressed the disparity in their ages quite so much. Before she could think of a reply he went on, 'Well, we mustn't detain you any longer, Miss Kingston. I know what a busy lady you are.' He bowed, tucked his companion's gloved hand more securely under his arm, and together they went on their way.

Olivia continued to stand there, watching their retreating backs. Lizzie Hunt looked ravishingly pretty in her rose-pink pelisse edged with white fur, her gleaming curls peeping enchantingly from beneath a matching pink bonnet. As they walked away the young girl raised her face to the American, her expression one of dewy-eyed adoration.

Minx! thought Olivia, then she turned her attention to the Captain's broad shoulders. What on earth is a man of his age doing with a chit of a girl like Lizzie Hunt? she wondered. She is scarcely out of the schoolroom.

The foolishness of the American's behaviour and his unaccountable taste in female companions occupied her mind for quite some minutes. When she came out of her reverie she was astonished that she should have wasted her precious time on such subjects. She was also puzzled at the suddenness with which the bright winter sun had lost its power to cheer, and taken with it all of her recent light-heartedness. The idea that the true cause might be her encounter with Miles Gilbert in the company of a pretty young girl caught her unawares.

'Nonsense! That has nothing to do with it!' she declared vehemently. Then she was startled to realise she had spoken aloud, and passers-by were looking at her curiously. Crimson with mortification she hurried into the shop to purchase the stockings.

There was a surprise awaiting her, upon her return home.

'Come for you ten minutes since. All tied up with ribbon,' Abbie informed her, indicating the bouquet of hot-house roses which rested on the hall table.

It had been years since anyone had sent her such flowers, and she looked at them in surprise. Conscious of an unexpected surge of happy expectation, she found that her hand shook a little as she picked up the accompanying card:

'I anticipate the pleasure of our next meeting, when I hope to have the twin privileges of being in your company and hearing you play.'

She did not need to look at the signature. Only one man could have thought of such a clumsily-phrased message. So Joseph Dunsford had returned from Plymouth, and was determined to continue his courtship. A suitor *and* a bouquet! She should have been pleased and flattered. Instead she felt only disappointment. She had no idea whom she had hoped had sent her the flowers, she only knew she did not want it to be Mr Dunsford.

CHAPTER FIVE

'Now that Mr Dunsford has returned we can have our supper-party,' said Mrs Kingston with satisfaction. 'Wednesday would seem a most convenient time, do you not think so, Olivia?'

'Wednesday next would be quite suitable, Mama.'

'Good. Then I will call upon Mrs Jenkins this afternoon. Now, what shall I wear? It is so long since we had an evening engagement I declare my wardrobe is sadly wanting. Perhaps I can refurbish my mulberry-and-cream striped satin. I suppose you will put on your blue silk yet again?'

'Of course. What else have I?'

'What else indeed! I declare you must be quite sick of that dress. It is high time you bought a new one.'

'The blue silk will do very well. It is only a small party.' said Olivia.

'Surely you could purchase a length of something pretty? There would be time enough for us to make it up. It must be years since you had anything new.'

'There you are mistaken, Mama, for I bought myself some new stockings this very day.'

'Stockings? I do not count stockings! They are a necessity, not to be considered as something new.'

'The stockings will suffice for now,' said Olivia.

Mrs Kingston looked as though she had not done with the subject, but at that moment Captain Gilbert entered the room, and her face brightened.

'Why, Captain, dear, here we are, discussing clothes and in you come with a new coat,' she cried. 'Oh, how splendid you look!'

'Do I not, ma'am!' said the Captain, striking a pose. 'This is how the prisoner of fashion is dressing this year. Not what I would have chosen if given a completely free hand, perhaps, but considering it was an emergency I don't think the fit to be too bad. I couldn't go on relying upon Mr Kingston's kindness any longer.'

'It is a remarkably good fit,' agreed Olivia, regarding the brown broadcloth garment critically. 'You were fortunate to find such a presentable coat immediately.'

'I was!' The American regarded himself in the mirror over the mantelpiece. 'It had been ordered by a gentleman who failed to honour his obligations. Seemingly he was last seen hurriedly leaving town on the Modbury coach, pursued by creditors. I had to bargain for it, mind. I had to persuade the tailor that it would be a long time before another customer of such perfect proportions came his way, and therefore he should drop the price.'

'I wonder he didn't charge extra, seeing that his former customer of the same size proved so untrustworthy?' Olivia laughingly pointed out.

'Oh, how can you say such a thing to the Captain,' protested Mrs Kingston. 'Any one can see he is a model of respectability.'

'How kind of you to say so, ma'am,' said the American gravely. 'But just in case the poor man was at all anxious I paid in cash.'

'Do you think that was wise?' Olivia's mother looked doubtful. 'These shopkeepers, once they get out of the way of giving credit there seems no going back for them.'

'It was the only way I could persuade him to part with it, ma'am, and since I was in particular need, having a pressing engagement at the Mayor's house this afternoon, I had no choice.'

'No doubt you know best, Captain dear. You have got it in good time, for our supper-party is to be on Wednesday. You are free on Wednesday evening, are you not?'

'Madam, I am free every evening,' said the Captain with a bow.

'How foolish of me, of course you are!' Mrs Kingston gave a little laugh. 'Now I must be off. I cannot stand talking all day. I have a thousand things to do.'

'Do not tell me you are playing billiards with the Mayor this afternoon?' said Olivia, after her mother had departed.

'I doubt if His Worship could spare the time. No, today I take tea with the ladies of the Mansion House.'

'Oh . . . !' Olivia had a sudden picture of pretty Lizzie Hunt pouring tea for the Captain, handing him cake, laughing and talking with him.

'You sound as though you disapprove. You would prefer that I played billiards instead?' asked Miles Gilbert quizzically.

'Certainly not, nor do I disapprove of you taking tea with Mrs Hunt and her daughters. I would not presume to do so,' said Olivia swiftly. What did she care if he took tea with a dozen Mayors' wives and a hundred daughters?

Captain Gilbert continued to regard himself in the mirror with dissatisfaction. He gave an exaggerated sigh.

'What was that for?' asked Olivia.

'I am regretting the passing of my naval uniform. There is something dashing about gilt buttons and gold braid. I shall cut a very poor figure in this,' he declared tragically.

'You are quite dashing enough for the ladies of Dartmouth as you are, sir,' laughed Olivia.

'Oh, Miss Kingston! A compliment! The first you have ever paid me!'

'It was nothing of the sort,' Olivia replied. 'It was a remark of censure.'

This was not completely true. Secretly she could not help thinking that the brown coat, cut as it was by a country tailor, suited him rather better than his naval jacket had done. It was an interesting observation. As the Captain had remarked a uniform added a certain quality to most men. Why he should be the exception Olivia could not fathom. There was no denying that, with the light-brown coat as a foil to his red-gold colouring, the American captain looked splendid, and not at all diminished by the loss of his uniform.

'Why should you wish to censure me, simply because I've bought a new coat?' he asked, trying to sound aggrieved.

'Because I am well aware that you intend to attract the attention of the ladies of Dartmouth. You know half of them are madly in love with you already. Now you wish to conquer the remainder. Such universal adulation will do you no good at all.'

'The adulation is not universal, Miss Kingston. I don't yet number you among my admirers.'

'Nor will you, sir. It is only right that one female should know your true character.'

'Then I beg that you keep the truth to yourself, and not spread it abroad among the other ladies,' he grinned. 'Otherwise my life will become exceedingly dull.'

'For a man so fond of female company I wonder you have managed to escape matrimony for so long. Have you never wished to marry?' she said, then stopped. 'Your pardon. That was a very impertinent question. I do not know why I asked it.'

'I don't think it is impertinent. I prefer to see your question as being perfectly natural. It is extraordinary that a man with my abilities and attractions should have had the skill and cunning to avoid scheming mamas and single ladies of marriageable age for so many years, is it not? I sometimes wonder how I managed it myself.'

'Do you think your modesty may have had something to do with it?'

'I wouldn't be at all surprised. I confess there have been a few ladies who have tempted me to contemplate matrimony. I was once even betrothed. Fortunately, for myself and for those delightful females who are still unwed, I never took the final step.'

'So you jilted the poor girl?'

'Certainly not. Would I behave so dishonourably? She jilted me.'

'You jest, sir.' Olivia stared at him. Then she was annoyed at her own surprise. Obviously there were other females of sense in the world, besides herself, who would not fall for Miles Gilbert's evident charms. 'No doubt you deserved it. You are remarkably cheerful about it,' she went on.

'No doubt I did. It was a long time ago, and we were very young.' He smiled at the memory.

'Being young is no protection against a broken heart,' said Olivia, suddenly serious. 'Young love can be as deep and abiding as the more mature variety.'

'I agree, but in our case there were no broken hearts, fortunately, simply much relief all round. We had known each other all our lives, and been childhood sweethearts. I think we grew so accustomed to one another that we simply accepted that one day we would wed.'

'And what changed your minds?'

'The passing of the years. What seemed idyllic when we were both sixteen looked less attractive when we reached twenty. Fortunately the young lady had the good sense to say so, and we broke off our wedding plans forthwith. We have remained the best of friends ever since. She is now married to a most excellent fellow, and the mother of a very lively brood.'

'And you have no regrets?'

'None at all. I confess I was beginning to feel most uncomfortable about the prospect of marriage, but naturally I could do nothing about it. Emma's commonsense saved us both from a lot of unhappiness.'

'But your families? Did they not object?'

'I think they were a little sorry; our parents had been close friends for years. However, they accepted that we were doing the right thing, and they supported us most admirably. Gossips always have a field day on such occasions, so to stop wagging tongues our families made a great thing of being seen together in public for weeks after the betrothal was ended. That puzzled the busybodies, I can tell you.' The Captain gave a chuckle.

'Then you were lucky,' said Olivia almost to herself. 'To have been saved from being an object of public comment. To be pointed out wherever you go is a hard thing to bear when you have nowhere to hide from your humiliation.'

'I think you were not so fortunate,' said Miles Gilbert gently.

'No, sir, I was not,' she answered very softly, then, because she feared he would ask further questions she said briskly, 'Are you going to make the ladies at the Mansion House wait much longer, sir? Their tea kettle will soon have boiled dry.'

'You are right, I should have left long ago.' He gave an irrepressible grin. 'Never mind. I am such a universal favourite in that household that I'll soon be forgiven.'

Olivia shook her head in amused disbelief.

'Be gone, sir!' she commanded, 'And take your inflated vanity with you!'

'I go! I go!' he cried, and she could still hear him laughing as he hurried down the stairs.

After he had left the house the smile slowly faded from Olivia's face. For a moment the past had come a little too close for comfort. The last thing she wanted was to remember those agonising days after Richard had jilted her. It had taken her years to learn to bury her bitter recollections, to push them to the darker recesses of her mind, and to present a cheerful face to the world. Only occasionally, as now, did they emerge and still have the power to hurt. For a moment she felt a return of her old animosity towards Miles Gilbert for having reawakened old memories, until she remembered that it was she who had started the conversation. She had only herself to blame.

Preparations for the party soon began in earnest. Although Peg Jenkins was to provide the feast, Olivia was determined that the Kingston household would not be found wanting as a venue for their supper. Every spare minute they had, she and Abbie polished and cleaned, swept and scrubbed. There was, however, one cloud on the horizon. Abbie flatly refused to have a day off and leave her kitchen in the charge of Mrs Jenkins's cook. No matter how Olivia begged, pleaded and threatened, the maid refused to budge.

Her parents were in the drawing-room when she returned from yet another tussle with the obstinate Abbie.

'Ah, there you are, my dear,' her father greeted her. 'The Captain is back, he'll be here directly.'

'Yes, I heard him come in,' she replied. 'As soon as he joins us we will have dinner—' She broke off, observing her mother curiously. 'That is a most becoming tippet, Mama. I don't recollect having seen it before.'

'Yes, it is extremely pretty, is it not?' Mrs Kingston fingered the swathe of delicate lawn with approving fingers. 'I think it will brighten my striped satin most admirably, do you not agree? In truth, I got it for the supper-party, but I could not resist putting it on for a minute or two, to show your Papa.'

'And quite delightful you look, my love. As pretty as the day I married you.' Mr Kingston fondly patted his wife's hand.

'La, husband, and you are still as gallant.' Mrs Kingston beamed back at him.

Olivia had not been paying attention to these fond exchanges of her parents.

'You got it, you say, Mama?' she said. 'Do you mean that it is new?'

'Yes, it is. I saw it on my way back from Mrs Jenkins this afternoon, and could not resist it. Is it not splendid? Miss Sheppard is willing to give us credit again! I was quite delighted, there are a host of things I sorely need and—'

'You obtained it on credit?' asked Olivia, her stomach contracting suddenly.

'Did I not say so? She had the sweetest lace caps in, too, but I was pressed for time. I will go back tomorrow so that I may pick one out at my leisure.'

'No, Mama, I beg you not to buy anything else!' said Olivia. 'If you go back tomorrow it must be to return the tippet.'

'Return it? Are you mad? It is quite charming. I am not at all dissatisfied with it.'

'Mama, we can't afford it.'

'I know we cannot, daughter, I am not stupid! That is why I was careful to buy it on credit.'

'But, Mama, even so, we must pay sometime.'

'Yes, but we need not bother ourselves about it just yet.'

'Mama,' said Olivia evenly, controlling her dismay with difficulty. 'We already owe Miss Sheppard a considerable sum, which I have been endeavouring to pay off, little by little, whenever funds permit. I have managed to clear much of the debt, although it has taken years. Now you are building it up again, and we have not the resources. We really have not!'

'Then why did that wretched woman accept my credit, if it was to cause all this fuss?' demanded Mrs Kingston tearfully. 'I have forgotten how long it is since I bought anything for myself. And I was most economical! The tippet is of lawn, which costs nothing!'

'Perhaps not the lawn, but what of the lace trimming it?' Olivia prompted gently. 'That is best Branscombe if I am any judge, and you can't say that it cost nothing. I'm sorry, Mama, we really cannot afford it.'

'I only wanted something pretty to wear at the party, and it is a very little tippet,' wept Charlotte.

'Is there no way your Mama could keep it?' asked Edward Kingston anxiously. 'Can we not buy on credit this once?'

Olivia thought of the scrimping and saving she had done to reduce their debt at Sheppard's, and the time it had taken. Now her parents wanted to sweep away all her efforts, and she longed

to cry out in protest, but she knew it was no use. Her parents
did not understand finance. Throughout most of their lives they
had shown a blatant disregard for economy, and they were incapable of learning now.

'I am afraid not, Papa,' she said, as kindly but firmly as she
could. 'We agreed a long time ago, did we not, that now we
would pay cash for everything. Using credit got us into a lot of
trouble in the past, and we are still trying to clear ourselves of
those early debts. It would be sheer folly to build up new ones.'

'What you say is very sensible, I know, my love,' said her
father. 'But your mother has set her heart on that scrap of
lawn, and I would so like her to have it. You know how she
loves pretty things, and goodness knows she has had few
enough these last years. Now, surely there is some sacrifice we
can make, some little luxury we can do without, that would
enable us to buy her the tippet?'

The force of his pleading and her mother's sobs were making
Olivia feel like a hard-hearted monster. How she wished there
was some way that her mother could keep her confection of lace
and lawn. She was all too conscious of how hard it must be for
her mother to do without.

'Very well, Mama,' she said. 'We'll manage somehow. Of
course you must keep the tippet, but it will be paid for immediately.' There was one vital question she had to ask. 'You did
not obtain anything else, did you?' To her profound relief her
mother shook her head. 'Very well . . . I had best tell Abbie to
serve dinner.'

Olivia was glad to be out of the room. Although she had said
her mother could keep the tippet she had no idea how they were
going to pay for it.

Despite the upheaval and the problems Olivia found that she
was looking forward to the supper-party more and more. Not
for a long time had she been in such a happy state of anticipation. Mrs Jenkins and her servants were constantly in and out
of the house on the day of the party, adding to the air of
cheerful confusion.

On the night of the party, choosing what to wear was a simple matter. As she had pointed out, Olivia only had one suitable gown, her blue silk. Putting it on she looked at her
reflection in the cheval glass. It did not fit her very well, it hung

so loosely on her slender figure. It had suited her once, when she had been younger and more plump. Now she thought it was rather *jeune fille* for a woman of her years.

She scrutinised her reflection in the mirror more critically. Something in her wanted her to look her best tonight, and she acknowledged that it would be no easy task in faded blue silk which was splitting with age. It was the overall youthfulness of the dress which disturbed her most. It went ill with her neat governess-like hair-style. In the old days she had worn her hair in a softer manner, not scraped back from her face as she did now. Acting upon a sudden impulse she pulled out the pins and shook her head until her hair, freed from the tight braids, cascaded onto her shoulders in deep waves. Trying to remember how she had dressed it all those years ago, she tied it back, letting her dark curls fall naturally. The result was better, but still not quite right. Her face looked too sharp, too drawn, it needed a softer frame. In desperation she took out her sewing scissors and snipped away at the front locks, twisting them round her fingers so that they curled gently onto her brow and her cheeks. She stood back and gasped at the effect. It was the other Olivia who stared back at her; the Olivia who had loved laughing, who had not known the meaning of responsibility; the young Olivia . . .

She felt quite self-conscious as she left her room, and even more so because the first person she encountered was Captain Gilbert.

'Miss Kingston, if I can have the cellar key—' he began, then stopped, his eyes taking in Olivia. She felt her colour rise. There was something in the frankness of his gaze which made her feel uncomfortable, yet pleased at the same time. If she had been more vain, or more fanciful, she might have thought it was admiration. As she was neither she was at a loss to recognise it.

'You were about to say, sir?' she prompted.

'Was I? I forget what it was. I only know that I dare not say what is in my mind at the moment. It would only make you angry.'

'"I can think of nothing concerning the cellar keys that would vex me.'

'Cellar keys?' He looked puzzled. 'Oh, the Devil take those keys! I'm talking about something else.'

'You are talking in riddles.'

'Yes, I am, for if I don't I might be tempted to say how truly delightful you look. Then you would get annoyed with me. Worse still, you wouldn't believe me.'

'You are right. I wouldn't.'

He gave a brief sigh.

'I feared it would be so. One day I intend to make you not only like me, but believe me, too.'

Olivia knew she should inform him brusquely that neither of his ambitions had any hope of success, but the prospect of the evening ahead was so pleasant she could not bring herself to spoil it.

A commotion downstairs heralded the arrival of Peg Jenkins. She entered the room unannounced, in a flurry of laces, plumes and jangling bracelets, making further conversation between them impossible. Her arms were filled with flowers.

'What a journey I had from my house!' she declared. 'I had these blooms so prettily arranged for the table, and just look at them! The wretched fellows came near to tipping up my chair, flowers and all, as we turned into Higher Street. They will take that corner at a run, and it is downhill. There will be a sad accident one day. I keep telling them so.'

'Here, let me take your burden from you, Mrs Jenkins, while you compose yourself,' said the Captain, taking charge of the somewhat travel-worn blooms. 'Shall I place them on the dining-table? Then you can give them the benefit of your skill and artistry when you are recovered.'

'Bless you, Captain, dear! What a treasure you are, to be sure!' Peg Jenkins beamed at him, giving him the full benefit of her porcelain smile, then she turned her attention to Olivia. 'My dear, you look quite ravishing tonight! And I think I can guess why? Quite where the wicked man has got to I can't tell. One minute he was beside my chair, and the next we had left him behind . . . But never fear, I think he has just arrived.' A sharp rap at the front door prompted Mrs Jenkins to simper coyly, and playfully jab Olivia in the ribs with her fan.

Olivia's heart sank a little. She had no wish to appear attractive to Joseph Dunsford. A moment later the man himself entered. He was wearing a superbly tailored coat, his breeches fitted to perfection, his neckcloth was immaculate, yet some-

how he still contrived to look as though he had come determined to haggle for a good bargain sooner than enjoy himself
among friends.

'Your pardon for entering in so informal a fashion,' he said,
'but your maid refused to come up and announce me.' From his
expression Olivia guessed that no servant would have dared to
behave so eccentrically in his house.

'Just a small domestic upheaval in the kitchen, nothing to be
concerned about,' said Mrs Kingston entering the room. 'We
are delighted to see you again, Mr Dunsford. Do come in and
take a seat. Yes, the one beside Olivia. We are wild to hear
about your trip to Plymouth. Olivia has talked of little else all
week.'

Olivia winced at her mother's lack of subtlety, but smiled
politely as the newcomer took his place beside her.

'I hope you are well, sir,' she said.

'In splendid form, thank you, Miss Kingston. I scarcely need
to ask if you are in good health for I can see you are looking
radiant. Positively radiant.'

'Thank you, sir.' She decided she had better choose her
comments with greater care, or she was likely to inspire Joseph
Dunsford to lavish more of his hefty compliments upon her.
The thought of a whole evening of exercising such caution was
a dismal one, not made any easier by the amused glance Miles
Gilbert shot in their direction.

'We only lack the company of Admiral and Mrs Ranscombe... Ah, here they are now,' cried Mrs Kingston, as the
pair in question entered.

'Good evening to you all!' exclaimed the Admiral cheerily.
'Your pardon for entering unannounced, Mrs Kingston, but I
fear there are signs you may have unrest below decks.'

'Oh dear, do you think so?' Charlotte Kingston's pretty face
looked troubled. 'Olivia, will you... Oh no, perhaps not!'

'I will go!' Mrs Jenkins made to heave herself out of her
chair. 'Though I never could handle your Abbie.'

'Ladies, with your permission I will go downstairs and see
what is happening,' said Captain Gilbert. 'There's no need for
Mrs Jenkins to trouble herself, and as for Miss Kingston, she
looks so comfortable where she is it would be a shame to disturb her.'

The look he gave Olivia was pure mischief, and she glowered back at him.

'Would you, Captain dear?' Her mother was delighted at the idea. 'Abbie can be very difficult, goodness knows, but if anyone can get her to behave it is the Captain.'

Miles Gilbert was back in a few minutes, grinning all over his face.

'I wouldn't recommend any of you ladies going near the kitchen,' he said. 'The language has made my ears red, not to mention my cheeks. But the smells emanating from there are delicious. And I saw no bloodstains on the floor. I suggest we leave well alone unless we hear gunfire.'

'Very wise, my boy,' agreed Mr Kingston with a chuckle. 'We'll have our supper first and then call in the Watch if need be, eh?'

'It need not come to that, sir. Such action might frighten the ladies,' broke in Joseph Dunsford. 'I am happy to offer my services, should they be required.'

'I think Captain Gilbert and my father were joking,' Olivia told him gently. 'I don't think there will be any real problems. We have both Mrs Jenkins's cook and our maidservant in the kitchen at the moment, and though they profess to hate each other, I think they are enjoying themselves tremendously, exchanging insults.'

'Ah, I see...' Joseph Dunsford did not actually say that he disapproved of such goings-on among the lower orders, but his expression left no doubt of his true feelings.

'Our apologies for being late,' said Admiral Ranscombe, accepting the glass of wine offered to him. 'I had to await the arrival of a messenger.'

'I sometimes wonder if my dear Ranscombe has any leisure,' said the Admiral's wife, looking at her husband fondly. 'He never seems to be off duty. The slightest bit of trouble and he must be informed.'

'Of course I must, my love,' said the Admiral, 'else all this is merely adornment.' And he ran a hand over the gold epaulette on his shoulder.

'There has been some trouble, Admiral?' asked Mr Kingston.

'There has indeed.' Admiral Ranscombe paused for a moment. 'Oh, since it will be common knowledge in the morning I see no harm in telling you all now. We fancy this area is being used as an escape route for French prisoners. We were informed that four from Ashburton had broken their parole and disappeared. Their trail headed in this direction, and earlier today a small boat was found drifting off Blackpool Sands. It was intact, complete with oars, so we think it may have been used to take the Frenchmen out to a ship in the Channel. It isn't the first time we have suspected that prisoners have used Dartmouth as a port of departure.'

'How disturbing!' cried Mrs Kingston. 'You may depend on it, smugglers will have a hand in this treachery somewhere. And to think it is happening under our noses.'

'And under my nose in particular, since I have a post of responsibility,' smiled the Admiral wryly. 'And I agree with you concerning the involvement of our local night-runners. They seem to have found themselves a very nice little extra source of income.'

'I would shoot the lot of them! And the deuced Frenchies!' growled Mr Dunsford. 'Nay, that would be a waste of good lead. Hang 'em! I have never understood why we need to take prisoners at all!'

There was an uncomfortable silence as everyone tried not to look in Miles Gilbert's direction.

'It is just as well we do, sir,' said Olivia hurriedly, 'otherwise the musical entertainment after supper would be meagre.'

'Indeed it would!' cried Peg Jenkins, in support. 'If you knew how I've been looking forward to hearing you sing, Captain, dear, why it would make you blush more than…than overhearing the exchanges between Abbie and my Sukie downstairs.'

'Madam, I am quite covered in confusion,' replied the Captain, in tones of such mock modesty that everyone laughed.

The tension was eased further by the door being flung open and Abbie announcing, ''Tis ready, for any of you as can bear to eat food cooked by that bladder of lard.' And she disappeared again, slamming the door behind her.

Mrs Kingston gave a whimper of distress at her servant's behaviour.

Olivia rose to her feet. 'I think that is Abbie's way of announcing that supper is served, ladies and gentlemen,' she said.

'You have to admit that Abbie's style of servitude is unique,' said the Captain, rising too. 'Can you imagine how splendid she would have been at a banquet given by the Borgias?'

'What a dreadful thing to say, you wicked man,' declared Peg Jenkins, taking his proffered arm, clearly not thinking him either dreadful or wicked.

'Who are the Borgias? Do we know them ...?' asked Mrs Kingston.

'Miss Kingston, I do hope I am to be allowed the extreme privilege of taking you in to supper?' asked Joseph Dunsford.

'I would be honoured, sir,' replied Olivia, choosing a more honest turn of phrase than saying she would be delighted.

The dining-room was not large, and it took some careful manoeuvring by Captain Gilbert to get Mr Kingston's chair into position at the head of the table.

'That's fine, my boy, I thank you,' said Edward Kingston. 'I am comfortable now. Pray don't neglect your fair partner any longer on my account.' And he nodded towards a simpering Mrs Jenkins, whose vast plumes fairly quivered with delight.

On his route back to his seat the Captain had to squeeze through the narrow space behind Olivia's chair. In doing so his hands rested briefly on her shoulders for a moment. It was a fleeting gesture, but the pressure of his touch was warm through the thin silk of her gown. There was something very pleasant in the sensation. It would have been so easy to interpret the gesture as a sign of friendship, admiration, affection ... Fortunately, her common sense asserted itself. He was acknowledging her support after Joseph Dunsford's *faux pas*, nothing more. All the same, the incident had its effect. In some indefinable way it added to her enjoyment of the evening.

Olivia regarded the scene with growing delight. The gleaming silver and sparkling Venetian glass were reflected in the polished wood of the table, and the candle flames struck myriad points of light from every shining surface. In the centre of the table the vivid colours of the hot-house flowers glowed against the richness of the mellow walnut. Appreciatively she drank in their delicate perfume.

'Oh this is so nice, to entertain properly again,' breathed Mrs Kingston, ignoring the fact that the glassware, the cutlery and most of the fine embellishments had been provided by the good-hearted Peg Jenkins.

Olivia had to agree with her mother. It was very pleasant to be in such company. In spite of everyone's misgivings the food proved to be excellent, the wine was good, and the conversation, on the whole, was entertaining. Only when Joseph Dunsford held sway did it flag. The man had a talent for being boring far beyond the ordinary. She was trying her best not to yawn during his lengthy and dull explanation of the effects of the present wars upon the Baltic timber trade when by chance she caught Miles Gilbert's eye. She had not meant to look across the table in his direction, only, somehow she found her gaze wandering towards him with uncomfortable frequency. He was a man who naturally drew attention, of course, and she wondered, not for the first time, how a man with such a plain face could be so attractive. Yet he was! She could not deny it!

As she looked at him he gave her a surreptitious wink. It was an impertinent gesture, and she attempted to glare at him disapprovingly, but her attempt was singularly unsuccessful.

'Ladies, shall we withdraw and leave the gentlemen to their port?' suggested Charlotte Kingston.

'We shall go, but don't tarry here long over your pipes and your gossip, else I shall be quite out of temper with you,' said Peg Jenkins. She addressed all four gentlemen, but it was Miles Gilbert whom she rapped sharply on the arm with her fan.

'They'll not be long, you mark my words,' she said, as the ladies settled themselves in the drawing-room. 'Mr Dunsford will see to that.'

'He will? Why?' asked Mrs Ranscombe.

'Because of Olivia, that is why! Did you ever see a man so dying of love? And Sly Puss, here, is pretending to be so calm about it, when I'm convinced her heart is in a turmoil.' Mrs Jenkins's fan made a sharp assault on Olivia's ribs.

'I have seldom seen a man look less like pining away than Mr Dunsford,' smiled Olivia. 'And as for my heart, I fancy it is keeping to its normal rhythm most satisfactorily.'

'Olivia and Mr Dunsford!' said Mrs Ranscombe in some surprise. 'I had no idea! He seems a worthy young man.'

Worthy! Yes, that described Joseph Dunsford exactly, in Olivia's opinion, and she certainly could not see him dashing away from masculine company to be by her side.

She was wrong. In a surprisingly short time the men joined them.

'We couldn't keep away from you lovely creatures, could we?' cried Mr Kingston, as the Captain wheeled his chair in.

'No, indeed,' said Mr Dunsford, sitting himself down heavily beside Olivia. 'With such beauty awaiting us, how could we stay away?'

Olivia knew her father's remark had been light-hearted, she feared Joseph Dunsford had been deadly serious.

'How gallant you are, sir,' she said politely, ignoring the knowing looks which were passing among the others.

She wished heartily that she could move and have some other companion for a while, but it would have been impolite. Also, she was committed to dispensing the tea, and was hemmed in by the tea-tray.

'May I hope that we are to hear you play now, Miss Kingston?' asked Joseph Dunsford, when the tea-tray was removed.

'A capital idea!' cried Mrs Jenkins, before Olivia could reply. 'Olivia and the Captain!'

'It seems we are to be the entertainers, Miss Kingston.' Miles Gilbert held out his hand to her. 'Come, let's give these good people a feast their ears will never forget.'

'I am sure I shall never forget a single note of Miss Kingston's playing,' cried Mr Dunsford, again failing to recognise a joke.

Olivia did not reply. Captain Gilbert, in leading her to the piano, had given her hand a conspiratorial squeeze, and she bit back a laugh. So someone else shared her opinion of Joseph Dunsford.

It seemed fitting that on such an enjoyable evening the music should prove more than ordinarily delightful. Olivia felt she had seldom played better, and the Captain's singing was superb. She tried to analyse just why he was so good. It was more than simply a naturally fine voice, or a masterly knowledge of music. It was the warmth and emotion he could get into the simplest piece. When he finished by singing one of the Italian love-songs he performed so well it was as though he were singing it to her alone. She wondered if the other women in the room felt as moved as she did whenever he sang. She was surprised to note that, though they had undoubtedly enjoyed his performance enormously, no one else showed signs of the tears she was battling to hold back.

As soon as the musical interlude was over Joseph Dunsford claimed her attention once more, much to Olivia's regret. His stolid conversation jarred the pleasantly sentimental mood evoked by the Captain's singing. Much as she tried to be polite and focus her attention solely on him, all too often she found her gaze wandering.

More than once her eyes met those of Miles Gilbert as he regarded her steadily. Then he winked at her again, slowly and deliberately. A rising tide of merriment swept over her. Mr Dunsford was in the middle of a discourse on how a ship should be loaded safely. Long and involved as it was, its very tediousness struck her as funny. One glimpse at the American's face told her that he, too, was having difficulty in maintaining his gravity.

How much longer she could have held back her laughter she did not know. Fortunately her mother saved the situation by exclaiming, 'Now, how shall we amuse ourselves? Has anyone any good notions?'

Captain Gilbert had! He proved to have a fund of puzzles and games and conundrums, each more nonsensical than the last. Olivia guessed he was making them up as he went along, but so brilliantly that she could not prevent herself from supporting him. Still borne up by laughter and high spirits, she took the lead in giving ludicrous solutions to his conundrums and totally impossible answers to his puzzles. The rest of the company followed suit with such hilarious results that the proceedings were frequently halted to give the contestants time to get their breath back.

'No, Miss Kingston, this will not do!' cried Captain Gilbert with pretended severity at one of Olivia's more fanciful replies. 'I can't accept the name "woofle fly". I fear you aren't taking this game at all seriously. That answer was one of your own inventions, and so does not count.'

'Do you know that for certain, sir?' demanded Joseph Dunsford indignantly. He was the only one not laughing. Instead he seemed vaguely bewildered by the general mood of gaiety. 'I'm convinced Miss Kingston would never deliberately make up an answer,' he went on. 'I suggest that we look up the species. Have you a book on entomology to hand, ma'am?'

Charlotte Kingston, to whom this question was addressed, and who had not the vaguest idea what entomology was, replied, 'Certainly not, sir! We are Church of England!'

This was too much for the rest of the party, who collapsed into helpless laughter.

'I don't recall a more entertaining evening, really I don't!' declared Admiral Ranscombe, when he had recovered.

'I am most gratified to have amused you all,' said Mrs Kingston, 'though I cannot imagine what I said that was so funny.'

'I think, ma'am,' began Joseph Dunsford in his ponderous way, 'it was because you confused entomology, which is the study of insects, with—with—' Here he stopped, unable to think of anything that could have been confused with the topic.

This would have sent everyone off into fits again if Olivia had not intervened. She was enjoying herself so much she felt sorry for poor dull Dunsford, who had understood none of the jokes and failed to get the hang of the simplest parlour game. She decided it must be dreary enough being Joseph Dunsford, without being the butt of everyone's laughter.

'Shall we have more music?' she suggested. 'Songs which we all know. If I play and Captain Gilbert leads then you can join in.'

'A capital idea!' cried the Captain. 'Play on, Miss Kingston. We are yours to command.'

He rose, and with a flourish, took her hand and led her to the piano. As he did so she caught the same expression in his eyes that she had noticed earlier, the one that came close to being admiration. She felt her colour rise once more—and promptly blamed her rosy cheeks on the warmth of the room and the excellence of the wine.

If she had hoped to involve Joseph Dunsford in the singing, she failed dismally. He proved to know no song beyond the first line. When she played his supposed favourite 'The Mallow Fling' he floundered long before the end of the first verse. In contrast, Miles Gilbert was in his element, and everyone else in the room sang lustily, if not tunefully, until the lateness of the hour brought the party to an end.

'I thank you for a most enjoyable evening.' Joseph Dunsford did not sound like a man who had just enjoyed himself. 'If you will forgive me taking my leave of you so promptly, Mrs Jenkins's chair has arrived, and I intend to speak firmly to the men. They were most careless in their manner of bringing her. I am determined they will behave better on the return journey.' He bowed politely and went downstairs, accompanied by Admiral and Mrs Ranscombe.

Peg Jenkins watched until he was out of earshot, then she gave Olivia a playful prod in the ribs.

'What a clever puss you are, my dear,' she beamed. 'I'd no idea you could be so cunning. Well done!'

'In what way have I been so cunning, ma'am?' asked Olivia with a smile.

'Why, in your behaviour towards Mr Dunsford. Making him jealous in such a way was exactly right. It does no man any good to let him think he has a clear path. Mark my word, our Mr D will be more mad for you than ever now.'

'I'm not sure I want him to be mad for me, and I certainly have no recollection of making him jealous,' Olivia replied.

'No? So you can't recollect flirting with the Captain all evening, eh?' teased Mrs Jenkins. 'A likely story! Never mind, the secret of your little ploy is safe with me. Oh, is that dear Mr Dunsford calling to me? He'll talk about you all the way home, I do not doubt it.'

Olivia bade farewell to her, then turned round. Miles Gilbert was standing in the doorway. His face was grim, the glint in his eyes was icy. She had never seen him look so angry. 'What is wrong?' she asked in surprise.

'Why should anything be wrong, Miss Kingston?' he replied coldly. 'I appear to have served a very useful function this evening. I'm glad to have been of service!' And he stalked up to his room.

Olivia stood still, completely bewildered, unable to account for his swift change of mood. Then she realised that he must have overheard her conversation with Peg Jenkins. But surely it could not have been that? What had there been in their words to cause such fury? Only Peg's teasing accusation that she had been flirting with the Captain. She had not been flirting with him, had she? Certainly it had not been her intention, though now, when she thought of it, she supposed it was an interpretation that could have been put on her behaviour... By a man accustomed to women admiring him, she amended to herself... By a vain man...

Then she remembered his challenge! How could she have forgotten it? So it was more than bruised vanity that was annoying Miles Gilbert! It was also pique. He had imagined that he had won, that he had made her like him at last. Then Peg Jenkins's remarks had told him otherwise. Olivia felt quite triumphant. She would have to be more cautious in the future, though, and steel herself more strongly against the Captain's all-too evident charms. She had withstood him this time, but it had been a close run thing. Just how close she refused to admit, even to herself.

CHAPTER SIX

NEXT morning brought the sense of anticlimax which so often follows celebrations. Mr Kingston kept to his bed, after being forced to acknowledge that the party had tired him more than he liked to admit. Mrs Kingston trailed about the house bewailing the fact that she had now nothing to which she could look forward. And Captain Gilbert was unusually silent at breakfast. Olivia surmised that this was more because he was still peeved with her than because of the aftermath of the feasting.

One thing she hoped for was that Joseph Dunsford might now be discouraged from paying her such marked attention. She was doomed to disappointment. Breakfast was barely over before a messenger arrived bearing a large basket of fruit for her parents and an opulent box of sugarplums for herself. Accompanying them was a letter from Mr Dunsford, in which he thanked them effusively for their hospitality. He also expressed a heartfelt wish that he might be permitted, in the near future, to call once more upon Mr and Mrs Kingston and their most charming daughter.

The 'most charming' Miss Kingston was hard put to it not to groan aloud. What did it take to deter the man? He had clearly not enjoyed himself at the supper-party. It must have been evident to him that he had little in common with her, her family or her friends. Yet still the man persisted. It was puzzling.

'Oranges, apples, hot-house peaches, a pineapple!' Mrs Kingston was delightedly taking stock of the fruit basket. 'I cannot remember the last time I tasted pineapple. What a treat we shall have at dinner! Dear, dear Mr Dunsford! I must take this to show your Papa.'

Picking up the basket she left the room, leaving her daughter regarding her sugared fruits in their expensive waxed-paper wrapping. Olivia wished she dared return them to their sender. Would such a snub penetrate Joseph Dunsford's thick hide? She had her doubts.

'I see you are to be congratulated!' Captain Gilbert's voice made her look up. She had forgotten he was sitting in the armchair, reading.

'Upon what am I to be congratulated, sir?' she asked.

He rose, and came over to her, dwarfing her with his height.

'Why, upon the success of your scheming last night. I see it has borne fruit, if I may use a most appropriate phrase!'

'You may not, sir!' she replied. 'I don't know what nonsensical notion you have got in your head, nor what right you think it gives you to be so discourteous to me.'

'The right of one who was innocently involved in your plotting. I tell you, ma'am, I don't like being used as a stalking-horse for you to attract rich suitors.'

Olivia gasped with fury. 'I'll tell you what you really don't like, Captain Gilbert!' she cried, facing up to him squarely, 'And that is having your own schemes thwarted. Under the cover of the light-hearted atmosphere last evening, you thought to trick me into actually liking you. Don't deny it, for I am wise to every little ploy you used. The amusing chatter, the charming smiles, the attentiveness. But I saw through your chicanery and played you at your own game.'

'And are you saying you wouldn't ensnare Joseph Dunsford if you could?'

'That, sir, is none of your business!' Olivia retorted. 'Only be certain of one thing—never let yourself be deceived into thinking that I was attracted to you.'

'I promise you I won't. I don't know whether to offer my commiserations to Dunsford or to hope you make a match of it, for he is the most boring man I have ever met!'

'I much prefer a boring man to a vain one, which is what you are!'

They were toe to toe, glowering at each other in belligerent silence. Then, unexpectedly, Miles Gilbert gave a shame-faced grin.

'I can't remember shouting at a female in such a manner since one of my girl cousins broke my hobby-horse,' he said.

'It is no comfort to learn that the intervening years have seen no improvement in your manners,' said Olivia warily. She did not trust his sudden change of mood.

'On that occasion I received a sound thrashing from my father for not behaving like a gentleman.'

'Don't worry unduly. I fear my father is incapable of thrashing you!'

'Nevertheless, I didn't behave well. I apologise. Will you forgive me?'

'What is there to forgive?' said Olivia, relenting in spite of herself. 'I fancy I wasn't especially polite to you, so honours are even.'

'I think you may mean dishonours,' he smiled at her.

'I think I may.'

Only after she found herself smiling back at him did she realise, with annoyance, that she seemed to have fallen for his persuasiveness. But by then it was too late!

That evening it was Abbie's turn to be ill-tempered. She stamped up the stairs to the dining-room and proceeded to be so heavy-handed with the crockery that Olivia feared for what was left of the dinner-service.

'What has annoyed you?' she asked. 'For pity's sake tell us, before we lose every plate in the house.'

''E'm back!' The maid fairly spat the words.

'Who is back?'

'That dirty bit of scum! That—'

'Abbie! I beg of you, moderate your language!' implored Mrs Kingston.

'My language be moderated, compared to what I'm thinking! Brung 'is wife, 'e as . . . The poor soul's six months gone if 'er's a day . . .' Abbie's words were punctuated by the dishes crashing onto the table. 'That'll be seven babes in seven years . . . Disgusting, I calls it.'

'Whom do you mean?' demanded Mrs Kingston. 'You really are too trying! Olivia, can you tell what this foolish creature is talking about?'

Olivia did not speak. She was too shaken to reply. She knew very well to whom Abbie referred.

Mention of Olivia's name turned the servant's attention in her direction. ''E was never good enough for you,' went on the maidservant relentlessly. 'I thought so from the fust, and I think so now. Don't waste no tears over 'e!'

'Abbie! That will be all!' said Olivia quietly.

'No it won't!' Abbie glared at them fiercely, then she said, quite mildly, 'There idn't no gravy. I'll go and fetch un.'

Captain Gilbert had been examining the handle of his dinner-fork with unusual concentration during Abbie's discourse. Now he looked up.

'Are you all right, Miss Kingston?' he asked. 'You have gone very pale.'

Olivia took a long slow breath, and, with a superhuman effort, replied calmly, 'I'm perfectly well, I thank you.' But she was not. Inside she felt as though a knife was turning in her heart. So Richard Hayter had returned! Richard Hayter, the man she had loved to distraction eight years ago, and who had rejected her so cruelly.

Throughout the meal her attention strayed. Her thoughts sped back eight years, as she went over the great joys she had experienced, and the even greater pain.

'...I cannot think what is the matter with you,' her mother's voice brought her back to the present. 'That is three times I have addressed you without receiving a reply.'

'Your pardon, Mama.' Olivia rose, pushing back her chair. 'If you will excuse me, I will withdraw. I have a headache...'

She was vaguely aware of consternation on the faces of her parents, and of concern on that of the American. She heard her mother protest 'But Olivia never has headaches' as she left the room. She could not help it. She could not bear to sit there another minute, pretending that all was well when it was not. Richard Hayter had come back, and she did not know what to do.

Olivia left the house next morning filled with dread. Dartmouth was a small town, and she knew it was almost inevitable that she would encounter Richard eventually. To meet him on his own would be bad enough, but if he had his wife with him...

To her relief she reached her pupils' house without catching a glimpse of the man who once had been the whole world to her. On the road home she met up with, not Richard Hayter, but Miles Gilbert.

'How do you feel this morning, Miss Kingston?' he asked. 'Has your headache gone?'

'Yes, thank you,' she said briefly. She was uncomfortable about the lie she had told, although it was just a small one.

'Good. Which way are you taking? Down Pinny's Lane? Then, may I walk with you?' Without waiting for her approval, he fell into step beside her, and together they began to descend the steep slope. 'And who were you teaching this morning?' he asked.

'The two youngest children of...' Olivia's voice trailed away and she stood stock still.

A man and a woman were making their way up the hill. Even at some distance it was evident that the woman was pregnant, and finding the slope difficult. Her companion, though he supported her on his arm, seemed somewhat impatient, as he urged her to move more quickly.

To Olivia this was her worst nightmare realised. Richard Hayter and his wife were heading towards her, and in this steep narrow lane there was no way of avoiding them.

'Miss Kingston, is something amiss?' asked Captain Gilbert.

Olivia could only shake her head, and resume her journey down the hill. She was vaguely aware of the American looking firstly at her, and then at the approaching couple. The next thing Olivia knew he had taken her hand and tucked it under his arm, so that she was obliged to move closer to him.

'Right, Miss Kingston, here we go!' he cried, setting off downhill at a cracking pace.

Olivia had no option but to run with him, trying to protest, while with her free hand she held onto her bonnet. They had to stop when they reached the oncoming Hayters, the way was too narrow for them to pass easily, but when she faced Richard Hayter it was with her cheeks glowing and her eyes bright from the sudden exertion.

Richard looked quite startled. 'Miss Kingston—er—Olivia!' he said hesitantly. 'Can it be you?'

She was not sure she could speak. Her heart was pounding, and she feared her knees were about to give way. Then Captain Gilbert gave her hand a friendly squeeze. The gesture was remarkably reassuring.

'It can, Richard,' she replied, 'It is good to see you after so many years.'

'Yes, it has been quite a time, has it not? A good eight years, by my reckoning.'

'Surely not? Who could believe the years could fly so quickly.' She pretended to be amazed, she even managed a little laugh.

'Will you not introduce me, Richard my love?' asked his wife timidly.

'Oh, yes. Bella, this is Miss Kingston, a friend from my youth.'

A friend? Was that how he remembered her? Olivia was hard put to it not to wince openly. Instead, she took the hand proffered by Bella Hayter. So this was the wealthy heiress Richard had married! She was not as grand as Olivia had expected. In fact she looked fatigued, and decidedly unwell. Only when she smiled shyly was there any hint of the prettiness that must have been hers before years of child-bearing had drained her looks.

Olivia became aware of Richard's eyes straying questioningly towards Miles Gilbert. She suddenly felt glad that she had the American as a companion. It was quite satisfying for Richard to meet her when she was in the company of such an undeniably attractive man.

'May I present Captain Gilbert, of the United States Navy?' she said. 'Captain, I am happy for you to meet Mr Hayter, who was a playmate in my childhood, and his wife, Mrs Hayter.' If Richard wanted to make their relationship into nothing more than a boy and girl romance, then she would go one step further!

'I can't equal the honour you enjoy, sir, of having known Miss Kingston from childhood,' said Miles Gilbert. 'But I hope newer friendships can claim their own privileges.' To Olivia's astonishment he smiled down at her in a way that could only be described as fond. Not quite sure what he was up to she smiled back at him, then turned to Richard.

'Do you intend to remain in Dartmouth long?' she asked.

'A few days only. I have some matters of family business to attend to.' There was frank admiration in his light-grey eyes as they swept over her, and also puzzlement, as if he could not make her out.

How had he expected her to be, after all these years? Shrivelled and faded? If anyone was faded it was his poor wife, who stood meekly at his side.

'And is this your first visit to our town, Mrs Hayter?' she asked.

'It is, Miss Kingston.'

'And does it please you?'

'Oh yes!' For the first time Bella Hayter's face showed animation. 'It is exceedingly pretty. I wish we could stay longer. I find the air quite delightful; I'm much better here than at home. Only, Mr Hayter says we must return.'

'Of course we must,' said Richard, somewhat pettishly. 'You know I have a deal of business on hand, awaiting my attention. Besides, the children need you,' he added as an afterthought.

'Let us hope you can bring your children on your next visit, and stay longer, perhaps when the weather is warmer,' said Olivia.

'What a splendid idea!' Bella Hayter's face brightened visibly. 'Could we, my love?'

'You can, I dare say, and the children. I doubt if I'll be able to get away. I'm far too busy!' Richard Hayter spoke in the irritable voice he seemed to reserve for his wife.

Mrs Hayter's wan face brightened even more. It occurred to Olivia that after seven pregnancies in seven years, the poor soul might welcome some respite from her husband. She became aware of Captain Gilbert looking at her. He raised his eyebrows in a silent enquiry. Yes, she wanted to go home. She had astonished herself with her ability to converse politely and reasonably, but she was not sure how much longer she could keep it up.

'This talk of warmer weather is doing little to take the edge off the wind,' said the Captain, as a chilly gust funnelled its way up the narrow lane. 'I think we have kept you ladies standing long enough.'

'I'm thankful for the rest, truly I am,' said Mrs Hayter shyly.

'But it wouldn't do for you to catch cold, ma'am. And as for you and I, Miss Kingston, I think some exercise is needed to restore our circulation.' He tucked her hand through his arm once more and gave it an affectionate pat. 'I'd be a sorry fellow if I let you grow chilled, would I not? I fear we must be on our way.'

The farewells Olivia exchanged with Ricahard were polite, formal, courteous. If he retained any fond memories of their old love he gave no sign of it. Still clutching the American's arm, she took her leave, and walked away from him without a backward glance. She even managed to chatter merrily to Captain Gilbert as she went. Only when they turned the corner, out of sight of Richard Hayter, did she stop, forced to lean against a wall for a moment, to recover herself.

'Let me help you into one of the shops, where you can sit down until you feel better,' said Miles Gilbert with concern.

Olivia shook her head. 'No, I thank you. If I can but have a minute I will feel better.' She took in great gulps of air... 'There, sir. I am fit to carry on our journey home. It was only a momentary indisposition.'

'But if you feel faint...'

'I never faint!' she informed him.

'No, I don't suppose you do.' He grinned at her briefly. 'In that case, I offer you my arm once more merely for the pleasure of your touch, and not for any support it may give you.'

She would have declined his offer if her legs had not felt so shaky she feared they would not hold her. The sight of her own front door was very welcome. Captain Gilbert had been uncommonly tactful as they walked along, not mentioning the Hayters nor asking awkward questions. He opened the door for her.

'Shall I fetch your mother, or Abbie?' he suggested.

'Oh no, thank you. I don't want anyone to be troubled by my silliness. If I can only sit quietly somewhere, until I am recovered. The music-room will do very well. I need nothing else.'

Miles Gilbert did not take her quite at her word. He disappeared, and returned a few moments later with a glass of brandy.

'Don't worry, I poured it while your father's back was turned,' he informed her. 'He doesn't know that anything is amiss.'

'Nothing is amiss!' Olivia retorted fiercely and took a hefty sip at the brandy. The result was a fit of coughing and spluttering, but when it was over she felt she had a legitimate excuse for the tears that were coursing down her cheeks.

'I think you have been considerably distressed, meeting Mr Hayter so unexpectedly,' said the Captain softly. 'I don't mean to pry. If you have no wish to talk then I will remain silent, although sometimes it helps to speak of things which disturb us. You and that gentleman were once very close? Have I guessed correctly?'

Olivia nodded. 'There is no reason why you shouldn't know,' she said. 'The rest of Dartmouth does! Richard Hayter and I were to be married, but before our betrothal could be announced the full extent of my father's business problems became known. In short, Papa was ruined! Richard's reaction was to go away. He abandoned me in the midst of all my other troubles. He had not the courage to tell me to my face that there was now no prospect of marriage between us. He sent me a letter.'

'He was no doubt very young at the time.' Miles Gilbert sought to find excuses for Richard's behaviour. 'Perhaps his family put pressure upon him—'

'No!' cried Olivia. Then more gently, 'No... No one who had ever loved could have written such things.' Every word of that dreadful letter was still scored upon her heart. She went on, 'He hadn't even the consideration to choose his timing with compassion. It arrived on the morning of my eighteenth birthday. The very day when we were to have announced our betrothal.'

'How could he?' demanded the American indignantly. 'To have behaved in such a way towards you, when he professed to love you!'

'I fear it was the prospects of Miss Kingston's fortune, not Miss Kingston herself that he loved,' said Olivia. She managed a little smile. 'Perhaps my father's ruin proved to be a blessing in disguise, or Richard and I might have been wed before...' She tried to say, Before I discovered he did not love me, but her throat tightened, and the words would not come.

'I agree with Abbie completely! He is totally unworthy of you!' He paused. 'Your pardon. I shouldn't have spoken so vehemently. It must have given you pain.'

Olivia shook her head. 'You haven't distressed me, sir, but, if you please—if I could be alone for a little while?'

'Of course. I will leave you in peace.'

He had started to go out of the room when Olivia said softly, 'Captain Gilbert . . . ! Thank you.'

'There is no need for thanks. I've done nothing.'

His denial was useless. She felt grateful to him. She realised just how accurately he had summed up the circumstances. Now she saw the reasons for his attentiveness: he had been deliberately playing the suitor so that Richard Hayter would not get the impression she was a dowdy spinster, of no interest to any man. Because of him she had not been at a disadvantage in this confrontation with her former love.

His perception surprised her. Was this the secret of his charm? she wondered. This sensitivity to other people's feelings, and the ability to act upon it swiftly? Doubtless that was how he managed to get his own way so frequently— But no! She was ashamed of the thought! On this occasion Miles Gilbert had had no ulterior motive for his actions other than kindness.

He had probably left the room thinking that she wanted to be alone to mourn her lost love. How far that was from the truth! Much of Olivia's distress stemmed from bewilderment. She still could not work it out herself. After years of being convinced that Richard Hayter was the only man she could ever love she had faced him to find that she felt . . . nothing! It had been like looking at a stranger. A pompous irritable stranger, with a receding hairline, a plump waist, and jowls that were definitely beginning to droop. The past years had not been kind to Richard. He could not be any older than Miles Gilbert— most likely he was a year or so younger—yet middle age, no hint of which had touched the American, had a firm grip upon Richard.

Oddly enough, it was the face of Bella Hayter which lingered in her mind. Exhausted, timid, sickly. Was that how she might have become, if circumstances had been different? She could not believe that she had talked to Richard's wife and referred to his children without a single pang of anguish. If she were truthful, the only emotions she felt at the moment were bewilderment—and relief.

Olivia sat in the music-room for as long as she dared. It was the risk of her parents missing her and sending to see what was wrong which finally prompted her to move. Slowly she ascended the stairs, removing her cape and bonnet as she went, conscious that, because of that one chance encounter, her whole life had altered.

The change in her inner self was so great it was almost surprising next morning to wake to the ordinary tasks of an ordinary day. Yet even this day had something unusual to offer. When she returned home after her teaching she found Captain Gilbert waiting for her.

'Miss Kingston, is that you?' he called from the top of the stairs.

'Yes. Were you expecting someone else?'

'No, you are exactly the person I was hoping would come.'

'Oh, then that means you want a favour of me!'

'How did you come to be so harsh? Or come to know my character so well?' he chuckled.

She regarded him cautiously. There was an air of excitement about him she did not understand.

'What is it that you want?' she asked.

He did not answer her directly.

'I am right, am I not? You have no more lessons in the latter part of this afternoon?' he asked.

'Not after half past two. Why? Have you found me another pupil?'

'Better than that. How would you like to form a musical partnership?'

'With whom?'

'With me, of course.'

'No.'

'You haven't heard what it is.'

'I don't need to hear what it is. The answer is still no.'

'Despite your stubbornness I will tell you, all the same. I'm asking you to accompany me at the piano when I sing at Mrs Holdsworth's at-home this afternoon.'

'You don't need me. You are perfectly capable of accompanying yourself.'

'Ah, but I wouldn't perform as well as you, and in addition, I would find your presence so reassuring. It is no easy matter, standing up before an audience.'

'It doesn't bother you one jot, and well you know it!'

'Please don't reject the idea out of hand.' He had stopped joking now, and was serious. 'Can you not force yourself to tolerate me for an extra hour? It means much to me, and will be for our mutual benefit.'

She was more wary than ever now that he was being persuasive. Miles Gilbert in a persuasive mood was a truly formidable force.

'I don't see how it would benefit me,' she said.

'Surely your share of the fee must be some inducement?'

'Fee? But do you not visit the Holdsworths' as a guest? How can you ask to be paid?'

'Quite easily; I am totally without funds at the moment. And if I am not mistaken you would not be averse to the extra two and a half guineas.'

'Really, sir, my financial state is none of your business.'

'Come, Miss Kingston, admit it. You need the money and so do I. Oh, I know in polite English society one does not discuss anything so degrading as money. Fortunately, in America we take a much more realistic view of the topic. If you need money there is no point in pretending that you do not! If I recall aright, at one time you actually recommended me to sing at street corners, it being a more honourable way of earning my bread than playing billiards.'

'So I did, though at the time I didn't know I would be required to stand with you and hold the collecting-cup. In spite of what you say, I won't change my mind. I don't perform in public, and not even a share in the two and a half guineas will tempt me.'

'You misunderstand. The two and a half guineas will be yours. Mrs Holdsworth has agreed to pay five guineas. You will be in the public eye for less than half an hour. Surely it is worth it, for all you will have to endure my company for rather longer? Think how many piano lessons you would have to give to earn that sort of money!'

Olivia was thinking! To be paid so much for so little!

'I still don't see why I am necessary,' she said. 'Why do you not accompany yourself? And pray don't repeat those fairy stories about my ability.'

'If I tell you the truth you will accuse me of being vain once more. However, I will take the risk. Sitting at the piano doesn't show me off to my full advantage, nor can I gaze into the eyes of my audience. I have decided that, since the company will be mainly comprised of ladies, both of these requirements are necessary. If things go as I hope, then this afternoon will be only the beginning. Where Mrs Holdsworth leads the wives of Dartmouth's other principal citizens are bound to follow. Therefore I intend to appeal to as many female hearts and eyes as possible.'

'You are incorrigible!' gasped Olivia, not certain whether to be shocked or amused.

'So you see now why I am beseeching you to come to my aid.'

Olivia did not reply immediately. Her dislike of playing in public was not the only reason for hesitancy. She felt that Captain Gilbert was right when he said that other hostesses in town would follow where Mrs Holdsworth led. She could see the ladies clamouring to engage him, for himself as much as for his voice. And that would mean she would be in his company a great deal, and she was not sure it would be a prudent move. If ever there was a time when her hostility towards him wavered it was when he sang. She acknowledged that their mutual love of music made her vulnerable, and she was reluctant to put that vulnerability to the test. But then she thought of the money. At last she would be able to pay for her mother's tippet.

'I agree,' she said. 'I have no alternative.'

'Splendid. You won't regret it, I promise you. Now, would you have a few minutes to spare in order to choose a programme? We must make it a good one. Let us give the ladies of Dartmouth a treat.'

The ladies of Dartmouth were going to be delighted, Olivia decided. She had to acknowledge that he looked more than ordinarily attractive as he sorted out the music. Not handsome, he would never be that, but dashing. Moreover, there was some mysterious appeal about him which drew people to him. Herself apart, she doubted if many other ladies at the at-home would be able to resist him.

'If you would be a favourite this afternoon you must certainly sing one of these.' She handed him the book of Italian love-songs.

He looked at the title with a smile.

'These will be the most affecting to female hearts?' he asked.

'Absolutely guaranteed!'

'There, I knew I had chosen my business partner well. I can see your advice is going to be invaluable,' he declared delightedly.

The expression of pleased approval on his face made something stir uncomfortably in the region of her heart, a region she had felt to be a vacuum since her encounter with Richard. She found herself hoping that Lizzie Hunt would not be among the guests at Mrs Holdsworth's.

'Here, my dear! You must have the loan of my lace tippet,' insisted Mrs Kingston, as Olivia prepared for the afternoon. 'It will brighten up that old crape of yours. I think it is good that you are going out into society once more.'

'I'm not going as a guest, Mama. The Captain and I are hired entertainers.'

Charlotte Kingston winced at the ugly word 'hired'.

'Nevertheless, you must look your best. Who knows, you might meet some of our friends from the old days who would be eager to renew our acquaintance.'

'If their friendship has been absent for eight whole years I doubt if my appearance this afternoon will make any difference. All the same, I will wear it, with many thanks.'

'Are you ready, Miss Kingston?' Miles Gilbert entered. He looked elegant. The intricate folds of his neckcloth showed up snowy-white against the light-brown of his coat, and his hair gleamed with the rich lustre of old gold. Olivia felt she must look quite dowdy beside him, but a chance glimpse in the mirror proved unexpectedly heartening. Although her snuff-coloured gown was old the crape was of fine quality and draped well against her slender figure, and the pale softness of the lace tippet about her shoulders was flattering to her clear complexion. With her dark hair dressed in a more soft and becoming manner the overall effect was certainly muted, but far from dowdy.

'I'm ready, sir,' she said. 'Though I will be glad when this is over.'

'You have no need to be nervous. You are an excellent pianist, I promise to sing superbly, so there is nothing to worry about.'

'And I don't suppose the ladies will notice whether I am there or not, eh? Oh, one moment, Captain!' She had spotted a flaw in his otherwise immaculate appearance. 'If you are intent upon breaking hearts do not do so with cat hairs all over your sleeve. You shouldn't allow Tibby such liberties. You know she is not permitted upstairs.' She took a clothes-brush from the drawer of the hall table and began to remove the offending hairs.

'Like every other female she finds me irresistible.'

'Almost every other female,' Olivia corrected him.

'Ah yes, I nearly forgot.' He sounded almost serious. She looked at him questioningly, but he was regarding his now impeccable sleeve.

'What a clever fellow I am,' he remarked. 'Along with my other numerous talents I have the ability to choose outstanding lodgings. Not only is my bed comfortable, the food superb and the company incomparable, I am also provided with a valet.'

'Before your vanity gets too overwhelming I think we ought to give Admiral Ranscombe some credit.'

'The Admiral? What has he to do with anything?'

'It was he who chose your lodgings. I don't recall you having any say in the matter.'

'Surely it is unusual, an admiral concerning himself with such a thing?' He looked at her, suddenly serious. 'I thought Captain Roberts was the billeting officer.'

'Normally he is, I suppose, but in your case the Admiral took an interest. Perhaps because you are the only American. Perhaps because he wanted to help us. Does it matter? You look quite grave.'

'Of course it doesn't matter. I was simply surprised.' Yet, despite his denial, he was uncommonly quiet the entire way to the Holdsworths' house, and she felt that, for some reason, the discovery of the Admiral's intervention had disturbed him.

That Captain Gilbert was no stranger to the household became evident the moment they stepped inside. The butler greeted him by name and with approving deference. The pretty maid who showed them to the ante-room where they were to wait also greeted him by name, but instead of deference treated him to some saucy looks from under her eyelashes; she hardly acknowledged that he had a companion.

Olivia relaxed. It seemed she was right, all eyes would be on the American, no one would notice her. True enough, when they were announced and she took her place at the piano she might have been invisible.

Once the performance began she was too occupied to feel uncomfortable. Concentrating upon her playing and upon the melodic richness of the Captain's voice left no opportunity for self-consciousness. In no time the final notes of the last song were dying away. It was one of the love-songs suggested by Olivia herself, and was greeted with yearning sighs from a score or more female bosoms, before the assembled company erupted into applause. The American took his bows with complete assurance, and, as he turned to acknowledge her, he gave her a confiding wink. She was left marooned upon the piano-stool as the ladies surged forward to offer their congratulations, and she found she was grateful for that wink. Somehow it set her aside from his flock of admirers.

The idea of a flock proved particularly apt. Despite Olivia's hopes, Lizzie Hunt was present among the guests, looking young and delightful in a gown of forget-me-not merino. Clearly Miss Hunt's air of simple innocence was misleading, for as Olivia watched, she rose from her chair and forced a way for herself through the seemingly impenetrable wall of female bodies. She then proceeded to edge the Captain out of the crush with the skill and cunning of a well trained dog cutting a sheep from the herd. What the girl had to say to him was impossible to hear. It involved a great deal of stretching up on tip-toe so that her rose-bud mouth was close to his ear, and much clutching at his arm to maintain her balance. From his expression Miles Gilbert was enjoying himself enormously!

He is welcome to her, Olivia thought sourly. I have always considered that Lizzie to be a hussy. They should suit one another perfectly.

Just as she was wondering when they would be allowed to withdraw an all-too-familiar voice said, 'Miss Kingston! This is an unexpected pleasure.'

'Mr Dunsford,' she said faintly. 'I had no idea you were here.'

'I am not really a guest at the at-home. I was conducting some business with Mr Holdsworth when we heard the music.

Noting my interest he kindly said he was sure the ladies would not object if we joined them for few minutes.'

Olivia was certain they would not object. Not those with marriageable daughters, at any rate. She hoped that some ambitious mama might come and carry off Joseph Dunsford, but no one did.

'...Imagine my surprise and delight. I had no idea it was you playing.' Mr Dunsford was talking again.

'And did you enjoy our little concert?' she asked, hoping to give the impression she had been listening intently to what he had to say.

'Very much. Though in my opinion it would have been improved if you had played on your own.'

'It is kind of you to say so,' said Olivia, rising.

'Oh, is it time for you to leave? Am I to be permitted to escort you home?'

'There is no need for you to trouble, I thank you. I go back with Captain Gilbert.' She glanced hopefully in the American's direction, without success. He continued to be absorbed by Lizzie Hunt's conversation.

If she expected Joseph Dunsford to be put off she was doomed to disappointment there, too. If anything, he seemed more enthusiastic.

'Then you shall have two cavaliers to protect you, instead of one. You wish to go now?' To her surprise, at her nod, he strode over and brusquely broke up the *tête-à-tête* between Lizzie and the Captain.

'Your pardon, Miss Hunt,' he said, butting in without a by-your-leave. 'Captain Gilbert, Miss Kingston wishes to go home!'

Such stunning rudeness made Lizzie Hunt go an unbecoming red. Olivia watched the girl change colour with satisfaction—she could almost have liked Joseph Dunsford at that moment. The Captain, too, looked furious. Then he made his farewells to his pretty companion in a pantomime of regret.

'I hope I have not kept you waiting.' Miles Gilbert bowed stiffly to Olivia, at the same time glowering coldly at the other man.

'Mr Dunsford has kindly offered to walk with us,' said Olivia.

The American looked less than delighted at the prospect.

'In that case shall we go?' he said curtly.

'If you feel you are not depriving your worshippers,' she replied.

The Captain's stern expression lessened a little, as he answered, 'They have had enough for the moment. We mustn't spoil them.'

'I don't see what can be spoiled if we leave now,' said Mr Dunsford, puzzled.

Olivia did not feel like enlightening him. 'You are quite right, sir. Let us be on our way.'

They walked briskly through the darkening streets, the shop lamps casting pools of light on the gleaming cobbles. Olivia, from her position sandwiched between her two escorts, steeled herself for more of Dunsford's clumsy gallantry. To her relief, and the American's evident annoyance, he seemed more inclined to talk to the Captain. In fact, he just about ignored her until they were outside the Kingstons' house.

'Well, here we are at your home, Miss Kingston,' he went on, addressing her almost for the first time. 'Don't invite me in, I pray you. The disappointment of having to decline would be too great. I have another appointment within the quarter-hour, otherwise nothing would have given me greater pleasure.'

'We must look forward to your company on some other occasion,' said Olivia, who had been hoping she would not have to put up with him for much longer.

'Until that happy day, farewell.' Joseph Dunsford bowed, and strode off back to town.

'Have you and Dunsford quarrelled?' demanded the Captain when they went indoors.

'Not that I know of. Why do you ask?'

'He had so little to say to you on the way home. But now I see his method. He was sounding me out, trying to determine how much of a rival I am for your affections.'

'Oh really!' exclaimed Olivia in exasperation, surprised that the aftermath of the supper-party still rankled with him. 'I hope you gave Mr Dunsford some satisfactory replies. I would hate my scheming to go for naught.'

The Captain continued to glower. Then he exclaimed, 'Let's change the subject and forget Dunsford! This afternoon was a

great success, was it not? I was right. More than one lady is
eager to engage our mutal talents. A plague on this curfew! But
for it our scope would be much greater. I will be glad when the
spring comes and it is extended to eight o'clock. In the mean-
time, here is your share of the proceeds. I know you found little pleasure in earning it, but I hope you agree with me that it
is good to be affluent.' And he dropped the coins into her palm.

She certainly agreed with him about the money. The two and
a half guineas seemed like riches to her. The performance, too,
had been less arduous than she had expected. It was the prospect of being so much in Miles Gilbert's company that she had
doubts about.

As for the Captain himself, his dislike of Joseph Dunsford
had clearly soured his pleasure in becoming solvent again. As
he went up to his room he looked decidedly glum.

'I hear you were a great success at Mrs Holdsworth's at-
home,' said Mrs Jenkins, when she came for tea next day.

'Captain Gilbert was a success, ma'am. I was merely there,'
smiled Olivia.

'I dare say you were most splendid, too. But speaking of the
dear man, where is he?'

'No doubt charming some unsuspecting lady into engaging
us to entertain her guests,' replied Olivia.

'Really, how can you speak so?' scolded her mother. 'I do
not approve of this performing in public, not even with the
Captain. I do not approve at all.'

'I see no harm in it, as long as they go only to the best
houses,' said Mrs Jenkins, rising to her feet with an effort.
'Well, I can't wait for that lovely man to return. I must be on
my way.'

It was growing dark and, as Olivia drew the curtains after
their guest had departed, she paused in the window. Although
she was reluctant to admit it to herself, she knew she was
watching out for Miles Gilbert. He had only to be late, it only
needed the clock to be approaching five, and she was conscious of a feeling of anxiety. Not until he returned home did
she relax.

She screwed up her eyes to penetrate the gathering gloom.
Then, to her relief, she saw two familiar figures approaching
from the direction of the town. Captain Gilbert was walking

with Lieutenant La Fontaine, and she smiled at the contras
between the two. The stocky Frenchman with his sailor's gait
and the tall American with his long athletic stride ... Then sh
looked again, puzzled. Why had she never noticed it before? N
seaman of her acquaintance walked as easily and evenly a
Miles Gilbert. From Admiral Ranscombe to the old sea-do
who plied the ferry across the river, without exception the
moved with a characteristic roll, still compensating for th
heaving of the decks long after they had left the sea.

There was no hint of a roll in Captain Gilbert's walk, no ev
idence that he had ever had to cope regularly with a ship toss
ing and wallowing beneath him. But he was a captain in the
United States Navy. At least, that was what he claimed to be.
Yet now she considered it he did not seem like a seaman. She
had never heard him talk of life on board ship, for example, or
speak of any seaborne adventures, save his capture by the Royal
Navy. To her recollection he had never even mentioned the
name of a single ship upon which he had served. In her experience, such reticence among sea-going gentlemen was rare. It
was true that he was well-travelled, though of course one did
not have to be in the navy to travel. And besides, his talk of
other countries had always been in relation to music, never the
sea.

He was standing outside Mrs Passmore's now, still talking to
the Lieutenant. As she watched, Olivia felt an increasing sense
of unease. The more she thought of it the less she felt Miles
Gilbert to be a seaman, and her unease deepened into disquiet.
What reason could this well-educated, much travelled American have for passing as an ordinary sea captain? And an enemy one, at that!

The one word 'enemy' stuck in her brain. Britain and
America were at war, and Miles Gilbert, for all his fine manners and winning ways, was on the other side. If he chose to
masquerade as someone else, then, in wartime, the reason must
surely be a sinister one.

Olivia found that she had gone cold, and she felt more than
a little sick. No, she was being silly and fanciful. If Miles Gilbert was playing a part then it had to be for some innocent reason such as ... such as ... It was no use, she could not think of
a single advantage he would enjoy through being a naval cap-

tain instead of a private individual, not even in prison. The more she dwelt on her suspicions the more likely they became. Miles Gilbert was not who he claimed to be, and he was up to no good.

She was aware of a strong feeling of betrayal, on her own account rather than on England's. In spite of her misgivings, she had trusted him, and all the time he had been deceiving her. Anger began to grow in her; at the American for his treachery, and at herself for having been taken in by him.

He was in the house now. The front door slammed and she heard him coming upstairs, two steps at a time. She stalked out to confront him, determined to discover what he was about.

'There is a most appetising smell coming from the kitchen,' he greeted her. 'I shall do justice to whatever it is, that I promise you!'

He was smiling broadly, and it was his smile which checked her. It was so open, so lacking in guile. Surely, no man with a guilty secret could have such a good-humoured smile? Disarmed, she let him go past and up to his room without a word. Her gaze followed him, as she tried to summon the strength of will to challenge him. No words came.

A knock at the front door made her jump. When she opened it she found Admiral Ranscombe standing on the doorstep. For some reason the sight of him made her nervous.

'Good evening to you, Miss Kingston,' he said, saluting her with exaggerated formality. 'I have two reasons for calling at this most inopportune moment. One is to hand in the Exeter newspaper for your father. The other is the delight of feasting my eyes upon you.' His tone changed to one of concern. 'But you look pale, my dear Miss Kingston. Are you unwell?'

'Pale, sir?' Olivia started. 'No, I am not unwell. I—I think I may be a little fatigued, that is all,' she added hastily.

'You do too much, young lady. You should treat yourself with some of the consideration you show to others.'

'An early night, that is what I need. Nothing more,' she replied. Politeness demanded that she invite him in, yet her instinct longed for him to go away. 'I thank you for the *Flying Post*. I am not sure if my father is resting, but if you would like to come in . . .' The Admiral shook his head.

'Not on this occasion, I thank you, much as it would please me. I have had strict instructions to be home in good time tonight, and I will not risk being clapped in irons by being one minute late. I bid you farewell for the present.' Saluting again, he departed.

Such overwhelming relief swept through Olivia that, after she had shut the door, she leaned against it weakly. Thank goodness he had not come in! Then she roused herself sharply. Why would it have been so terrible for Admiral Ranscombe to have entered the house? Normally she enjoyed the visits of the cheery little man. Why was this occasion so different? Because she suspected Miles Gilbert was an imposter?

Slowly Olivia sank down and sat on the stairs. Surely the one person to whom she should have reported her suspicions was the Admiral? He was a man of authority, he was also a friend. Above all, he had been there, in front of her, talking to her. Yet never once had the thought entered her head. She had been far too preoccupied with protecting the Captain! Denouncing him had never occurred to her. The reason for her silence came as a shock. There could only be one! She was in love with him!

CHAPTER SEVEN

OLIVIA got precious little sleep that night. She could not tell which gave her the most anguish—the fact that she had fallen in love with Miles Gilbert, her suspicions about the man, or the way in which she had protected him when surely it had been her duty to denounce him. But denounce him for what? As far as she knew impersonating a naval officer, even an American one, was not a crime. It was not as if he had done anything wrong— or had he? The burning of the frigate had happened since the American had been in town. And then there was the matter of the escaping prisoners of war. Someone must have organised that. The local smugglers were unlikely to have contacts as far away as Ashburton who would send them extra business in the shape of absconding Frenchmen.

'Fanciful nonsense!' Olivia muttered, pummelling at her pillows. 'You are becoming one of those people who see spies behind every bush!'

But the idea, once it had entered her head, would not go away. What better cover for a secret agent than already being a prisoner of war, particularly one on parole who had consid- erable freedom of movement. True, Captain Gilbert was an American, but the Americans were allies of the French, and anyway, might they not have spies of their own?

What had begun as a fanciful notion began to seem more and more probable as the night wore on. By the time morning came Olivia had at least solved one problem. She knew which of her torments was bothering her the most. It was loving Miles Gil- bert. Without that she would have had no other troubles. She could have gone to Admiral Ranscombe in confidence and told him her suspicions, and that would have been that.

As she rose to begin her morning's work she found herself wishing she had only the normal miseries of love to contend with—things like doubts, and hopelessness.

Olivia's heart pulled her in one direction, her conscience in another, until her life was made a misery. At times she tried to watch the Captain surreptitiously, just in case he did anything suspicious. At others she would so dread discovering any definite proof against him that she would do her utmost to avoid him. Her whole existence became difficult, and her temper grew short.

'Have I done something to displease you, Miss Kingston?' he demanded one day, when she had been particularly snappy towards him.

'No more than usual,' she retorted.

They had been trying some new songs together in the musicroom, and the practice had gone badly. She had found herself fumbling over the keys, disagreeing with him about the timing, and had finished by declaring he was impossible to work with.

'Perhaps our musical enterprise isn't such a good thing,' he said.

'How can you say that? We've a host of engagements during the next few weeks.'

'But I wonder if it isn't all too much for you. Already you work so hard.' He took her hands in his own, his fingers curling about hers. 'We'll abandon the whole idea.'

The softness of his touch was more than she could bear. Roughly she pulled away from his grasp.

'Neither of us can afford to do that,' she retorted. 'There's no need to stop out of consideration for me. I can carry on quite easily.'

'Then what's wrong? What's happened?'

'Nothing has happened. I keep telling you so.'

They were sitting side by side on the long piano-stool. She could feel the warmth of him against her, the gentle pressure of his long limbs against hers. She wanted to feel his arms about her, to be pulled against him, and know the soft caress of his lips against her skin. She wanted all this from a man whom she feared was trying to destroy everything she held dear.

'But you aren't happy. Is there nothing I can do?'

'Only to go away and never come back. That would make me happy!' she cried.

He flinched at the harshness of her tone, and moved away from her.

'Your pardon, Miss Kingston,' he said stiffly. 'Lately I thought you were coming to approve of me more. Now I see I was wrong.'

'That you were, sir! And I'm too well aware of your efforts to get into my good books. Do you think I've forgotten your declaration? What were your words? "I'll make you like me more before I'm through, I swear I will." You would have me added to your list of conquests, like a gamekeeper's trophy, for no better reason than to please your vanity. Well, you can go on trying. I wish you joy of it, but you won't succeed.'

'No, I won't!' he replied, suddenly angry. 'And do you know why? Because you are cold! There's not one vestige of real warmth or tenderness in you. I nearly said your heart is of flint, but one can at least strike sparks from flint. And your mind is as rigid as your heart. Once you decide upon something there's no swaying you. You were determined to dislike me the minute you saw me. You took no pains to try to discover my true character. You simply marked me down as unworthy from that first moment. I've tried since to alter your opinion of me. Heaven only knows how much I've tried! I should have known it would be so much wasted effort. Just once in your life, Miss Kingston, try to consider other people's feelings before you trample on them quite so effectively.'

He rose abruptly from the stool, pushing it back with such force that she was obliged to clutch at the piano for support. Then, without a backward glance, he strode out.

Olivia sat very still, going over his words again and again. He had been so angry, and something more . . . Had he been hurt? That he could cause her distress was never in doubt. His stinging words about her coldness and hard-heartedness had hit at her like blows, yet it seemed as if he actually cared about her good opinion of him.

She had almost allowed herself the luxury of hope when a cautionary inner voice intervened. If, as she suspected, the American was in the pay of Bonaparte, then subterfuge and deceit would be part of his stock in trade. Such a man would

regard deceiving her, a provincial spinster, to be child's play.
Why he should bother to pretend he had some regard for her
she could not imagine, unless he wished to involve her in his
duplicity. Did he intend her to be a shield of respectability behind which he hid other, more sinister activities?

'Oh, I don't know what to think!' she cried, putting her
hands to her throbbing head. 'Why, oh why did he come here
to torment me?'

In spite of everything, she could not stop loving him. If only
she could put aside her doubts and suspicions she knew that
being with him was the greatest happiness she would wish for.

No matter what her emotional turmoil she still had duties to
perform, and lessons to give. Forcing herself into some sem-
blance of calm she went upstairs.

'Maria will be here for her lesson in half an hour, Papa,' she
said. 'Is there anything you require before she arrives?'

'Ear plugs?' suggested Mr Kingston wickedly.

'Apart from that!'

'Would you have time to fetch my medicine from the apothecary? It should be ready by now.'

'I'll go straight away. I can be back long before Maria gets
here. Is there anything else?'

'No, thank you, my dear. I am quite content with my telescope, looking at the traffic on the river. Ah, I was right. It is
the *Marigold* coming in. Such a battered old ketch! I sometimes wonder how she stays afloat. Do you know, the last time
she was in the Dart the Captain referred to her as a brig. Yet,
anyone can see she is ketch-rigged.'

'Perhaps things are differently named in his part of the
world,' Olivia replied shortly.

The fact that Miles Gilbert could not identify shipping merely
served to confirm her worst fears.

Mr Kingston regarded his daughter with a quizzical smile.
'You are looking very pretty today, my dear. Is that a new
gown?'

'No, it is not, Papa. It is a very old one, refurbished with a
few pennyworth of trimming,' she replied, feeling the colour
rise in her cheeks.

So her father had noticed that she had been paying more attention to her appearance lately! She could not do much, for

she had neither the time nor the means, but she had begun dressing her hair in more flattering ways, and softening the neckline of her gown with a muslin fichu. It had been some time since she had bothered much about how she looked. She was not exactly sure why she was making the effort now, except that it made her feel better. The notion that she might be trying to attract the eye of Miles Gilbert was too futile for consideration.

'Old or not, your gown looks extremely fetching,' observed her father. 'Now, off you go. Don't let me detain you.'

Olivia left the house, stepping over the puddles left by the recent rain. She was passing her neighbour's house when the door opened, and Lieutenant La Fontaine emerged.

'*Bonjour*, Mademoiselle Kingston,' he greeted her. 'You permit I walk with you?'

'I will be glad of your company though I'm not going far,' she replied.

'You go to give a music lesson, I think?'

'No, not this time. I'm off to fetch my father's medicine. I do have a pupil in a few minutes, but she is coming to the house.'

'I think I am very lucky to live beside you. So much music.'

Olivia wondered if he would feel the same if he knew that the music was to be played by Maria.

'I hope we don't disturb you,' she said, with concern.

'Oh no, it is very pleasant. I know it is not polite to listen, but it gives me much pleasure. Because of the curfew I must spend many hours in my lodgings. My landlady is kind, but she is old. Also, she does not hear well. It is difficult to speak with her, so the winter nights, they often seem long.'

'They must indeed,' said Olivia sympathetically. 'I am glad the music from our house doesn't intrude.'

'I like it very much. It reminds me of my wife. She, too, plays the piano. Not well, like you, but very prettily. When I am at home it gives me pleasure to hear her.'

'Have you had the letter you were expecting from her yet?'

'Alas, no. I wait and wait, and it does not come. I am most anxious. You see, mademoiselle, my Lucille was expecting our first child when I left. The baby, it was to have been born in late summer. So many months, and I have heard nothing. I am anxious. I fear things have not gone well.'

The Frenchman's distress was evident, and Olivia felt sorry for him.

'Don't despair because you've not received a letter,' she said. 'It means nothing. We heard naught of my brother, who is imprisoned in Verdun, for over a year. We were distraught, convinced he must be dead, then two letters arrived from him within the week. They'd been dispatched months apart. Your letter will come, never fear.'

'You are kind, mademoiselle. You make me cheerful again.' Despite his words the Frenchman's visage still registered anxiety. 'You permit I show you a picture of my wife?'

'I would be honoured.' Olivia held out her hand for the miniature he took from inside his coat.

The face smiling back at her from the scrap of ivory was pertly pretty, the dark eyes full of laughter.

'Your wife is lovely!' she exclaimed.

'Yes, she is.' The Lieutenant gazed at the picture with great longing before returning it to its resting place next to his heart.

Olivia was moved by his plight. The poor man must be having a miserable time, especially since he was worried about his wife and child.

'It would be good if you could come and spend an evening with us occasionally,' she said. 'It seems silly, you being by yourself, when you are just in the next house.'

'You are kind to think of it, mademoiselle.'

'Is there no way you could come so that no one would see?'

'I could, perhaps, climb over the garden wall? Then I will not be walking on the streets, so I do not break my curfew. No?'

'That seems an excellent scheme, sir,' she laughed. 'Can we look for you at about seven this evening?'

'That will be very pleasing. I thank you. My landlady, she hears nothing. She does not know if I am in or out . . . Oh, we are at the shop of the apothecary.'

'So we are, sir. I thank you for your company.'

'No, mademoiselle. It is I who thank you, for your kindness.' The Frenchman bowed.

Olivia went into the shop, still smiling at the way he proposed to evade the curfew. She had not expected the Lieutenant to be so devious. Clearly, he was not as quiet as he seemed.

She had barely returned home again before Mrs Rowden and Maria arrived.

'Why, Mrs Rowden, what has happened to distress you?' she asked.

'You mean you don't know, Miss Kingston?' Maria's mother's bosom heaved with agitation as she fanned herself energetically with her hand. 'The whole town is in an uproar. That Bonaparte has been abroad again. I tell you, I had to think twice about whether it was safe to bring Maria out for her lesson today. I quite feared we'd be murdered on the street, that I did.'

'How strange. I have only just come in from town, and I observed nothing unusual. What has happened?'

'Why, the French have attacked the castle!'

'Surely not! We heard nothing.'

'It is true, I assure you, Miss Kingston. My neighbour, who was on duty there with the Volunteers last night, said that they shot at a prowler.'

'Couldn't he have been an ordinary thief?'

'What is there for an ordinary thief out there? And what ordinary thief would tackle a place so well guarded when he can have easier pickings elsewhere? No, the fellow was a Frenchman, you mark my word!' Mrs Rowden was determined not to be robbed of her bit of drama. She dropped her voice to a theatrical whisper. 'My neighbour reckons that he's living here among us.'

'Who? Bonaparte?' asked Olivia, a little startled.

'No, one of his devilish minions! My neighbour said the rogue headed off back towards town along the foreshore, as if he knew exactly where he was going. Believe me, Mr Rowden is going to be in such a fury with me for not keeping Maria indoors when danger is stalking the very streets of Dartmouth, but then she does so love her music. And I believe a true gift should always be encouraged.'

'Shall I begin playing now, Miss Kingston? Before Boney gets here?' asked Maria, her round face alight with eagerness.

'Yes, do,' said Olivia.

As the child thundered out the first notes of the scale it occurred to her that Maria's playing might prove a very effective deterrent against any invading force. In truth, though, she did not feel like joking. Mrs Rowden's story had been exaggerated, of course, but she feared there must have been some substance to it. The incident sounded sinister. In one point the bootmaker's wife had been right—it was unlikely that any ordinary prowler would have tackled the well-guarded castle. Inside Olivia felt a cold feeling of dread at the prospect of more espionage in the town. Try as she might she could think of no way to prove that the Captain had been the intruder, just as she could think of no way to prove that he had not.

With Maria playing it was difficult to concentrate on anything else. Olivia was relieved when the dying chords of 'Shepherd's Hey' finally echoed off the music-room walls, and the Rowdens departed. She was thankful, too, that Lieutenant La Fontaine would be with them that evening. Having a visitor would ease the strain of being in Captain Gilbert's company.

Her family took the news that they could expect the Frenchman to arrive, via the garden wall and back door, with surprising aplomb.

'The more the merrier!' declared Mr Kingston. He turned to Captain Gilbert. 'It must be deuced dull for you fellows, being confined to the house in such a way.'

'Yes, it must be most tedious, almost as though you were back in the nursery,' commiserated Mrs Kingston.

'Not quite, ma'am,' said the Captain gravely. 'I can't imagine myself back in the nursery unless I can picture a beard, and no one in this house sports such a thing.'

'I do not understand, sir.' Charlotte Kingston was perplexed.

'Well, my nurse had a splendid one. My father was extremely jealous of it, I remember.'

'Oh, Captain, you are funning!' Mrs Kingston gave a delighted laugh. 'What a pleasant winter we are having. I declare usually I hate this season, it is so dull and cold, but this year we have you, dear Captain, to cheer us.'

Olivia took care not to look in Miles Gilbert's direction. She was gaining precious little cheer from his presence. The feeling appeared to be mutual, for his manner towards her, of late, had

been restrained. She did not know whether to be glad or sorry.
It would have been easier if she could have stopped loving him,
but she did not know how. If fears of his duplicity and treachery could not achieve it, what hope had anything else?

'I shouldn't expect over-much cheerfulness from this
Frenchman,' cautioned Mr Kingston. 'By the looks of him
there is not a deal of laughter in him.'

'You never know, Papa. I fancy he may have hidden depths,'
Olivia said, with a slight smile.

Lieutenant La Fontaine proved to be an unexpectedly pleasant guest. He was still quiet, it was true, and apologised for his
poor command of English more than once. Yet he was appre-
ciative of the music provided by Olivia and the Captain. And
if his understanding of the language failed him, then Miles
Gilbert interpreted most expertly. This ability of the American
to speak fluent French did nothing to soothe Olivia's peace of
mind. It seemed to be one more confirmation of her suspicions.

From then on the Frenchman became quite a regular visitor
to the house, almost as regular as Joseph Dunsford, who
seemed to haunt the place. Olivia grew to dread every knock on
the door, lest it proved to be her unwanted suitor.

'Mr Dunsford would be a very good catch,' remarked her
father, one day.

'Yes, he would,' she agreed, without enthusiasm.

'He does seem to be paying you particular attention. Had
you noticed?'

'Yes, Papa, I had,' she replied, her enthusiasm waning further.

'Have you given any thought to your answer, if he should
make you an offer? Marriage to him would improve your situation considerably, not to mention . . .' He stopped, looking a
little awkward.

Olivia could guess what he had meant to say. More and more
recently, as Joseph Dunsford had become an increasingly fre-
quent caller, she had been forcing herself to face distasteful reality. If Mr Dunsford proposed to her she would have to accept,
for her parents' sake. Her own inclinations in the matter must
count for nothing. As Mrs Dunsford she would be able to restore her mother and father to the sort of life to which they were

accustomed. It would be within her power to give them all the comforts they so sorely missed. She tried to imagine a life bound to the stolid merchant, and found she had to suppress a shudder at the prospect. Nevertheless, plenty of other women had been forced to accept much more distasteful marriages in order to ensure security. She would be far from unique. Nor would she be the first woman to have married one man when she loved another.

'I consider it highly unlikely that Mr Dunsford will make me an offer,' she said, trying to sound cheerful. 'If he does, I will naturally give it serious consideration.'

Was it her imagination, or did her father expel the faintest sigh of relief?

She had a busy afternoon, giving lessons first at a house in the town, and then at another high up on the hill at Townstal. The steep slope, combined with the distance and the sheer effort she put into her teaching, made her particularly weary as she returned home. She pushed open the front door, and was at once struck by the unusual silence. There was something ominous about such quiet, and she began to hurry along the passage, discarding her cape and bonnet en route.

'Miss Kingston! Thank goodness you've come!' Miles Gilbert was leaning over the bannisters, looking worriedly down at her.

'What has happened? Is someone ill? Papa! Has something happened to Papa?' She started to run up the stairs.

'No, it isn't your father. I fear it's your mother. I was about to go for the doctor.'

'Mama!' She pushed past him into her parents' room, where she found her mother lying prostrate on the bed. Her father was positioned in his wheelchair at the bedside, holding his wife's hand.

'Olivia! You are here at last!' he exclaimed when he saw her.

'What happened?' She leaned over her mother, noting the closed eyes and the pallor.

'I'm not sure. I only know that your Mama was taking tea in her boudoir with Peg Jenkins—I didn't join them, there was a vessel going out whose progress I particularly wanted to follow. The next thing I knew there was a great commotion. I confess I was very alarmed. Then your Mama came rushing in to me, in such a state and promptly swooned. What would have happened if the Captain had not arrived soon after, and carried my Charlotte in here, I don't know. Of Peg Jenkins there was no sign. And I rang and rang for Abbie, without results.'

At that moment Mrs Kingston stirred and groaned.

'Lie still, Mama. You will be better by and by,' said Olivia soothingly, as she laid a handkerchief soaked in lavender-water on her mother's brow.

'No!' moaned Mrs Kingston weakly. 'I will never be better again! Not ever! I cannot bear it!'

'You're in pain?' Olivia asked in alarm. 'We'd best send for Dr Puddicombe.'

'No, I want to see no one! No one, do you hear? How could she? How could she have done such a thing?'

'Do you mean Peg Jenkins, my love?' asked Mr Kingston solicitously.

'Peg! My best friend! My only friend! And now she is lost to me! She must be turned off this instant, without a character!'

Olivia straightened up. She was beginning to recognise a familiar note in her mother's hysteria.

'What has Abbie done this time, Mama?' she asked.

'Do not ask me! Do not torment me so! It is too horrible to contemplate!' And Mrs Kingston went into such hysterical paroxysms that it took all her daughter's skill and experience with hartshorn and the smelling-bottle to dispel them.

At last Olivia was able to leave her mother's bedside.

'How is Mrs Kingston? Is there anything I can do?' Miles Gilbert was anxiously waiting on the landing.

'She's suffering from an agitation of the nerves, nothing more. She simply needs peace and quiet.'

'What can have happened to cause such a thing?'

'That,' said Olivia, with determination, 'is something I mean to find out.'

She stalked downstairs, the Captain in her wake, and flung open the kitchen door. Abbie was sitting huddled by the fire. At their entrance she looked up, guilt and defiance etched on her wrinkled face.

''Er wants rid of me, don't 'er?' she demanded.

'My mother did mention something of the sort.'

'Well, I idn't going. Not unless 'er pays all my back wages!'

'Abbie, what did you do?'

'Nuthing!'

'You must have done something. What was it? Were you rude to someone?'

'No, I wadn't!' The denial came out fiercely.

'Oh dear! And to whom were you rude? Not Mrs Jenkins, I hope.'

'I keeps telling you, I wadn't rude . . . ! I were trying to be 'elpful.' Abbie's aggression dissipated swiftly. 'You'm idn't going to turn me out, be you? I don't want to die in no poor'ouse.'

Olivia's annoyance faded. Through the maid's belligerence she could detect real fear. They both knew Abbie would never get another situation, she was too old and her reputation for being cantankerous too well known. Of all the servants in the Kingston household, she had been the only one to remain after their financial ruin. In truth, it was because no one else would have her—even then her eccentric behaviour had made her unappealing to any prospective employer. Yet in the ensuing years she had been loyal, hard-working and honest. In spite of her trying ways, Olivia was genuinely fond of their unconventional servant.

'You won't go to the poorhouse,' Olivia said gently. 'But you must tell me what happened.'

'Peg Jenkins's teeth!' said Abbie darkly. 'They was the cause.'

'You didn't make some remark about them, I hope. You know how sensitive Mrs Jenkins is about them.'

'I didn't make no remark, I tells you! I was being 'elpful!'

'And what form did your helpfulness take?' Olivia's trepidaton was increasing by the minute.

'I'd made a bit of gingerbread, only it didn't turn out proper. Fire wadn't drawing or summat. Anyway, it was a might sticky, so when I took the tea in to yer ma and Peg Jenkins I thought of they teeth of 'ers, and what they cost. Being considerate, like, I give 'er an extra plate. "Yer, missus," I says, "Put they teeth of yourn along yer, else they'm going to get proper stuck." Well, 'er starts a yelling and a scritching, and saying 'er've never been so insulted—'

'What happened next?' asked Olivia, conscious of strange spluttering sounds coming from the Captain behind her.

'Well, 'er goes on about 'ow every tooth in 'er 'ead be 'er own. 'Ow that woman'll look the Vicar in the face come Sunday is more than I can fathom! Everyone knows 'er paid seventy pound down Plymouth for un. Seventy pound! A man could keep a family real 'andsome for a year on that! I don't know why 'er wadn't content with gums. I manages well enough with gums. There idn't nothing I can't manage with they. 'Er own teeth, indeed. I minds 'er own teeth! Gurt yaller things 'er 'ad! Like Joshua Crowther's donkey!'

This description proved too much for Captain Gilbert. He made a hurried exit.

So much for any support I might get from him, Olivia thought tartly. Aloud she said, 'Abbie, doubtless you were trying to act for the best. Unfortunately, you seem to have caused an upset. My mother is very distressed, so I insist that you keep out of her way for the next day or two. As for poor Mrs Jenkins... It'll require careful thought, deciding what must be done there. It's a most delicate problem.'

'I knowed you wouldn't let me go to no poor'ouse, not really.' Abbie beamed at her fondly, pink gums gleaming in the firelight.

Shaking her head in disbelief at this latest domestic crisis Olivia left the kitchen. She found Miles Gilbert in the music-room. He was leaning on the piano, his head resting on his folded arms, and he was sobbing with laughter.

'It's distasteful to see a grown man cry,' she snapped.

'I...I know...but...' he gasped, then collapsed again.

'You were no help. No help at all,' Olivia stated angrily. 'Nor are you now, laughing away like someone fit for Bedlam.'

With great difficulty the Captain struggled to control himself.

'I can picture it exactly,' he gasped, fishing in his pocket for a handkerchief. 'A plate! Dear heaven, can't you see Abbie handing the unfortunate woman a...plate for...her...teeth? I'd have given a fortune to have been there, truly I would.'

'And no doubt you'd have behaved just as stupidly!'

'How did...did she describe Mrs Jenkins's teeth? Great yellow things, like someone's donkey's?' Recalling the description nearly overset his composure again.

'Joshua Crowther,' supplied Olivia. 'He owns a string of pack animals.' She paused, thoughtfully. 'I must admit, Abbie has a point there. I can remember Mrs Jenkins's er—original teeth quite clearly, too, and they did...did have a...decidedly horsey look...' Her lips started to quiver as she pictured the scene... Abbie bringing the plate especially... being so solicitous about the welfare of the false teeth... Poor Peg's indignation... It was too much. Laughter rose up in her and refused to be quelled. Soon she was laughing as heartily as the Captain, until, eventually, she collapsed against him, helpless with mirth.

They clung to each other, paralysed by hilarity. Then gradually Olivia's laughter faded away. She became conscious of his arms about her. He was holding her hard against him. Startled, she looked up and saw the laughter die away from his face, too. His eyes, changeable as the sea, looked down into hers. Slowly, of their own volition, her arms found their way about his neck, her hands began to caress his hair. The pressure of his hold on her tightened, so that she could hardly breathe. Then, with great deliberation, his mouth came closer. She rose up to meet him, until the warmth of his lips crushed against her own. That warmth flowed through her, melting away the last remnant of reserve within her, and with it the empty, barren years. The taste of him against her mouth, the sweeping joy of his body so close to her, these became the only realities in her world. She gave herself up to the sweet ache of love, something she had thought lost to her for ever.

The tumult of passion within her receded as swiftly as it had arisen, leaving behind harsh reality. Appalled, she let her arms fall to her sides. Taking a step back, she broke his hold on her. His face was grim, as he stared back at her, as though he, too, had been caught unaware by the force of such emotion.

'Miss Kingston—Olivia—' he began,

'I don't recall giving you permission to address me by my Christian name,' she said, through trembling lips.

'What can I say?'

'There is no need to say anything. Do not think to chalk this up as a triumph, sir. My opinion of you is what it has ever been. Your efforts were in vain.'

'It wasn't like that at all!' he protested.

'No? Tell me, would you have behaved like that towards Miss Hunt?'

'Certainly not!' he cried. 'Because—'

'There's no need for explanations or excuses. All I require is your assurance that such a thing will never happen again.'

'You have it, ma'am.' He spoke in a low voice. 'Just as you have my heartfelt apologies for my behaviour.' He bowed curtly, then left the room without a backward glance.

With iron control Olivia listened to every one of his footsteps as he went up to his room. Only when she heard his door close and knew she ran no risk of encountering him again, did she move. Even then some tight self-discipline forced her to walk slowly up the stairs to her room. She closed the door with great deliberation, then, and only then, did she give way to anguish. Sobs tore through her uncontrollably. It was for her own humiliation that she wept. For those few minutes she had abandoned all restraint, allowed her passions full rein. She had let her love pour out of her, raw and vulnerable. And to what purpose? She knew very well that to Miles Gilbert it had been no more than a game.

CHAPTER EIGHT

OLIVIA wished she could remain in the comforting privacy of her bedroom. The thought of having to face Miles Gilbert again filled her with dread, but she knew she had to emerge from her dark haven sometime. Washing her face and re-doing her hair did little to make her feel calmer, inside she still felt shaken and distressed. As she went about preparing the dinner her mind was consumed with dread. To be confronted by him day after day! Memories of their encounter in the music-room continued to send a scalding flush sweeping over her. How could she have been so weak and foolish?

It was the worst meal Olivia could remember. She was so tense with nerves she could not stop shivering, and her mouth went dry. To make things worse her parents had decided to dine in their room, so she was obliged to sit at table alone with the American. She found it an effort to say such mundane things as 'Can I help you to some pie, sir?' or 'Would you be kind enough to pass the salt'.

To her surprise he appeared to be equally ill at ease. She had half expected to see some glint of triumph in his eyes, at having made her betray herself so positively, but there was none. His manner was stiff and formal, and she noted that he picked at his food in a way quite unlike his normally healthy appetite.

'Will you take tea or coffee, sir?' she asked, when the ordeal of dining was nearing its end.

'Neither, I thank you.' He rose and bowed abruptly. 'By your leave, I'll withdraw. I'm only too aware how much distress my presence causes you.'

With another curt bow he left the room, leaving Olivia staring after him.

Next morning Mrs Kingston felt strong enough to get up. This made extra work for Olivia. As well as her usual duties, she had to organise matters so that her mother and Abbie did not meet, no easy thing in such a small house. To her relief Captain Gilbert left the house as soon as the curfew would permit. In fact, during the days that followed, he spent remarkably little time at home. When he was in her company they treated each other with a chilly politeness that prompted her father to ask her if they had quarrelled. She was forced to deny that they had, she could not tell the truth without being involved in painful explanations.

The other emotional undercurrents in the household were gradually resolving themselves. Charlotte Kingston deigned to resume talking to Abbie, which was a great relief to Olivia. Acting as intermediary during their dispute had been both wearing and time consuming. Making the peace with Peg Jenkins was a more protracted matter. Then news came that Mrs Jenkins had taken to her bed with a particularly virulent cold. Seizing the opportunity, Olivia called upon the lady. Her timing was superb. The invalid, ever a convivial person, was almost at the end of her tether through boredom. Desperate for company, she greeted Olivia's arrival with such delight that all hostility and injured dignity were forgotten.

One benefit of the resumption of the friendship with Peg Jenkins was that the Kingston household was once more *au fait* with the latest news from town. When Dartmouth was set buzzing by further activity by Bonaparte's agent it was Mrs Jenkins who supplied the details.

'Would you believe the audacity of the man?' she cried. 'To go into the house of Mr Holdsworth himself, our Member of Parliament and Governor of the Dartmouth Castle, and steal his keys!'

Olivia did not want to believe this latest development.

'They could simply be mislaid,' she said hopefully.

'They were stolen.' Peg Jenkins was quite definite. 'I had it on the best authority that the keys were in Mr Holdsworth's desk-drawer yesterday morning, and by evening they had gone.'

'And were these keys important?' persisted Olivia. 'Might they not have been to his wine-cellar, or something like that?'

'If so, then why has the locksmith been working out at the castle since first light? Not that it will do any good.' Mrs Jenkins leaned forward to give her words emphasis, the feathers on her ornate bonnet bobbing earnestly. 'It's too late to change the locks now. Boney's man will have been there already. Aye, been and gone! You mark my word!'

Mrs Jenkins's news stirred up all sorts of doubts for Olivia. Doubts which focused upon Miles Gilbert.

'And where is the dear Captain this afternoon?' asked Mrs Jenkins, as though reading her thoughts.

'He is taking tea with the Mayor's family,' Mrs Kingston informed her.

'With Lizzie Hunt, you mean?' said Mrs Jenkins, giving a knowing smile. 'I fancy that young lady is quite bewitched by our dashing American. Her own mother told me, in strictest confidence, of course, that her girl positively dotes on the man. And if I read the signs correctly the Captain is far from indifferent to little Lizzie's charms. He was certainly most attentive at the charity tea yesterday, the one in aid of widows and orphans. I was there a full half-hour, and he never left her side once.'

Olivia's spirits tumbled. So Miles Gilbert had been paying court to Lizzie Hunt! As if that was not enough, she knew that the tea had been held at Mr Holdsworth's house. The Captain had been in the building on the very day the keys had disappeared.

So, too, had dozens of other people, she argued silently. But no amount of reasoning would remove the cold feeling round her heart.

Distressing though it was, Olivia doubted if there was much she could do about Lizzie Hunt, but her fears that the Captain might be a spy were quite another matter. She knew she should report her suspicions to Admiral Ranscombe, and her failure to do so troubled her conscience very much.

But what should I report? she asked herself, more than once. Some circumstantial evidence, nothing more.

It was the indecision that she found hardest to bear, not knowing whether Miles Gilbert was a spy or not. It troubled her so much that she felt she could tolerate it no longer. The only solution was to tackle the Captain about it openly. She would be clear and concise, so he would be in no doubt of what he was accused, and she would accept no vague evasions.

Actually finding the opportunity to speak to Captain Gilbert alone proved to be a difficult matter, there never seemed to be an appropriate moment. Eventually, she encountered him one morning, as he was about to leave the house.

'Sir, I would speak with you, if you please,' she said.

He had already opened the front door, and he stood there, regarding her with ill-concealed impatience.

'Your pardon, Miss Kingston, will this take long?' he asked. 'I have an urgent appointment.'

He still held the door open, letting a cruel draught whip along the passage. Olivia shivered. An urgent appointment, when it had only just turned half-past eight? She shivered again and glanced out at the weather. Winter was having one last final fling before giving way to spring, and a cold, heavy rain lashed down. Miles Gilbert was ill-equipped for such conditions. He had his umbrella, it was true, but no cape or greatcoat. He would be soaked and frozen before he got a hundred yards.

'Do your friends always welcome you this early in the day?' she asked.

'I've much to do. I like to make an early start,' he replied evasively.

'At what? Billiards? Cards?'

'Miss Kingston, you said you wished to speak with me,' he said curtly.

'Yes, I do.' Another rain-laden blast swept into the house, and Olivia's resolve broke. 'Oh, for pity's sake, there's no need for you to trudge about the town on such a day!' she cried. 'I know you do it to keep out of my way, but you'll be frozen if you go out in this weather so ill-clad. I wouldn't have your death from lung fever or consumption upon my conscience, and that would be the result.'

'I've no wish to inflict my presence upon you,' he said, his voice only a shade less cold than the wind outside.

'We need see little of each other. I am giving lessons for much of the day. Close the door, if you please, before we freeze.'

'If you are sure.' He sounded uncertain, but he closed the door.

'I am sure. Now go up where it's warm, and keep my father company!'

'I confess I wasn't relishing the thought of going out in such rain,' he said, with a faint smile. 'It'll be much more pleasant to sit by the fire playing chess with Mr Kingston.' He paused, awkwardly fidgeting with the umbrella he held in his hand. 'I fear I've been more than brusque with you of late. I apologise. If you want the truth, I am still ashamed of my behaviour towards you. I—'

'I would prefer we didn't speak of the matter. Let's agree to share the blame, and have done.'

'But, Miss Kingston—'

'Please!' she begged. 'Neither of us has any cause to be proud of ourselves. Let's forget the whole sorry business.'

'If that's what you want, then the incident is wiped from my mind.' He looked far from convinced, but at least there was now a truce between them, albeit an uneasy one.

Olivia's satisfaction was short-lived. She had not confronted him with her suspicions, and so nothing was resolved. She was still in as great a state of confusion as ever, but at least, she did not know for certain that Miles Gilbert was a spy. A sense of relief remained with her. It betrayed how much she dreaded finding out that her worst fears were true.

Relations between Olivia and the Captain became, if not exactly friendly, at least more relaxed, as winter faded and the spring arrived.

One afternoon, soon after the midday meal, the peace of the household was shattered by an urgent hammering at the front door. Hurrying to open it, Olivia was confronted by an excited Lieutenant La Fontaine on the doorstep.

'Mademoiselle Kingston! I had to tell you! I am a papa!' he cried, waving a letter in his hand.

'What splendid news!' exclaimed Olivia in delight. 'Is it a boy or a girl? How is your wife? Oh, do come in and tell my parents.'

'A girl. Since six months I am papa!' The Frenchman was far too excited to settle. 'She writes herself, does my Lucille, and says she is well and the baby, she flourishes. *Mon Dieu,* I am mad with joy!'

'Our heartfelt congratulations, sir! Such splendid news after your long wait!' Mr Kingston exclaimed.

'Congratulations? Why, what has happened?' Mrs Kingston came in to see what was the cause of the commotion. 'Oh, Lieutenant La Fontaine! I did not know you were here.'

'I think I intrude, madame. Your pardon, I had to share my news,' said the Frenchman.

'Of course you did, sir,' said Olivia. 'Mama, Madame La Fontaine has been safely delivered of a daughter. Is that not splendid?'

'Oh Lieutenant! I am so happy for you!' Mrs Kingston clasped her hands with pleasure. 'And the baby? How does she fare?'

'Very well, I thank you, madame. My wife, she writes the baby is so good. Already she sleeps through the night!' declared the proud father. 'See! My wife she has had a picture made. *Mesdames, messieurs,* this is my daughter!' With great reverence the Lieutenant handed round a small watercolour sketch. It was of a pink blob surrounded by a vast amount of frills, which the Frenchman had no hesitation in recognising as his offspring.

'A decidedly handsome child!' stated Miles Gilbert gravely, examining the picture. 'She doesn't resemble you much, La Fontaine.'

'No, she is the image of her mama.'

'What am I thinking of! We should be celebrating this happy event!' cried Mr Kingston. 'Captain, can I ask you to go down to the cellar? I should still have a couple of bottles of champagne left down there. If you would be kind enough to bring them both up. Olivia, my dear, would you get some glasses.'

'Our French friend is near off his head with delight!' Miles Gilbert remarked as he accompanied Olivia downstairs. 'Such is the power of fatherhood.'

'He was extremely worried about his wife.'

'Yes, he was, though how he could say the babe resembled his Lucille I can't imagine.'

'Why, you, yourself, said she was a handsome child,' protested Olivia.

'I could scarcely tell the man that his long-awaited progeny looked exactly like a pink blancmange, now could I?'

'Sir, I believe you are a dissembler. In future I shan't believe a word you say,' laughed Olivia.

'Perhaps you would be wise, Miss Kingston,' he replied, and she was surprised to detect a note of seriousness in his voice.

The champagne was poured, but the toast not yet proposed when another visitor arrived.

'Why, Mr Dunsford! How delightful! Olivia, my love, see who has come?' cried Mrs Kingston.

Olivia had no option but see who had come, for Joseph Dunsford stood there, solid and vast in his caped greatcoat. She wished she could share her mother's pleasure at the arrival of the newcomer.

'Sir, this is an unexpected surprise,' she said.

'I am happy to see you in such blooming looks and evident good spirits, Miss Kingston,' replied Joseph Dunsford with a bow. 'However, I have no wish to interrupt.' And he eyed both the champagne and the Frenchman warily.

'You do not interrupt, sir,' said Mr Kingston. 'Indeed, you must join us. Olivia, another glass for Mr Dunsford. We celebrate, as you see. Our good friend, Lieutenant La Fontaine, has just learned he is a father. You do know each other, I trust, gentlemen?'

'Sir.' Mr Dunsford gave the briefest of nods in the direction of the Frenchman. That he disapproved of the French prisoner's presence was evident, though Olivia could not understand why. He seemed to accept Captain Gilbert readily enough.

'I know Mr Dunsford by sight. *Mon plaisir*, monsieur.' The Frenchman bowed politely.

'Now, a toast! To the new Mademoiselle La Fontaine. May happiness, health and prosperity be hers,' exclaimed Mr Kingston.

After the toast was drunk Mrs Kingston turned her attention to Joseph Dunsford and asked, 'Have you been on your travels again, Mr Dunsford? You seem to be often coming or going.'

'My business dictates that I visit many places, ma'am. I have recently returned from London.'

'A fine city, I think,' said Lieutenant La Fontaine. 'Some day I hope I can visit London. I would see if it is more beautiful than Paris.'

'Paris cannot compare, sir, I assure you,' said Joseph Dunsford promptly.

His snub was so obvious that for a moment there was a hush. It was Captain Gilbert who stepped into the breach again.

'You think not?' he said. 'I consider Paris to be a very fine city. As to making a comparison, I'm not really in a position to judge, since I visited London only briefly once, some years ago.'

'Do you know Paris well, Mr Dunsford?' asked Olivia, annoyed that he should have been so rude to a guest in her house.

'Not well. In fact, I have never been,' blustered Joseph Dunsford. 'I do not need to go. It stands to reason London must be the better place.'

'How delightful it would be to visit both!' sighed Mrs Kingston, unconsciously easing the tension. 'The shops, the balls, the entertainments. Perhaps one day... Now, can we persuade our two visitors to dine with us?'

'I regret I have another engagement, madam, much as I would like to continue in the company of you and your very delightful daughter,' stated Mr Dunsford. 'As for the Lieutenant, by my reckoning he has but three minutes to the curfew bell. He should be getting to his lodgings quickly.'

Olivia fumed silently at such rudeness. She hoped the Lieutenant's English had been too poor for him to have appreciated Dunsford's lack of courtesy. Miles Gilbert knew it, though, and his mouth tightened angrily.

'Mr Dunsford is most kind to remind me.' Lieutenant La Fontaine rose. 'I must bid you *au revoir* with my thanks. Again you have been all kindness.' He bowed as he took his leave.

Although the Frenchman had gone, Mr Dunsford made no attempt to depart. He looked so settled by the fire that Mrs Kingston asked, 'Are you sure you will not take your mutton with us, sir?'

'No, I thank you. I fear I cannot, for truly I am expected elsewhere. Your pardon if I seem to prolong my visit. My excuse is that I would enjoy your company for as long as possible, since tomorrow I will not have the opportunity to call upon you.'

'Oh, for shame! We shall miss you!' cried Mrs Kingston.

Olivia's regret did not match that of her mother. The sense of relief she felt was not made any easier by the fact that Miles

Gilbert was regarding her keenly, as though waiting to see her reaction to Joseph Dunsford's announcement.

'You are forced away on business?' she asked, honesty preventing her from expressing a disappointment she did not feel.

'Not exactly, Miss Kingston. The fact is I'm going to look at some plots of land. I have decided it is high time I had a decent house built for myself.'

'Are you indeed?' Mrs Kingston sat up attentively, and exchanged such a blatantly meaningful glance with her husband that Olivia flushed.

'Yes, I have been considering it for a while. My present apartments are getting too small. Living close to my wharves and warehouses does well enough for me at the moment, but adequate as they are for a bachelor existence, my rooms have their limitations. They are not fit to offer hospitality to you ladies, for example. So I decided it was time I had a proper dwelling. Besides, few men of business live over their counting-houses any more these days.'

'And you have got as far as considering sites, you say?' asked Mr Kingston.

'I have two or three in mind. I intend to visit them tomorrow, and scrutinise them most thoroughly. That is if the weather doesn't break again. I don't relish the prospect of struggling through acres of mud. There are so many points to be taken into consideration when choosing a location. What do you think, Miss Kingston? In your opinion, what is the most important factor in deciding a suitable place to build a house?'

Olivia was alarmed at being asked such a crucial question. If she gave an ill-judged answer it might be misconstrued as a wish to live in the proposed dwelling. She replied carefully, 'I should think that, after the recent rains, somewhere well above the level of spring tides and flood-water might be an immediate asset.'

'Do not be flippant, dear,' said her mother reprovingly. 'I am quite certain Mr Dunsford does not intend to do anything so imprudent as build his home at the water's edge.'

'No, indeed not,' agreed Joseph Dunsford.

'In that case I suppose a location that is light and airy would be best, maybe on a hill,' said Olivia.

'You don't think such a site would be cold and draughty?' asked Mr Dunsford. 'One of the places I intend to view is in a valley, steep but sheltered.'

'Damp!' declared Mrs Kingston firmly. 'Damp and poor drains!' Then, warming to the subject, she put forth her own ideas on a suitable site.

Olivia prudently decided to remain silent, but she became uncomfortable when her mother's discourse touched upon growing families, and having a suitable space in which the children could play.

'Of course, Olivia is desperately fond of children,' said Charlotte Kingston, confirming her daughter's worst fears. 'She positively dotes upon them.'

All eyes now turned to Olivia, who, certain that her mother's innuendo had not been lost on anyone, felt herself go a fiery-red. Unexpectedly, it was Captain Gilbert who came to her rescue.

'Your business must be flourishing, sir, if you can contemplate such a major undertaking,' he observed. If there was one thing guaranteed to divert Joseph Dunsford's attention it was the word 'business'.

Olivia heaved a sigh of gratitude.

'I will admit to having been fortunate in my business dealings of late,' said Mr Dunsford, with self-satisfaction.

'You are fortunate indeed,' said the Captain. 'This war has been the ruination of many good men.' There was a note of irritation in his voice, and, although he remained as courteous as ever, Olivia sensed his continuing dislike of the other man.

'Far too many who fail put the blame on the war, when the fault lies with themselves,' said Joseph Dunsford complacently. 'I simply refuse to allow myself to be intimidated by a lot of Frogs. Who could be frightened of a nation that allows itself to be governed by a fat little Corsican, who can't even speak its own language, eh?'

'You exaggerate there, Dunsford,' protested the Captain. 'One must be both fair and accurate. I'll admit that Bonaparte is not tall, and that he is stout. Also, I believe that as a child he spoke only Italian, but to claim that he can't speak French intelligibly now is nothing more than a foolish tale.'

'You say so, Captain?' Joseph Dunsford was patently displeased at being contradicted. 'And upon what authority can you be so certain?'

'Why, the evidence of my own ears, of course! I had no difficulty whatsoever understanding his French, I wasn't even aware of an Italian accent.'

There was a profound silence as everyone stared at the American in shocked awe.

'Are you saying that you have met Napoleon Bonaparte, and spoken to him?' asked Olivia.

'Certainly I have.' Captain Gilbert gave a laugh. 'Really, Miss Kingston, there's no need to regard me in that startled fashion. It was only Bonaparte whom I met, you know, not the Devil incarnate. Just as I didn't detect any Italian accent, nor did I note signs of horns and a tail.'

He spoke jokingly, yet Olivia fancied he was ill at ease. His encounter with Bonaparte was something he had let slip inadvertently.

'How did it come about? Captain dear, you must tell us.' Mrs Kingston had recovered from her surprise, and was agog.

'I'm sorry to dash your hopes, ma'am. It was nothing grand, simply a very ordinary reception.'

'A very ordinary reception! With Bonaparte himself there! Will you listen to the man?' cried Charlotte Kingston in disbelief. 'Where did it happen? And how did you come to be there? And what did he say to you? Oh, there is so much I want to know.'

Olivia was growing more and more convinced that Captain Gilbert was regretting his indiscretion. Earlier he had come to her rescue, so she decided to come to his. 'Mama, shall I ring for Abbie to bring some more tea?' she asked.

'Tea? Who can think tea now, when the conversation has taken such a fascinating turn?' exclaimed Charlotte Kingston, dismissing her daughter's suggestion with a wave of her hand. 'Captain dear, I have never known anyone who has met a famous person, and to have someone in our house who has met Napoleon Bonaparte. I declare I shall go into a decline from sheer curiosity.'

'I can't let you do that, ma'am. Not when it's within my power to prevent such a catastrophe,' said Miles Gilbert, giving Olivia a grateful look. 'Now, which of your questions shall I answer first? Ah, yes... The assembly was in Paris, two years ago. You know the sort of affair. Too many people in too small a room, and not enough to eat or drink. Very boring.'

'Boring? How can it have been boring? I shall go distracted, I know I shall,' declared Mrs Kingston excitedly. 'How did you come to be invited?'

There was a brief hesitation before the Captain replied.

'Ah, you know us naval men, ma'am. We are such an ornamental lot that no function is complete without us to decorate it.'

'And did you have a long conversation with Boney?' Now it was Mr Kingston who could not curb his curiosity.

'It was scarcely enough to be called a conversation, sir. He asked me where did I come from, and how long had I been in France, and how did I like the country. Nothing profound. Only the conventional sort of remarks that the great bestow upon the lower orders.'

'Great? You can call that villain great?' demanded Joseph Dunsford. He had been listening to the Captain intently, and now was unable to maintain his silence.

'I do, certainly.' Captain Gilbert answered calmly. 'When one remembers his relatively modest origins, and then considers what he has achieved in such a short time—I don't know how else to describe that other than greatness.'

'How you can approve of such a rogue is more than I can understand!' Mr Dunsford seemed about to explode with rage.

'I didn't say I approved of the man,' replied the Captain. 'Far from it. Quite apart from anything else this emperor business sticks in my craw. I believe that all men are created equal, and conquering a large slice of Europe is no excuse for putting a crown on a fellow's head. Having said that, I don't have to like a man, or his actions, in order to recognise his attributes.'

'You disapprove of the man, yet you go running to one of his receptions the minute he calls.' Joseph Dunsford's anger was increasing, until Olivia feared he would leap out of his chair and attack the American.

Fortunately, Miles Gilbert relieved the tension by smiling. 'I didn't run, I promise you. I went in an exceedingly rickety carriage. As for attending the reception, you forget, sir, I was in a foreign land, and, as a representative of America, I was bound to show its ruler every respect out of common courtesy. Nor was I free to follow my own inclinations. I had to obey the orders of my superiors.'

His reasonable reply had the desired effect upon the other man's temper.

'I suppose you are right,' Mr Dunsford conceded more quietly. 'Your pardon for being so hot-tempered. I should not have given way to my feelings so in front of the ladies, particularly you, Miss Kingston, whom I know to have the most delicate of sensibilities. Only, I have to admit, that if one name can provoke my ire it is that of Napoleon Bonaparte.'

'You are not alone there! Why, I feel quite faint at the merest mention of him,' cried Mrs Kingston, forgetting her recent curiosity.

'In that case, I think we should talk of something else,' suggested the Captain.

'I regret I can't stay to be a part of any further conversation,' said Mr Dunsford, rising to his feet. Olivia noted that now his temper had cooled there was a strangely satisfied air about him, as though he were very pleased about something. He continued, 'I really must be on my way. How light the evenings are becoming now that we are in April. It is a month of special significance to you, I believe, Captain. And one day is of extra importance. Monday next, perhaps?'

'How do you know that?' Miles Gilbert looked astounded. 'You are to be congratulated on your sources of information, though I can't claim it to be of importance to anyone save my family and myself.'

'What is this special day? Can we be allowed into the secret?' asked Mrs Kingston excitedly.

'It is only my birthday, ma'am. I shall have reached the great age of one-and-thirty. No cause for celebration.'

'Nonsense, we must certainly mark the day in some way.' Charlotte clapped her hands with pleasure.

'Your birthday! Quite so!' Joseph Dunsford nodded his head approvingly. 'Well done, sir! Well done!'

Olivia could not think why reaching one-and-thirty should deserve approval. Nor could she imagine how Mr Dunsford had found out such a fact. She had no chance to question him further, however, for he was moving purposefully towards the door.

'I bid you farewell,' he said. 'Perhaps you and I will meet on Monday, sir. In which case we will have a drink together in honour of your—er—birthday.'

'Sorry though we are to see you go, we have no wish to keep you from your house-hunting, Mr Dunsford.' Charlotte Kingston gave a trilling laugh, then added briskly, 'Olivia will see you out, will you not, my dear?'

Olivia was only too thankful to show their visitor to the door. He had long outstayed his welcome. To her consternation, once in the passage he paused.

'Miss Kingston, there is something I must say to you,' he said.

She felt herself go pale. After all the talk of building and new houses, surely he was not going to propose? Not here? Not now?

'Yes, Mr Dunsford?' she said through dry lips.

'Your pardon if I am impertinent,' he began. 'Can I ask if that Froggie visits you often?'

'Froggie?' Olivia could not think what he was talking about.

'Yes, the French prisoner.'

'You mean Lieutenant La Fontaine? Yes, he calls upon us from time to time.'

'Take my advice, dear Miss Kingston. Do not encourage him. They are a tricky lot, the Frogs, and not to be trusted.'

'I thank you for your advice. I'll give it consideration,' said Olivia, keeping her annoyance under careful control.

As she closed the door on Joseph Dunsford she regretted that she had to continue being polite to him, but she knew she must. It seemed more and more likely that he would make her an offer of marriage, and she dared do nothing to discourage him. The thought caused her stomach to churn.

Her mother and father were in high spirits when she returned to the drawing-room. The subject exciting them was far closer to their hearts than the pros and cons of Bonaparte's character; it was the behaviour of Mr Dunsford.

'Did you notice, husband?' Mrs Kingston was saying. 'That delightful man wanted to know Olivia's preferences concerning houses most especially. It must mean something.'

'I fancy it was simply polite conversation, Mama,' said Olivia, attempting to dampen her mother's enthusiasm.

'Polite conversation! Do you hear our daughter, sir? Why would a man think of building a house if he were not considering taking a wife? And why would he ask the opinions of an eligible young lady if he did not intend to make her an offer?'

'Oh, Mama, I wish you wouldn't say such things!' cried Olivia in distress.

'Why not, when it is as plain as the nose on your face? Do you not agree, husband?'

Mr Kingston was more cautious. 'I don't think we should assume too much,' he said. 'I can understand our daughter's agitation. It is not kind to raise her hopes, no matter how optimistic we are.'

He did not understand. It had not been prim modesty that had made her cry out, it had been panic. To add to her perturbation Captain Gilbert stood up.

'Can I offer my felicitations in advance?' he said, his voice quiet, his face pale and set.

Before Olivia could protest he had left the room.

'There, the Captain thinks it is a foregone conclusion too,' said Mrs Kingston in delight.

Olivia barely heard her. These days it seemed that her anxieties aways came in twos. Today it was Joseph Dunsford's increased attentions, and the Captain's revelation. Despite the way Miles Gilbert had tried to make nothing of his meeting with Bonaparte, she fancied that ordinary sea captains did not usually get invited to receptions given by emperors, not even in countries bound by liberty, equality, and fraternity. The incident was one more indication that the Captain was in the pay of the French. In her opinion it was the most damning so far.

Loving him was proving to be too agonising and too confusing. She felt she could bear it no longer. She wished Joseph Dunsford would propose to her soon, then she could say 'Yes' immediately, and solve her problems once and for all!

CHAPTER NINE

NEXT day Olivia sat alone in the drawing-room, grappling with the quarterly accounts. It was a tedious business, for despite her efforts, expenditure threatened to exceed income. She had just started at the top of the column of figures yet again, to see what could be deleted, when Miles Gilbert entered, carrying a book.

'Your pardon, I thought the room was empty.'

He hesitated uncertainly in the doorway, then said again, 'Your pardon,' and began to leave.

'Captain Gilbert,' she called after him. 'If you are seeking somewhere to read your book then for goodness' sake stay!'

He stepped back into the room.

'That was my intention,' he said. 'The light is so much better in here... If you are sure I don't disturb you?'

He did disturb her! By simply entering the room, by filling it with his presence, by just looking at her he had disturbed her, though she could not say so.

'You won't bother me,' she said. 'I hope to be finished soon.'

'Thank you.' He crossed the room with exaggerated stealth, and sat down. Although he opened the book on his lap he did not look at it.

'Your reading won't interfere with my work,' she prompted him. 'Not unless you propose to read aloud.'

'No, I promise not to do that.' Obediently he turned his attention to the book, and Olivia went back to her accounts.

'Now, did Dr Puddicombe attend Papa once last month, or twice?' she wondered.

'Once.'

She started at his voice. 'I'm sorry, I didn't realise I'd spoken aloud.'

'It's of no importance. And, as I say, the doctor called upon Mr Kingston once, in the first week of the month. You're doing your accounts?'

'Yes,' she said, amending her figures. 'A troublesome task it is, too.'

'I'm surprised that you bother. Soon such matters won't concern you.'

'I don't understand.'

'It seems your plans are nearing fruition in a most satisfactory way. I only hope you're suitably grateful to me, for my part in the success of your schemes.'

Laying down her pen Olivia said, 'You're talking in riddles.'

'I'd have thought my meaning was obvious. A little more effort and you'll bring Dunsford up to the mark, you see if you don't.'

'Did you come in here simply to insult me?' she demanded.

'What's insulting about speaking the truth? I suppose you're looking forward to Joseph Dunsford whisking you off to this new house of his.'

'Mr Dunsford's house is no concern of mine. And as for your silly notion that I involved you in some fictitious scheme to ensnare him, that's nonsense. I hoped you'd forgotten about it long since. I must ask you not to make such comments.'

'You would have me mind my own business, eh? Won't you even accept my congratulations?'

'Your congratulations aren't required, sir. Nor are they likely to be,' she protested, her anger increasing.

'Are you saying you wouldn't have Dunsford if he offered?'

'Of course—' she began, then stopped. She had been about to say that nothing would persuade her to accept Joseph Dunsford, but it was not true. If he proposed to her she would have to say yes.

The Captain took her hesitation for confirmation. 'I thought so,' he said coldly. 'Dunsford's money must make him a good catch. I acknowledge that wealth can be a great influence on the heart.'

'Really, sir, this is enough!' she cried. 'You seem determined to pick a quarrel, and I don't know why.'

'No, you don't!' He rose abruptly from his chair and strode over to the window. Thrusting his hands deep into his pockets, he stared disconsolately out at the river below.

'I think I can guess why you're in a bad mood,' she cried. 'Have Lizzie Hunt's eyes begun to stray elsewhere? Is that it?'

'Lizzie Hunt has nothing to do with the matter!'

'Don't tell me some other lady of discernment has spurned you! That would be too bad.'

'You speak nonsense!'

'Nonsense, eh? And now where are the charming manners for which Captain Gilbert is so renowned? They disappear when anyone gets close to the truth.'

'You are about as far from the truth as you can get.'

'Am I? I think not. I only wish I knew her identity, so that I could congratulate her,' Olivia taunted him, rising to her feet.

'That would please you, wouldn't it? To know of someone else who dislikes me as much as you do!' he cried angrily. 'You're the most bothersome female it's been my misfortune to meet!'

They glared at each other in fury, tension mounting between them with each passing second. Suddenly Olivia realised how near she was to him; close enough to see the small pulse beating beside his mouth; close enough to smell the clean freshness of his skin; close enough to be in danger. Too late, she tried to step back.

Grasping her with fingers that bit into her flesh he pulled her to him. His mouth came hard upon hers as he held her tightly against him in an iron embrace. She could hardly breathe. His nearness made coherent thought impossible. This was not how she wanted things to be between them! How often she had ached to be held by him. But not like this. Not with anger and a whole tumult of passions she could not identify as the ruling emotions.

Then, abruptly, he released her.

'You deserved that,' he said in a low voice which was far from steady. 'I hope it gave you as little pleasure as it gave me.'

After he had gone Olivia began to shiver, her body trembling with emotion. She could not imagine why he had behaved in such a way, deliberately trying to hurt her. Even long after, when she was calm again, she was still unable to think of a reason. At first, in the aftermath of this extraordinary incident, she expected him to come forward with an apology or an explanation. When he did neither she was uncertain how to behave towards him. She was determined that any conciliation would not come from her. A cold formality appeared to be the only sensible course of action, and this she achieved with success. In fact, for a while, conversations between her and Miles Gilbert were so correct and so stilted they might have come straight from a book on etiquette.

'I trust you have not forgotten we are expected at the Mayor's reception this afternoon, Miss Kingston,' he addressed her with exaggerated courtesy.

'I had not forgotten, sir, though I thank you for the timely reminder,' she replied in kind.

The thought of the afternoon's engagement gave her no pleasure. She was tired of the tensions between them, and of her own conflicting emotions. She longed for an end to them. Judging by the lines of strain on his face, the American did not relish the prospect, either.

This was to be a very elegant gathering at the Mansion House, too grand for her usual simple crape gown. Instead she took out her blue silk. In the bright light of the April afternoon it looked decidedly tired. She wondered what Lizzie Hunt would be wearing. Not a gown that was eight years out of fashion, that was certain. Still, there was no point in being despondent. She put on her silk gown, spent extra pains in doing her hair, and, finally, round her neck she fastened a locket on a velvet ribbon, one of her few remaining pieces of jewellery.

With surprise, she regarded the undeniably attractive reflection which gazed back at her from the mirror. Her looks had certainly improved of late. It was more than the way she had dressed her hair, or the increased attention she had given to her dress. There was a brilliance in her eyes and an animation in her face that had not been there a few months ago. She knew the cause—the arrival of Miles Gilbert. For better or for worse, he had brought her back to life.

She was almost ready when the sound of voices downstairs heralded a visitor. Olivia breathed a silent prayer that whoever it was would not make them late. Feet sounded on the stairs. When she went to investigate she found Joseph Dunsford impatiently pacing about the drawing-room. He seemed taken aback at seeing her.

'Miss Kingston—er—how delightful you look,' he said uncertainly. 'Though, to tell the truth, it was Captain Gilbert I wished to see.'

'Indeed, Dunsford? How can I be of service to you?' Miles Gilbert entered the room.

'It's I who can be of service to you. I've a message of some urgency.' Mr Dunsford looked from the American to Olivia, and back again.

'You wish to speak in private? I'll leave you.' She made to go.

'That's unnecessary, Miss Kingston. I am sure Mr Dunsford has nothing private to say. I'd be obliged if you'd be swift, sir, for we've an important engagement this afternoon.'

'An engagement?' Joseph Dunsford seemed quite surprised at the idea. 'Oh yes, the Mayor's reception! That's it, eh?'

'Please, what is your message?' asked the Captain with growing impatience.

'Why, it's about that very reception. Yes, of course it is!' Dunsford seemed strangely disturbed, not at all like his usual stolid self. 'I've a message—a very important message. There's been a change of plans for the reception—it's to be held out at the castle instead.'

'The castle? Whatever for?' demanded Olivia.

'Er . . . because of a mishap at the Mansion House . . . a ceiling has come down, or something of the sort. Nothing serious—no one hurt—but quite impossible to hold the reception there.'

'That's inconvenient!' exclaimed the Captain. 'The way is decidedly dirty, we'll be over our shoes in mud. I'd best go and see if I can get a couple of horses.'

'I knew you'd understand.' Joseph Dunsford looked unaccountably relieved. 'There's no need for horses. A boat will take you out there, if you'll be at my wharf in half an hour.'

'That's most obliging of you,' said Captain Gilbert. 'Half an hour it shall be.'

'Good.' If anything the relief on the other man's face had increased. 'I'll bid you farewell for the present. Er . . . Captain Gilbert, you do understand my message, don't you? I want there to be no mistakes.'

'I understand perfectly, you have my word on it,' the Captain assured him patiently. But when Mr Dunsford had gone he shook his head in bewilderment. 'I can't make that fellow out,' he said, 'There are times when I think he must be inebriated, or else his wits are to let. Oh, your pardon, Miss Kingston. I shouldn't have spoken about Mr Dunsford like that in your presence.'

His swift apology was sincere. It was the first natural remark he had made to her in days, and she could not help smiling.

'He was most explicit in his instructions, was he not?' she said. 'I don't think either of us could have failed to understand.'

'No.' A slow smile crossed his face.

If ever Olivia had wondered why she loved Miles Gilbert his smile would have explained everything. It lit his plain features, transforming them from being irregular and ordinary into something that was more than handsome. At that moment it did not matter what he was—spy, shallow charmer, libertine—she would have forgiven him everything, with all her heart.

'We must finish getting ready,' he said. 'Have you got the music? No? Then I'll fetch it while you put on your cape. We don't want to keep Mr Dunsford waiting, do we?'

With the Captain as an escort, Olivia found herself enjoying the walk through town in the spring sunshine. The freshness of new growth brought colour to the surrounding hills, and the waters of the River Dart sparkled a crystal blue-green that was remarkably reminiscent of Miles Gilbert's eyes. The idea made her chuckle. She really was foolish, thinking such thoughts, like a girl straight out of the schoolroom!

'Your pardon, Miss Kingston. Did you say something?' he asked.

'No, sir, nothing at all,' she replied, thankful she was not obliged to reveal what was going through her mind.

Joseph Dunsford's collection of wharves lay on the far side of town, fringing the area known as Coombe Mud. Olivia had never been to the yard before, and looked about her with curiosity. Business, as Mr Dunsford was wont to boast, was evidently good. All about was hustle and bustle. Men and pack animals hurried back and forth, so that she constantly felt Miles

Gilbert's arm come about her to guide her to safety, out of the way of trundling barrows or clattering hooves.

'Be grateful Mr Dunsford has decided to build that new house,' remarked the Captain. 'I don't think living over his counting-house yonder would be at all comfortable.'

Olivia was in complete agreement, for the counting-house, an austere stone-walled building, was in the centre of the large yard, looking directly onto sombre piles of coal. She did not say so, though. The last thing she wanted just then was any discussion that might touch on her relationship with Mr Dunsford.

'Where will we find Dunsford, do you suppose?' Miles asked. 'Perhaps one of these fellows knows.'

'The maister be aboard the *Jenny*,' they were informed. 'She'm down the far end of the quay.'

The *Jenny* proved to be quite difficult to find, moored as she was in a secluded section of the wharves, among the warehouses. A trim, speedy-looking vessel, she was evidently ready to put to sea right away.

'Are you Captain Gilbert, sir? Mr Dunsford said to come straight aboard,' said the seaman, who had evidently been watching out for them. At least, he had been watching out for the American. He regarded Olivia with some surprise. 'He didn't say about any lady, though. Are you coming too, miss?'

'Of course the lady is coming too,' said Captain Gilbert, helping her along the narrow gangplank.

'I'll tell Mr Dunsford you're here.' Uncertainly, the sailor glanced once more at Olivia before he hurried below.

The mooring-ropes were let go, and, a short distance away, men in a sturdy boat bent over their oars. The hawser between the *Jenny* and the smaller vessel tightened, and slowly she began to be tugged towards the mainstream of the river-current, so that she could catch the wind.

'Where's our boat?' asked Olivia. 'Surely we aren't being taken out to the castle aboard this?'

'Maybe we'll be put ashore in something smaller,' suggested the Captain.

Olivia hoped not. Going over the side in long skirts and petticoats was not the most easy or dignified of processes.

Joseph Dunsford's head appeared above the companion-way hatch.

'There you are, Gilbert! What can you be thinking of, standing there? Come below...' His voice, at first so urgent, trailed away as he caught sight of Olivia. 'Damn it, man! Why have you brought her?' he demanded.

'Watch your tone, Dunsford! That's no way to refer to Miss Kingston,' replied Captain Gilbert in angry surprise.

'But what stupid game are you playing? Why didn't you come alone?' cried Joseph Dunsford, in a fury. 'Oh, the Devil take it! It's too late to put her ashore now!'

'There's no question of her being put ashore,' protested the American. 'Miss Kingston is to come with me.'

'You fool! You'd endanger everything for the sake of a woman? Oh, bring her below, for pity's sake, before anyone sees her!'

'I prefer to remain where I am,' said Olivia firmly. She was certain Dunsford was drunk, and she refused to go into any ship's cabin with a man in that state.

'You'll come now, if you know what's good for you,' snapped Dunsford, in a curt voice. 'And you, too, Gilbert,' he added.

'Either apologise to Miss Kingston, or I'll give you the hiding of your life,' threatened the Captain, taking a step towards him.

'Best do as you're told!' The seaman who had ushered them aboard was suddenly wielding a cudgel, and he gave the American a push with it. Miles turned angrily and knocked it out of the sailor's hand, sending it clattering to the deck. He would have sent the man after it if Olivia had not given a cry of warning. She had seen what he had not—the gang of sailors, all armed with hefty staves of wood, who had moved ominously close.

'Get below, the pair of you!' ordered Joseph Dunsford.

The men took another step forward.

Olivia glanced up at Miles Gilbert in alarm and saw that he shared her bewilderment.

'I don't know what this is all about,' he said quietly, moving closer to her protectively. 'But I think we'd better do as we're told for the moment.' Together they followed Joseph Dunsford down the companion-way, and into a sizeable cabin.

'What are you up to, Dunsford?' Miles demanded angrily. 'If this is a joke then it's decidedly unfunny. And I wonder at you involving Miss Kingston in this way. Now put us ashore at once. Dirty as the road will be, I think we both prefer to go to the castle that way.'

'Oh, stop your pretence,' said Joseph Dunsford unexpectedly affable. 'There's no need to carry on with your charade. We're getting nicely under way now and with this wind we should be at our rendezvous in mid-Channel in very good time. I confess I was taken aback that you should want to bring Miss Kingston with you, but if that's what you want, so be it. Will you take a glass of brandy?'

'I will not,' snapped Miles. 'I'd prefer a few explanations. So far you've been talking nonsense. I know nothing about any mid-Channel rendezvous. I know only that Miss Kingston and I are expected at the Mayor's reception in the castle.'

Joseph Dunsford shook his head, a sly smile on his face.

'Cautious to the last, eh?' he said. 'In our line of business that's a good thing. But I hope you appreciate my swift thinking, suddenly inventing a change of venue for the reception. It was the only way I could manage to get my message to you, with Miss Kingston there at your elbow and listening to every word. Of course, if I'd known how things stand between you...'

'What do you mean, "inventing a change of venue"?' Olivia demanded.

She was not only puzzled by this odd affair, she was beginning to feel really frightened. He was not drunk, she could see that now. Nor, if she were any judge, did he appear to be deranged. There was a tense excitement about him that she found threatening.

'I suppose it's safe to let her in on it now?' Joseph Dunsford grinned at Captain Gilbert in a conspiratorial way. 'I'm sorry to inform you, my dear Miss Kingston, that, at this very moment, Mr Hunt's reception is taking place at the Mansion House without your gracious presence. Without the Captain's, too, of course. But he never intended to be there in the first place, did you, Captain?'

Olivia's alarm increased. Whatever was happening, Miles Gilbert seemed to be a part of it. Then, under cover of the folds of her cloak, his fingers found hers and gave them a comforting squeeze. She relaxed a little, reassured.

'Of course I intended to be there,' he protested hotly. 'For heaven's sake explain yourself, and put us ashore!'

As he spoke the vessel gave a slight shudder. Then the motion changed as her sails filled, and she began to run before the wind.

'Sorry, Captain, it's far too late for that—as if you didn't know,' grinned Dunsford.

'No, I don't know!' yelled the Captain. 'I haven't the faintest notion what you're talking about, and nor, I'm sure, has Miss Kingston.'

The grin on Joseph Dunsford's face faltered. 'You keep up your pretence well,' he said, but his tone was less confident.

'I tell you, there is no pretence!' Miles Gilbert was almost beside himself with fury. He would have leapt at Dunsford, but two of the sailors pounced, seizing him by the arms. 'What's going on?' he demanded, still trying to shake himself free of his captors.

'You know all about it. I've had you marked out as my contact for weeks. You've a good knowledge of the area, as I was told my contact would have. You gave the right passwords more than once. There can be no mistake.' Dunsford was sounding less and less sure of himself.

'Contact? Passwords? I know nothing of these.'

'Yes, you do!' Joseph Dunsford was suddenly angry. 'Stop playing games! You are my contact! I know you are! Else, why would you have responded when I mentioned today as a special day? You knew I was informing you of our rendezvous with the French vessel, when you'll be the one to take these to Paris.' He opened a locker and snatched out a leather satchel, which he flung on the cabin table. 'You'll take these,' he repeated, tearing it open. 'All the information I have gathered over the past months, vital information, details of gun installations and . . .' His voice faded as he stared at Miles Gilbert. The colour drained from his face. 'You are the right man . . .' It was almost a plea.

There was a silence in the cabin, broken only by the creaking of the ship's timbers, and the slap of bare feet from the sailors on the deck above. Olivia felt a shiver run down her

spine. Joseph Dunsford was the spy who had been so active!
And he was trying to implicate Miles in his treachery. Tense and
terrified, she awaited the Captain's reply. Her suspicions of the
last few weeks were about to be confirmed or denied! So strong
was her dread that, for the moment, it overruled any surprise
and fear she felt at discovering Joseph Dunsford's duplicity.
She stared up at the Captain's face, unwilling to tear her eyes
away for a second. She had to know the truth.

'I don't know who or what you expected,' said Miles, his
voice suddenly very calm. 'But I am not your man. As for a
rendezvous—I know naught of the matter. I spoke the truth.
Today is my birthday.'

Olivia believed him! Her head whirled with relief, the stag-
ger she gave owed nothing to the motion of the ship.

'You lie!' Joseph Dunsford had gone white to his lips. 'I had
you down as my contact from the minute you came to Dartmouth. I spotted at once that you weren't what you claimed.
You had to be the man. Why else would I try to strike up an
acquaintance? I even courted Miss Kingston, here, to give me
an excuse to meet up with you—'

'Oh, really!' protested Olivia. 'Of all the insults...' She
stopped, too thankful at Miles's innocence to express indignation.

'Well, having discovered your mistake, I suggest you put us
ashore immediately,' Miles said.

'Don't be a fool. You know I can't do such a thing!' exclaimed Dunsford.

'Then, Miss Kingston—she needn't be involved.'

'She's involved, whether she likes it or not! It's your fault,
Gilbert. You shouldn't have brought her! Now she'll have to be
disposed of too.'

'Disposed of?' Olivia's voice cracked over the words.

'Of course. What else? I can't let either of you go. You know
too much.'

She gave a gasp of horror at his words.

'It's one thing to say, another to do. I'm not convinced you
could commit murder in cold blood, especially not a woman.'
How Miles was able to sound so calm she did not know.

'I can do it, never fear. Especially when it'll save my own
neck.'

Bewilderment and terror seethed within Olivia. He could not mean to murder them? Not this stolid man who had visited her home so often, and been so boring and dull. He could not mean it? Then she looked into his eyes. They were cold and opaque. And her fear increased.

'Think, man! There's no need for such brutality. You say you have a rendezvous with a French vessel? Well, hand us over to them. Or, at least, Miss Kingston. Do what you please to me, but you don't have to harm her!' Somehow Miles was still managing to sound reasonable.

Frightened as she was, she knew she did not want to live without him.

'No!' she cried. 'No, I won't go alone!'

'No, you won't!' stated Dunsford harshly. 'You'll both go together! Over the side, after you have had a good crack on the head. Do you think I want you to go blabbing to the French any more than I want you telling tales to the English? What do you think the Frogs would do to me once they knew I'd made such a blunder? There'll be a rope waiting for me on both sides of the Channel if I'm not careful. But I intend to be careful. That's why you both must die.'

He meant it! Olivia was in no doubt about it now! She looked frantically about her for some means of escape. The door at the far side of the cabin and the companion-way leading to the deck were both guarded by burly seamen. There was no way out.

'But not yet,' Dunsford amended. 'We're not clear of the river mouth, and there's too much shipping about. There's no hurry. I can wait until we're further in the Channel. Put them in the sail-locker.'

At his command the sailors moved forward to seize Olivia. She kicked and bit and fought, but the arms which held her were like iron bands. She was vaguely aware of Miles valiantly fighting off his assailants, until a blow to the back of his head floored him. They were bundled out of the cabin, and slung into a small, cramped compartment, and the door locked upon them.

Olivia felt the American's body slumped against her. He had been barely conscious after that blow to the head.

'Miles, are you all right?' she asked with concern.

'I-I think so,' came the hesitant reply. 'I believe my head is still on my shoulders. And what of you? They didn't hurt you, I hope?'

'A bruise or two, nothing more.'

'Thank goodness for that! A sail-locker, did he call this place? Well, there are no sails here now, but perhaps there's something which will be of help to us.'

She was conscious of him trying to move in the confined space.

'It seems empty,' she said. 'I can feel nothing save the ship's planking.'

'Nor can I.' There was a thump as he attempted to stand. 'Ouch!' He sat down hurriedly again. 'Now we know the height of the locker.'

'If only we had some light.' In spite of her efforts her voice shook.

'I fancy there would be precious little to see. Perhaps we're better as we are. Where's your hand?'

In the darkness she felt him take her hand and hold it tightly.

'We must get out,' she whispered. 'We can't stay here to be killed.'

'I agree. We'll get out of here, don't worry.' He spoke with such complete conviction she felt quite heartened. He continued, 'Our first priority is to get out of this box. If I put my feet against the door and push . . . Curse this lack of space! There's no room to get any leverage.'

'I'll help you!' Olivia wriggled round until her feet were also against the small door and her back against the wall, then together they pushed.

It was no use. They pushed and kicked until they were exhausted, the door did not give.

'Let us out! For pity's sake let us out!' Olivia yelled, beating against the planks with her fists in a burst of panic.

'Save your strength.' Miles's fingers wrapped themselves round her bruised hands. 'We will get out of here, I tell you, so save your strength for when you need it.'

She slumped wearily back against the wall, wondering if he was as confident as he sounded.

'Dunsford, a spy! I can't take it in,' she said.

'It is hard to believe. You must find it particularly distressing. He's behaved especially badly to you.'

'Apart from wanting to kill me, you mean? Well, he came a-courting under false pretences. It'll be a long time before I forgive him for that alone!'

In the darkness Miles laughed. 'Good girl! I'm glad to see that even Dunsford hasn't dented your sense of humour.'

'He might have done if I'd been obliged to marry him,' she said with feeling.

'Obliged?'

'Do you think I'd have had any choice in the matter? How many wealthy suitors come knocking at the door of a woman of my age? For my parents' sake I'd have had to accept him.'

'Ah, I didn't see it that way.' He sounded unexpectedly relieved.

'Men seldom do!'

There was a pause.

'If you are rested I suggest we make another attempt to get out of this place,' he said. 'The door seems to be secured by a drop-latch. If you'd sacrifice your hairpins I might be able to fashion a device to lift it.'

But although Olivia parted with her hairpins willingly, they did not prove rigid enough to lift the latch. An attempt to unscrew the bolts fastening the latch to the door met with failure too, as did their efforts to break the hinges. In the end, they fell back in the tiny prison, their fingers too torn and bleeding to do any more.

Olivia did not like the increased rolling motion the ship had adopted; it told her they were getting further out into the open Channel. It took every vestige of self-control to hold back her mounting terror. The darkness and the silence did nothing to ease her fears. She wished Miles would say something to give her confidence, he had been silent for what seemed an age.

'Are—are you all right?' she asked. 'You've gone so quiet!'

'Yes, I'm trying to think of a way to get us out of this mess. We've no weapons, and we're outnumbered, so we will have to use guile. Our best chance will be when they come to...' His words petered out.

'When they come to give us the crack on the head that Dunsford is so insistent about,' she supplied, with a bravado she did not feel.

'Exactly! I might have known there was no need to mince words with you,' he said, with approval. 'Can you scream loudly? Enough to really startle?'

'I think so. Do you want me to demonstrate?'

'Not at this moment. My idea is that we play dead. Then when we've got our guards thoroughly puzzled, at my signal— I'll squeeze your hand perhaps—we take them by surprise. You scream while I attack. If I can but get one weapon we can make a fight of it. What do you think of my scheme?'

Olivia considered.

'Well, is it not a good plan?' he persisted.

'No,' she said flatly. 'But under the circumstances it is by far the best chance we've got.'

'Yet you sound disapproving.'

'I'm thinking of you squeezing my hand. I'm wondering if I should allow you to take such liberties!'

He gave a bark of laughter. 'You are indomitable, you really are!' he declared. 'Just as you proved the ideal partner in music, so you are a splendid companion in danger. No swoons! No vapours! Simply a concern for propriety. I can think of no one else who could make me laugh at a time like this.'

'I'm gratified you find me amusing. However, if at some future date you require a partner to join you in a similar adventure, I must beg you to leave my name off your list of candidates.'

'You are not enjoying yourself?' he began. Then he stopped, suddenly alert.

There were voices outside. Olivia gave a gasp of alarm.

'So soon,' whispered Miles, his arms going about her protectively. 'Now we'll discover whether my idea works or not.'

They tried to hear what was being said beyond the locker door. It was impossible to catch the individual words, but something in the intonation of the conversation puzzled Olivia. It took her a moment or two to work out what it was.

'They are speaking French,' she whispered.

'They are?' He listened more intently. 'I believe you are right. This may give us a better chance than my plan. Dunsford certainly doesn't want us talking to any Frenchmen, so, at a guess, they don't know we're here. Maybe we can turn the situation to our advantage.'

'How? They are still the enemy.'

'Not to me,' he reminded her softly. 'Yell your loudest.'

They began shouting, and hammering at the door so hard that when it was finally opened they almost tumbled out.

'Mademoiselle Kingston! Captain Gilbert!' After the darkness the light of the solitary lantern was dazzling. Although Olivia could not make out the features of the man who spoke she recognised the voice immediately.

'Lieutenant La Fontaine!' she cried. 'Of all people, it's you!'

Gradually her eyes adjusted, and she saw the Frenchman's dark, serious face looking at her with concern. Behind him she made out two other men, French prisoners, too, by their shabby uniforms.

'Mademoiselle Kingston, what on earth are you doing here?' he demanded. 'And the Captain, also.'

'It's too incredible a story to tell just now!' she exclaimed. 'All we ask is that you protect us. Joseph Dunsford intends to kill us.'

'Kill you? But that's preposterous.'

'It's the truth,' said Miles urgently 'You'd best be warned. Dunsford was involved in some scheme to spy for France, but his plans have gone wrong, and he blames us for his stupidity. The only way he can think of to rectify matters is to kill us.'

'And how is Mademoiselle Kingston involved?' asked the Lieutenant with surprising calm.

'She was innocently caught up in this mess. La Fontaine, you've got to help us! I don't know what you're doing on board this ship, but you can't let that rogue harm Olivia!'

'You're wasting your breath, Gilbert. The Lieutenant and his friends are eager to get back to France. They won't help you.'

They swung round to see Joseph Dunsford descending the companion-way steps. The pistol he held in his hand looked exceedingly menacing.

'Now, you monsewers, get yourselves back to your quarters, if you know what's good for you,' he snarled. '*Allez-vous* back to *votre* cabin if you don't want a taste of lead. Dispatching three escaping French prisoners won't trouble me in the least. *Allez!* Maybe this'll make you understand English better.' And he leaned forward and prodded the Lieutenant in the chest with his pistol.

'That thing might go off,' said Lieutenant La Fontaine evenly, pushing away the pistol barrel with an unhurried movement.

Olivia noted with astonishment that his command of the English language had suddenly improved. Although he still spoke with a French accent, it had lessened considerably. Something else was different about him, too. Something about his demeanour. He was less self-effacing, more authoritative.

'Get back to your quarters, or I'll turn this ship round and deliver the three of you to the authorities at Dartmouth,' blustered Dunsford.

'What, and tie the noose round your own neck for being a spy? I think not,' said the Lieutenant contemptuously.

'Who said I was a spy? If it was the American, he was lying!'

'No one needed to tell me. I've known all along,' said the Frenchman. 'You're a fool, Dunsford, and a bungling one at that. Did you really think I was just another Frenchman eager to get home? Didn't you recognise me as your contact?'

'You?' Dunsford's jaw dropped. 'I was sure it was the American. He gave the passwords.'

'Imbecile! I was the one who said them. Comparing London with Paris! That was it, wasn't it? I introduced those words into the conversation at Miss Kingston's home, only you were too stupid to recognise them.'

'I didn't know— I thought—' Joseph Dunsford was taken aback, and visibly frightened.

Olivia did not blame him. There was something very cold and ruthless about the Frenchman. He bore little resemblance to the overjoyed young man who had rejoiced at the birth of his daughter.

'So, what's to be done, Dunsford? How do you propose to sort out the sorry mess you've made?' demanded La Fontaine.

'That's easy. We throw the pair of them over the side, after we've knocked them senseless.'

'We?' The contempt in the Lieutenant's voice was searing.
'I've done many things in the service of my Emperor, but never
once have I killed a woman. Before we have any more disasters
I suggest you drop that pistol.'

'Oh, yes, and then what? I've no intention of being hanged
in France or in England. It should be an easy matter to get rid
of anyone who knows too much.'

Olivia's mouth went dry and her heart began to pound with
fear at the increasing menace in Dunsford's voice. She had
never imagined he could sound so threatening.

'Yes,' he continued, 'five to feed the fishes instead of two. I
can arrange that with no difficulty whatsoever. On deck, the lot
of you!'

'Don't be such a fool! You're no threat to us with an un-
cocked pistol,' snapped Miles.

Automatically Dunsford looked down at the weapon. It was
then that Miles leapt at him. The two of them fell to the floor
with a crash which sent the pistol spinning out of Dunsford's
hand, to land at Olivia's feet. She snatched it up and pointed it
at the struggling bodies. As they fought, now with Miles up-
permost, now Dunsford, there was no clear target, even if she
could have brought herself to pull the trigger.

'Shall I take that?' suggested La Fontaine, coolly removing
it from her grasp. 'It would be bad enough being shot deliberately, to be shot accidentally would be exceedingly galling.'

The other two French prisoners had been standing by, quite
as alarmed and astounded by the turn of events as Olivia. Now,
at an authoritative command from La Fontaine, they threw
themselves into the *mêlée*. Dunsford had no chance. He was
soon overpowered.

La Fontaine regarded him with scorn.

'I think I'll take you back to France with me,' he said. 'You'll
make an unusal souvenir of my stay in England. Until French
justice decides what to do with you.'

'No, shoot me now and have done,' yelled Dunsford.

The Frenchman merely shook his head.

'Do you think my crew'll stand for this?' Dunsford cried,
struggling even harder.

'Yes,' replied the Lieutenant. 'Once they realise that, without my say-so they'll get no money when we rendezvous with

the French vessel, I don't imagine they'll be too anxious about you. I think we'd better put you in the extremely inadequate accommodation you provided for Miss Kingston and Captain Gilbert.' He gave a nod, and the Frenchmen bundled Dunsford into the sail-locker.

'That was quick thinking on your part, Captain,' he continued, addressing Miles, who was still sitting on the floor, dabbing at a bleeding nose. 'I can see you are a useful man in a tight corner.'

'I'd no more wish to become fish food than you.' The American rose to his feet. 'What's to be done now?'

'We'll make our rendezvous as arranged. Nothing has changed. You look rather worn after your ordeal. *Le mal de mer* perhaps? It strikes us all at some time. A glass of brandy is what you need. And you, Miss Kingston. May I offer you some?'

'You're a spy!' exclaimed Olivia, the facts beginning to sink belatedly into her brain. 'You've taken tea with us, and sat with us, and you're a spy.'

Lieutenant La Fontaine considered her statement.

'I prefer to think of myself as a patriot and a loyal servant to my Emperor. I don't always like the tasks I am given, but someone must do them.'

'You deceived us as much as Joseph Dunsford did!' she cried.

'Oh no!' The Frenchman looked hurt. 'I told you no lies, Miss Kingston. I simply didn't tell you the complete truth.'

'Your wife, the baby and everything? That's all true?'

'Certainly it is. As was my anxiety when I got no letter from home. It's also true that I appreciate the many kindnesses you have shown me; which is why I am most concerned for your immediate future. The Captain is no problem. As an American he is one of our allies. When we rendezvous with the French vessel, which I anticipate will be in two or three hours, he can be taken to France and put ashore a free man. But you, Miss Kingston, what am I to do with you?'

'Turn round and take her back to Dartmouth,' urged Miles.

The Lieutenant shook his head.

'Much as I wish I could, such a solution is impossible. I must complete my mission; my two compatriots are eager to return home, and I understand there is a little business concerning cognac to be attended to when our two vessels meet. There are English lady prisoners in France, I know. I understand they're kept under reasonable conditions.'

'You can't contemplate imprisoning her!' Miles cried.

'No, I can't. The distress to Miss Kingston and to her parents makes that a course of action I am reluctant to take. I can think of only one alternative. We can put you ashore somewhere on the English coast. Somewhere fairly isolated, I am afraid, for we must be given time to make our escape before you raise the alarm. Would you be agreeable to that?'

'No she would not!' Miles interrupted before she could speak. 'It'll soon be dark. Olivia can't wander at night alone in an area she doesn't know.'

'Then can you think of some alternative, Captain?'

'Yes. I must be put ashore too.'

'You can't do that,' objected Olivia. 'If you go to France with the Lieutenant you'll be free.'

'The way the war is going I fancy I'll be free soon, anyway. Put us both ashore!'

'If that is what you wish, Miss Kingston?'

'No!' protested Olivia. 'I'll go alone. I've no objections.'

'But I have!' said Miles firmly. 'It's too dangerous.'

'Then I'll continue to France!' Olivia stated, determined he would not sacrifice his chance of liberty for her.

'Was there ever such a difficult female! I've experienced prison. Oh, I don't expect you'd suffer conditions like those at Mill Prison. I dare say La Fontaine, here, would do his best for you. All the same, it's no place for a woman. Besides, what effect would your sudden disappearance have upon your parents? How would they manage? What would the shock do to your father's health?'

It was an argument against which she had no answer.

'I think Captain Gilbert is right,' said Lieutenant La Fontaine. 'I confess I'd not be happy about putting you ashore alone. These are dangerous times. It's not wise for a lady to wander about the countryside by herself. Forgive me, Miss Kingston, but you have no say in the matter. Captain Gilbert is willing to go, therefore he'll accompany you. Now, if you'll excuse me, I'd better go and explain to the crew that this ship is under a new command.'

'I wish you wouldn't come, there's no need,' said Olivia after he had gone.

'Yes, there is,' said Miles. 'It's because of me that you got into this fix.'

'It wasn't your fault Joseph Dunsford got it all wrong.'

'Maybe not, but something I did or said must have misled him. I owe you for that.'

'You owe me nothing!' The last thing she wanted was for him to accompany her because of a sense of obligation. If he had said he would go with her because he could not bear to parted from her—that would be very different—different and impossible.

Footsteps on the companion-way announced the return of the Lieutenant.

'As I expected, the crew took the news of a new skipper extremely well,' he said. 'The only thing they were worried about was not being paid. Once I assured them they would be, all was fine. They even suggested a most splendid place for you to be landed, a beach a few miles from Dartmouth. It's backed by high cliffs. You'll be marooned there until low tide, I'm afraid. But once the tide has dropped there's an easy way into the next cove, from which you can walk to safety.'

'I can see I'll have no reputation left after this adventure,' Olivia observed, in an attempt at humour.

'I've considered that,' said the Lieutenant. 'I've said your abduction was a misunderstanding. I've also assured the crew that I still have eyes and ears in this place. If I hear any rumour of your good name being besmirched I'll be obliged to return.'

His words might have been ludicrous and overdramatic, if it were not for the manner in which he said them. Olivia felt her spine go cold. She reckoned it would be a dangerous thing to cross him.

It was dark when the boat was lowered over the side to take them to the beach. Olivia was glad. After so many mishaps and dangers it was still good to have her dignity preserved.

Lieutenant La Fontaine accompanied them ashore.

'I bid you *adieu*, Mademoiselle Kingston,' he said.

'And I wish you a safe journey, sir,' she replied, then wondered if she had said the right thing. Did one wish an enemy a safe journey, even if he had just kissed your hand?

'I'll tell my Lucille about your kindness to me, and I'll tell the baby, too, when she's old enough to understand.'

'Does your wife approve of what you do?' Olivia asked.

'She doesn't know!' La Fontaine sounded quite alarmed at the idea. 'She thinks I'm an ordinary naval lieutenant waiting for preferment. And that's what I hope to be when I complete this mission. Though, if my Emperor still has need of me I'll serve him. *Adieu* once more, Mademoiselle Kingston. *Adieu* to you, too, Gilbert, though in your case I think *au revoir* is more appropriate. I think that Dunsford may not have been as mistaken as he feared, eh?'

'What did he mean by that?' asked Olivia, as the oars of the boat crew dipped into the water, carrying Lieutenant La Fontaine away from the shore.

'I don't know. A French joke of some sort, perhaps.'

Olivia did not point out that La Fontaine was a man unlikely to joke. The Frenchman's words had reminded her of something. In her relief and joy at discovering that Miles was not a spy she had quite overlooked one point. The revelations of the last few hours did not alter the fact that he was not the American sea captain he claimed to be. Miles Gilbert was still a mystery.

CHAPTER TEN

THE crew on board the *Jenny* were well used to getting under way silently. Only the rattle of sheets through blocks, and the flap of canvas as the sails took the wind betrayed the fact that she was leaving.

On the beach Olivia and Miles stared out to sea, watching her shadowy departure. Then an incoming wave rushed perilously close to their feet, reminding them that the tide was still rising.

'Unless we want a soaking we'd better move,' said Miles.

Together they trudged up the shingle.

There was no moon, but a soft opalescent glow from the water relieved the darkness. Olivia was able to make out the heavy band of flotsam which marked the high-tide line. She was thankful to see it. A nagging anxiety had troubled her that, in spite of Lieutenant La Fontaine's assurances, the sea might reach right up to the sheer cliffs which backed the cove. If it had, then there would have been no refuge for her and Miles. As it was, although there was no way out of the cove without a boat, the beach appeared to be perfectly safe.

'At least La Fontaine didn't leave us without provisions,' Miles remarked, opening up the canvas-covered bundle that had been put ashore with them. 'Now, what have we here? A couple of blankets, some food, even a bottle of wine—trust a Frenchman to think of that! And what's this? Ah, a lantern! Very useful. He's even remembered to include the means with which to light it. Good fellow!'

He lit the lantern and placed it on a rock, where it cast a ring of brightness onto the multicoloured pebbles.

'There, that makes the place seem more like home.' He straightened up and looked about him far beyond the lantern's range. 'We should be safe and dry up here, I'm glad to say. I was pretty sure La Fontaine wouldn't play us false, but it's re-assuring to know for certain.'

So he had been sharing her fears.

'Now we've to wait until morning for the tide to drop,' said Olivia. 'That's if Lieutenant La Fontaine proves to be reliable to the end.'

'Until morning? You don't think we'll be able to get away until then?'

'He did say that the way to the next cove was only possible at low tide. I can just make it out vaguely, but I think our route must be by those rocks to the right—the cliffs at the other side are far too steep—and they're already surrounded by water. It'll be some hours before we can reach them; the tide hasn't yet turned.'

'This isn't the most comfortable of places to spend the night,' he observed, gazing thoughtfully at the sea. 'I'll swim round and fetch help, or find a boat or something.'

'Surely not in the dark, it's far too dangerous.'

'I think not. I'm a strong swimmer.' He took a step towards the water's edge, judging the distance he would have to go. 'Yes, it isn't far. I can manage it easily enough.'

'No, please don't,' begged Olivia, in a sudden panic. 'Didn't you notice the current that caught us as they brought the boat in?'

'I confess I didn't. But I'm prepared to try it, nevertheless, to save you from discomfort.'

'I don't mind having the pebbles for a bed, truly I don't. After having survived so much danger already today it would be foolish to throw your life away because you were too impatient to wait for the tide to turn.'

'Perhaps you're right.' To her intense relief he turned his back on the sea and walked up the beach. 'There seems to be plenty of driftwood lying about. If we're to be castaways then I suggest we make ourselves as comfortable as possible and build a fire. A passing ship might see it and come to our aid.'

'I approve of building a fire,' she said, 'But don't hope too much for rescue. I've an idea that this stretch of coast is a favourite haunt of the local smugglers. Any law-abiding ship's captain, seeing a fire on shore, is more likely to give the area a wide berth sooner than come and investigate.'

'Never mind, we'll have a blaze simply to cheer ourselves,' he laughed.

In a surprisingly good humour, considering all he had endured, Miles began to collect kindling. He seemed to have begun to enjoy the adventure.

Pushing back her long dark hair, in disarray now because of a lack of hairpins, she joined him in his search. For herself, she was glad of the activity. She was even more grateful for the leaping flames of the fire that they built. They gave her a feeling of security, as well as warmth. The sailing of the *Jenny* had had a strange effect upon her; it had seemed to empty the world of everyone save her and Miles. It was as if they were the last beings left in the universe, and a strange feeling of desolation had taken hold of her.

They sat warming themselves by the driftwood fire, the salty flames sending sparks shooting heavenwards. Then Miles decided to investigate the provisions left for them by the Lieutenant. Olivia was convinced she was not hungry, but once she had sampled the bread, cheese, and cold meat she found her appetite returning with a vengeance.

'You know, today has had one extraordinary outcome,' remarked Miles, helping himself to more wine.

'Only one?'

'Ah, I'm talking now of more personal matters, nothing to do with spies and secret agents.'

'Very well, don't keep me in suspense. What is this extraordinary outcome?'

'The fact that you've actually called me Miles. Aye, and more than once. Also, you've accepted me calling you Olivia without reproving me.'

Olivia considered. Yes, it was true. And it had happened so naturally that she had never noticed.

'In the circumstances formality does seem pointless at the moment,' she said. 'I suppose we may as well stay on Christian name terms until we get away from this place. Once we return to civilisation tomorrow, then we can go back to our usual forms of address.'

It was the thought of the morrow that did it. The idea of returning to normality after the perils and excitement of the last hours. It seemed very desirable, and very unattainable. Before she could stop them the tears were streaming down her cheeks, and her shoulders began to heave with unexpected sobs. In a moment Miles had gathered her in his arms.

'I don't know why I am crying,' she wept, her face pressed against his shoulder.

Gently his hand came up and smoothed the tangle of her hair.

'You've been so brave through all this,' he said, his lips against her brow. 'So very brave. I can think of no other woman who'd have come through this day's adventures with such spirit. It's no wonder you feel the need to weep now.'

'I don't like crying,' she wailed. 'I—I can't stop, and I'm making your—your coat wet.'

'Don't try to stop,' he said, sounding as though he were smiling. 'Cry until you feel comfortable again, and to the devil with my coat!'

He was right. As she wept she realised how much she needed the release of tears. All the while he cradled her close to him, stroking her hair, talking softly to her. She clung to him, drawing a comfort from his closeness which seeped through her like warmth. As she grew calmer she began to take in what he was saying. To her astonishment she realised that he was murmuring words of endearment and love. With her face still against the now soggy broadcloth of his shoulder she listened in wonder as he told her she was his brave love, his sweet Olivia, his darling girl—things she had never expected to hear him utter, not in her most hopeful dreams. It seemed only natural that she should raise her face to receive his kisses. Already they had shared so much—bewilderment, danger, fear. It was only right that they should share their love. Gradually the secluded beach became the centre of the world, bounded by the black cliffs and the dark silver sea. Beyond that everything ceased to exist.

His fingers entwined in the silken tendrils of her hair, as he drew her even closer, his kisses soft and urgent on her cheeks, her brow, her neck, her mouth.

'I knew it from the first, of course,' said Miles, tracing the curve of her ear with kisses.

She turned her face towards him, her mouth searching for his lips.

'And what did you know?' she asked drowsily.

'Why, that you were made for loving. The rest of the world may have seen the capable Miss Kingston, but I saw beyond to the soft passionate heart.'

'You did? Then I care not what the rest of the world might see.'

'Of course, that heart did have its stonier moments where I was concerned. I never believed any female could be so cruel and treat a poor fellow so.'

'It was for your own good,' replied Olivia, pretending severity. 'Far too many young women admired you openly, it was making you quite conceited. What you needed was a sensible female who was impervious to your charms.'

'Oh, is that what you were?' he demanded. 'And are you still sensible, eh?'

'Certainly I am,' she smiled, for his face was very close to hers.

'And are you still impervious to my charms, too?'

Now they were nose to nose in mock belligerence, and laughter prevented her from answering immediately.

'Can you doubt that I'm impervious?' she managed to gasp, at last. 'What interest can I possibly have in a worthless creature like you?'

'That's an intriguing question, one I propose to put to the test. Does this not interest you?' And he bent and kissed her full on the mouth.

'No, sir,' replied Olivia, when she got her breath back.

'Then what are your arms doing about my neck, pray?'

'I simply put them there to keep them out of harm's way,' she answered innocently.

'You're quite certain they don't denote the merest hint of interest on your part?'

'None whatsoever,' she assured him.

'Bother! That means I must make greater efforts!'

She gave a shriek as his grip tightened into a bear-hug, and he rained kisses down on her, until at last laughter and love exhausted them. Languid and content, she eventually fell asleep, her head resting against Miles's shoulder, her lips still savouring the softness of his mouth, happy in the knowledge that he loved her.

She awoke to the chill grey of an April dawn. Shivering, de spite her covering of a blanket and her cape, she sat up. O Miles there was no sign, though his coat still lay on the shin gle. Everything looked changed in the cold morning light. The tide had dropped to beyond the rocky headland at the en trance to the cove, robbing it of its sense of isolation. The tal cliffs, too, instead of offering a protective barrier, as they had in the night, now seemed only stark and forbidding. But these were mere details. They made no difference to the joy tha continued to glow within Olivia.

Miles loves me, she thought happily. He loves me!

The delight of being so loved threatened to occupy her mind to the exclusion of all else, until the urgency of getting back home as soon as possible asserted itself. She wondered where Miles had gone. At a guess, to reconnoitre the path from the next cove. Eager to be ready for when he returned, she hastily bathed in a small freshwater stream which gushed from the rocks. The icy chill of it made her gasp, and afterwards it proved no easy matter getting dressed when she had no means of drying herself properly. Wriggling uncomfortably as the blue silk clung clammily to her still damp body, she wondered at the young ladies of fashion in London, who, it was claimed, delib- erately dampened their muslin gowns to make them hug the figure more seductively. The peculiarities of fashion did not interest her, she was more inclined to dwell upon how wonder- ful the world had suddenly become.

Cheerfully she hummed to herself as she tried to smooth her hair into some sort of order. She was still humming when the crunch of feet on the shingle announced the return of Miles. Just seeing his tall figure round the rocky spur from the next beach was enough to make her heart start with joy. She had missed him! She had only been aware of his absence for a little while, yet she felt as if part of herself had been wrenched away. Now that he was walking towards her all was well once more. It was as if the sun had suddenly begun to shine.

'Miles!' She ran to meet him.

'Ah, you are awake at last,' he greeted her, striding up the beach.

'Yes, and what of you? Have you found the path from the other...' her voice faded.

She was close enough to see his face now, to make out the expression in his eyes. She had expected to see a pleasure in them which matched her own, a joy at being reunited. She wanted him to snatch her up and hold her close, to prove how much he had missed her in the short time they had been apart. Instead he avoided her gaze, and continued to walk up the beach, his shoes crunching on the pebbles. The arms she had extended to fling about him fell to her sides as she hurried to keep up with him, her face upturned to scrutinise him more closely. She could not believe what she saw. He suddenly seemed cold, distant. A stranger.

'Miles?' she said hesitantly. 'Miles, where have you been? I woke up and you'd gone.'

The smile he gave her was brief and bleak, and offered her no comfort. His whole manner had an awkwardness about it that was quite alien to his usual self-assurance.

'I wasn't far away,' he replied, with a forced heartiness. 'I'd only gone exploring.'

She waited for him to say something loving, for him to kiss her, or for him to give some sign that he remembered all that had happened between them. Instead he bent to pick up his coat and he put it on with unnecessary concentration.

'I found the path right enough,' he said, making a great play of brushing sand off his sleeve. 'It's an easy one, so we should have no difficulty leaving this place. I expect you'll be glad to go, eh?'

No, she would not be glad to go. It was here that she had experienced the greatest happiness she had ever known, a happiness she thought he had shared. She was wrong. She was beginning to recognise the emotion which shadowed his eyes. It was regret!

The cold reality of truth engulfed her. Miles did not love her after all. The tender endearing things he had spoken had been mere words, nothing more. And now he was regretting them! The hurt that beset her blotted out everything.

'Certainly, it'll be a relief to get home,' she said. 'Have you any idea how far we are from Dartmouth?'

'None at all, save that La Fontaine said we'd not be too far from town, if I recall.'

'Then perhaps we'd better eat the last of the food before we set out, to sustain us in case we have a long walk.' Was that really her voice sounding so brisk and matter of fact? So normal?

'A good idea. You're ever practical.'

Practical! She did not want him to think of her as practical!

The last thing Olivia wanted was food, she had only suggested it as a means of activity, anything to bridge this awful void that had opened up between them. Carefully she divided what was left of the bread, cheese and meat. Mechanically she ate, although the food had no more taste than ashes.

'If you've eaten enough I think we should set out,' he said. 'We want to avoid people on the road, don't we?'

'There's no need to be protective of my reputation,' Olivia retorted.

He drew in his breath sharply. 'I've broken my parole,' he reminded her quietly, leaving her wishing she had not spoken. Her words had sounded too much like a reproof.

The way round the small headland to the next bay was wet underfoot but easy enough. The cliffs were less sheer here, more tumbled, and with a well-worn path clearly discernible. As they were about to move from one cove to the other Olivia came to a halt. She had to make an effort, one last attempt to see if anything of the previous night's love could be rekindled. She knew that once they left the little beach behind her chance would be gone.

'Stop!' she pleaded. 'Stay for a moment, I beg you.'

Miles was a step or two ahead of her. He turned.

'Yes, Miss Kingston?' he said, his face impassive. 'Can I be of help to you?'

It was the 'Miss Kingston' that cut her like a knife. It was so cold and impersonal.

'I've—I've a stone in my shoe. I'll be with you directly,' she said, thankfully bending down to attend to the imaginary pebble. She feared her hurt was all too visible on her face.

They made their way across the other beach in silence, then, when they reached the path Miles turned round and offered his hand to help her over a steep rock. Olivia ignored it, preferring to scramble up on hands and knees sooner than feel the touch of him again.

He turned away from her and continued up the path. Olivia
followed behind, trying not to look at his broad-shouldered
figure striding ahead, trying not to love him.

With their backs to the English Channel it seemed sensible to
strike east, towards the rising sun. Although their voyage in the
Jenny had apparently taken them many miles from Dartmouth, the journey across country proved to be shorter and less
arduous than they had feared. Most of the way their route was
through country lanes, only occasionally did they have to avoid
a farm or cottage, or take cover until some labourer passed by
on his way to work. Here and there early blackthorn blossom
was turning the tops of the hedges white, while along the high
Devon banks pale sweeps of primroses lit the fresh green of new
growth. The beauty of the morning was lost on Olivia. For her,
all colour had faded from the world, leaving it a sombre grey.

The last mile of their journey, as they approached Dartmouth, proved the most difficult. The town was well astir by
the time they reached it, so they were forced to cut through
woods and fields to avoid meeting people. They approached the
Kingston house from the rear, descending from the lane at the
back and down through the steep garden to the kitchen.

Charlotte Kingston leapt to her feet as they entered the
drawing-room.

'Where have you been? Oh, where have you been? We have
been half out of our minds with worry!' she cried hysterically.

Her husband's reaction was more muted, but no less heartfelt.

'You are both safe! Thank God!' he said.

Olivia felt an anxious pang as she noted how white he looked,
and how heavy were the shadows round his eyes.

'We didn't mean to distress you! We didn't mean it!' she
protested irrationally, crumpling onto her knees and burying
her face in her father's coat.

She found she could say no more, so it was left to Miles to
explain.

'That's true,' he said, sinking wearily into a chair. 'The last
thing we wanted was to cause you anxiety. Unfortunately it was
beyond our control.'

'What happened? Where have you been? Oh, this has been
the most dreadful time! We had prepared a special supper as a

surprise, because it was the Captain's birthday, but it was ru
ined. And your gown is torn, Olivia!'

Mrs Kingston's voice ran on in agitation, until her husban
gently put out a restraining hand.

'Let us hear what they have to say,' he said quietly.

'It's so incredible I find it hard to believe myself,' said Miles
'It began as Ol— as Miss Kingston and I were preparing t
leave for the Mayor's reception yesterday afternoon. Josep
Dunsford called and said that there had been a major chang
in the arrangements...' He went on, telling of the extraordi
nary events that had befallen them.

Mr and Mrs Kingston listened aghast, tightly clasping eac
other's hands as the American recounted incident after inci
dent.

'That Dunsford! What a black-hearted, double-dyed rogue!
Edward Kingston cried at last, unable to contain himself. 'If h
ever comes within a mile of me I'll horsewhip him until he beg
for mercy, that I will.'

'I doubt if you'll get the chance, sir,' said Miles. 'I fancy tha
the French have more permanent plans for him.'

'The French! Ah, yes! Fancy young La Fontaine being a
master spy! I can't imagine it somehow. He seemed so plain and
ordinary. Still, maybe that was an asset to him sooner than a
disadvantage.' Mr Kingston shook his head in astonishment
'Give him his due, French or not, he behaved like a true gentleman.'

'Thank heavens he did, Papa!' said Olivia with feeling. 'He
saved our lives.'

'And for that I shall be eternally grateful to the dear man!'
exclaimed Mrs Kingston. 'After all, he cannot help being
French, can he? Now Mr Dunsford is quite another matter. I
was never so deceived by anyone! And to think, he was received into all the best houses!'

'I saw the *Jenny* go out, you know,' mused her husband. 'I
watched her progress out past the castle, never dreaming that
my own child was aboard and in such danger— My stars!
Admiral Ranscombe! I had forgotten all about him.'

'Admiral Ranscombe, Papa?'

'Yes, when it grew late and you didn't return, naturally we
became exceedingly anxious. We even sent a discreet enquiry

down to the Mansion House, in case you were still there. When we learned that you'd never arrived we knew things must be serious, so we sent Abbie along with a message to the Admiral. There's no better fellow in an emergency. We must send to the Admiral immediately, and let him know you are safe.'

'Yes, by and by, husband. First we must attend to these two poor creatures,' said Mrs Kingston, suddenly being practical for once. 'Food and rest is what they need, the pair of them. They both look worn to the bone.'

'I'm not hungry, Mama, but the thought of my own bed and a good wash ... I look like a hedgerow gypsy.' Olivia was indeed suddenly overwhelmed by exhaustion.

'Then off you go to your room, and you, too, Captain dear. And I, myself, shall bring you each something on a tray.'

'You are very kind, ma'am,' said Miles. He, also, sounded weary.

'Kind? Nonsense! We are just so glad to have you both back safely, are we not, husband?'

'Never in your life have you spoken a truer word, my love,' agreed Edward Kingston fervently. 'How thankful we are that, despite all your terrible adventures, you have both come home safely! Everything has turned out well in the end.'

Everything has turned out well in the end! Her father's words echoed in Olivia's head as she went to her room. If only he knew the truth, she thought.

One outcome of her adventures was that her blue silk gown was past redemption. She dropped the tattered garment onto the floor, summoning up enough energy to give it a derisory kick. Its demise was the only good thing to have happened, as for the rest ... For a brief spell she had thought herself to be truly loved and truly happy, but it had proved to be a fool's paradise—it had lasted for such a little time. She put on her night-gown and crawled into bed, pulling the bedclothes over her head to shut out the world. Tired as she was she feared her misery would not let her sleep, but when Charlotte entered the room ten minutes later, bearing bread and butter, and coddled eggs on a tray, Olivia was breathing deeply, oblivious to the world.

It was late afternoon when Olivia awoke. She rose and dressed. Splashing her face with cold water made her feel more refreshed, though it did nothing to relieve the ache in her heart. When she was ready she went downstairs to find Admiral Ranscombe sitting in the drawing-room with her parents. Of Miles there was thankfully no sign. The Admiral rose as she entered.

'My dear Miss Kingston, what adventures you've been having! How do you feel now, after your ordeal?' he asked with concern.

'Much better for having slept, I thank you.'

'Was there ever such a heroine! To make so little of it after being in so much danger! Thank goodness you're safe!' he exclaimed. 'I blame myself, you know. I've had my suspicions about Dunsford for some time. I even had the *Jenny* under surveillance. Would you believe it, your own father was keeping a watch on her for me, and neither of us suspected you were in danger.'

'Papa!' Olivia gazed at her father in amazement.

'Certainly.' The Admiral gave a chuckle. 'My friend Kingston, here, often keeps me informed about what is happening on the river. No one has a sharper eye, nor a better knowledge of the traffic on the Dart.'

'My knowledge was sorely astray this time,' said Edward Kingston gravely.

'There was no way you could have known, Papa.'

'Indeed not,' agreed the Admiral. 'Who would have guessed that that scoundrel, Dunsford, would have had the nerve to sail out on such a mission in broad daylight— Ah, who is this I hear? I think Captain Gilbert has returned.'

The tread of Miles's footsteps coming up the stairs gave Olivia time to get her emotions under control. When he entered the room she was in command of herself enough to greet him calmly.

'You've been out already, Captain? I admire your fortitude after our recent perils,' she said evenly.

'Ah, so you're awake at last, Miss Kingston. I hope your rest did you good.' His words were courteous enough, but cool. Swiftly he turned his attention to their visitor. 'For a second time I bid you good day, sir,' he said.

'A second time?' queried Olivia.

'The Captain and I have already met once today, when he gave me all the details of your ordeal,' said the Admiral. 'And now I see you have been taking the air, sir. I wish I had such stamina.'

'I went to take care of a small matter of unfinished business, to make our apologies to the Hunts for our non-appearance yesterday. I felt that some explanation was necessary if only to silence gossiping tongues.'

'How typical of you, Captain, dear,' cried Charlotte Kingston. 'I might have known you would be so careful of Olivia's reputation.'

'A wise move, my boy!' agreed the Admiral. 'We want no mention of Miss Kingston's involvement in this affair to leak out, do we?'

'And what did you tell them?' demanded Olivia, feeling herself grow tense. She had given little thought to the effect their adventures would have on her reputation, her mind and her heart had been concerned with other matters!

'I was most profuse in my excuses, I babbled on vaguely about mistaking the venue, which was close enough to the truth.'

'And did they believe you?' she asked.

'Oh yes, I think so. To be honest they seemed to have all but forgotten the incident. The entire household was agog at the escape of the three French prisoners.'

'So that tale has reached town already, has it?' commented Admiral Ranscombe.

'It certainly has, the streets are buzzing with it. Far from being annoyed that Miss Kingston and I weren't present at their reception yesterday, the Misses Hunt were much more interested in my acquaintance with Lieutenant La Fontaine. I left them fully persuaded that it was his eagerness to see his new daughter that had prompted him to break his parole and escape to France.'

'And is nothing being said about that dreadful creature, Dunsford?' asked Mrs Kingston.

'Not a word, ma'am. So far no one has missed him yet,' said Miles. 'I suppose that, at the moment, most people consider him to be away on business. His absence hasn't been remarked upon.'

'I'm amazed you suspected Mr Dunsford, Admiral,' said Charlotte. 'He seemed such a respectable young man. It was extremely clever of you.'

'Not clever enough.' Admiral Ranscombe gave a wry grin. 'I was caught out completely by Lieutenant La Fontaine. I'd not picked him out to be Dunsford's confederate. No, I had my eye on someone quite different for that.' And he gave a knowing smile which rested briefly on Miles. Olivia wondered if he had shared her suspicions about the American. If only she had known! It would have saved her much anguish!

'I can't understand why Joseph Dunsford worked for the French at all?' she said. 'He seemed always to despise them.'

'He didn't despise their gold,' said the Admiral with contempt. 'He's the lowest creature on this earth, the sort who'll betray his country for money. I hope the French give him the welcome he deserves.' He rose to his feet. 'Ah well, we can do naught about him now. Nor about La Fontaine, though I've less regrets on that score. They'll both be well away by this time. Nevertheless, I've sent word for the revenue cutter to go out after the *Jenny,* if we can't apprehend any French spies we'll have to make do with French brandy. I'll let you know what happens. Captain Gilbert, I'm afraid there'll have to be an official enquiry into all this, which you will be obliged to attend, if only to explain how you came to break your parole. Don't worry, it'll simply be a formality.'

'I'm at your service,' said Miles. 'I presume we both agree that Miss Kingston's name need not be mentioned?'

'Certainly we are! Before you're called we'll have a private word together, you and I, just to make sure of the details, eh?' The Admiral clapped the American on the shoulder in a friendly fashion as he passed.

'There, see how mindful the dear Captain is of your good name, Olivia!' exclaimed Charlotte. 'I confess we have been a little concerned, have we not, husband? We know that neither of you is at fault, and of course, dearest Captain Gilbert, never for one moment do we doubt that you behaved most properly throughout. All the same, you cannot blame us for being a little anxious for our only daughter. If one word of this ever leaked out then her reputation would be ruined.'

'I thank the Captain for his concern,' Olivia said, her eyes never leaving him. 'Though I don't think anyone need worry. News of our night together won't get abroad.'

'You are very kind, but I must beg to differ,' he retorted.

To her surprise he sprang to his feet and began to take measured strides across the floor, his head down, as though deliberating carefully on what he was about to say.

He went on, 'This question has occupied my mind for most of the day. Aye, and during last night, too. It's true that we were very careful not to be seen on our return home, and both Lieutenant La Fontaine and Admiral Ranscombe have done their best to protect Miss Kingston's good name. But I'm not convinced that it is enough. It would just take one farm worker to have seen us, or one member of the crew of the *Jenny* to speak carelessly and her reputation would be gone for ever.'

'I think you worry unduly, the chance is slight,' said Olivia uneasily. He was leading up to something, and she could not imagine what it might be.

'No, it isn't slight!' he protested. 'In my view it's too great to be ignored. There's one obvious solution. This, I know, is not an ideal moment, but under the circumstance I hope you will forgive me. Mr Kingston, I formally ask you for your daughter's hand in marriage.'

The silence that fell was profound.

'My dear boy!' exclaimed Mr Kingston. 'My dear boy—'

'How splendid!' cried Charlotte. 'Of course! It is the perfect answer. What could be more delightful or more satisfactory?'

'No!' exclaimed Olivia, recovering last. No one heard her.

'I know my finances are in a sore state at the moment,' went on Miles, his face wooden. 'I do assure you that it is caused entirely by my present situation as a prisoner of war. At home, on Rhode Island, I have a good estate of my own, plus an income more than adequate to keep a wife in comfort. My prospects, too, are good, for I am the only son of—'

'I don't care whose son you are! I won't marry you!' Olivia retorted.

'There, your nerves are getting the better of you,' said her mother soothingly. 'No wonder. The Captain's offer has taken us by surprise. Yet it is a most advantageous one, as you will realise after you have given it due consideration.'

'I don't need to consider. I know what my answer is. I thank you, Captain Gilbert, for the honour you have done me, but I must decline!' exclaimed Olivia, battling to keep her distress under control.

'Miss Kingston, I beg you to think about it.'

For the first time he looked her full in the face. If she had seen anything she could recognise as love... if he had even addressed her as Olivia, she might have reconsidered. As it was, she could only reply quietly, 'There is nothing to think about. My answer is still no.'

'Captain Gilbert, as far as I am concerned, I give you full leave to pay your addresses to my daughter with my blessing,' said Edward Kingston. He turned to Olivia. 'Come, my dear, you're being over hasty. Give yourself more time. I don't believe for one moment that you were ever really attached to that Dunsford scoundrel, so what other objections can you have to this match?'

She could think of a dozen reasons, every one of which was tearing at her heart. She was only capable of putting forward the least painful.

'I have no intention of becoming involved in some long legal tangle in order to marry,' she said, as calmly as she was able. 'Don't you recall the fuss when the daughter of the lodging-house keeper on the Foss wished to marry a French prisoner? The authorities were most uncooperative. The matter went on for weeks, and then she finished up being told that any such marriage wouldn't be legal in France. The gossips had a field-day, and I've no intention of providing them with another such target.'

'Your situation bears no comparison,' protested her mother. 'As you say, the girl was only the daughter of a common lodging-house keeper. Besides, it was a delicate matter of some urgency for her to be married promptly, as I recall. And, of course, the man she proposed marrying was a Frenchman. I dare say the laws on marriage are different in America. Is that not so, Captain?'

'I'm not aware of any American law making a marriage between a prisoner of war and an English lady illegal, ma'am,' said Miles stiffly.

'There, I was sure it would be so,' said Charlotte, with satisfaction. 'Besides, I expect you could always have a second ceremony once you got back to America, just to be on the safe side. So you see, Olivia, there can be no real objections. You would be properly married, and your reputation would be safeguarded.'

'Mama,' said Olivia, choosing her words with care. 'Nothing you say will make me accept Captain Gilbert. I'm sorry to be so blunt. He is only proposing because it is the honourable thing to do, yet there is no need. The situation was not of his devising, he was as much a victim as I. He didn't want to spend the night alone with me, he had no alternative. I don't consider my reputation so important that he must sacrifice himself for something which was not his fault. A woman's reputation is only of worth if she is still on the marriage market, and I am not. Therefore it is of no importance.'

'Olivia, how can you say such a thing?' cried Charlotte. She would have prolonged the argument if Miles had not cut in.

'I wouldn't have Miss Kingston urged to do something against her inclinations,' he said. 'I fear I've chosen my moment very badly, no doubt she's still feeling the after-effects of all she has suffered. May I suggest we continue this conversation tomorrow?'

Olivia wished he had not come to her rescue by being so reasonable. The hurt he had dealt her still stung savagely. It went ill with gratitude.

'The lad's right, my love,' said Edward Kingston. 'We've been most inconsiderate, trying to hold a discussion when the pair of them are still worn out. No wonder Olivia is overwrought. We'll say no more on the matter for the present.'

Olivia feared she could not contain her distress much longer. Making her excuses she hurried to her room and closed the door. She sat on the edge of the bed, her arms wrapped about herself for comfort, as the events of the last half-hour tore through her mind. Miles had proposed to her. Something she had never dreamed would happen. But under what circumstances! He had proposed out of a sense of honour, nothing more. She tried to imagine marriage to him, loving him desperately as she did, and knowing that he felt nothing for her. It was a dream become a nightmare. She could not bear it. She could have tolerated being the wife of Joseph Dunsford far more easily.

CHAPTER ELEVEN

OLIVIA knew, with an uncomfortable certainty, that Miles had not taken her refusal to marry him seriously. He was sure to ask her again! The eyes of her parents, which so often rested on her with hopeful speculation, increased her discomfort.

Just when she was congratulating herself upon having evaded him she found the American lying in wait for her next morning, in the drawing-room.

'You are up betimes,' she said coldly. 'Don't tell me you've another of your urgent early morning appointments.'

'Yes, I have,' he said. 'With you!'

'I'm sorry, I've nothing to discuss with you. Nor have I the time,' she replied.

She made to leave the room, but he was too quick for her. He reached the door first and barred her way.

'Olivia, we've got to talk,' he said urgently.

So he was back to using her Christian name again! He was too late!

'I'd prefer you to resume calling me Miss Kingston,' she said, her voice growing more icy.

'Don't go on about details, I beg you,' he protested. 'What I want to say is far too urgent and important. You must marry me!'

'Oh, must I? And on whose orders?'

'On no one's orders, just on my fervent entreaties.'

'You've made your offer and I've refused, and so released you from any obligation you might feel. There's nothing more to be said. Now please stand aside, and let me pass.'

'For heaven's sake hear me out!' he protested. 'If the slightest rumour that we spent a night alone together on a beach should ever leak out you would be ruined. That would mean the loss of your livelihood too, don't forget. Therefore you must marry me.'

Still there was no hint of love in his words or in his eyes.

'I seem to be experiencing great difficulty in making you understand,' she said, speaking slowly and evenly. 'I don't see why you should make such a sacrifice, or why it is necessary for us to marry. To be blunt, I have no wish to marry you.'

'I know you haven't!' he exclaimed. 'I know well enough what you think of me. I can only promise you that as my wife you'd be shown every kindness and consideration.'

'I won't argue. My answer is still no.'

'I'm a man of means in my own country. Your life would be much more comfortable. You would have an allowance that was more than adequate, and—'

'How dare you! If I would not marry you for the sake of my good name, do you honestly think I'd marry you for your money?'

'No, of course not. It seems that yet again I have expressed myself badly—' He stopped, unable to continue. 'You had better go,' he said, standing aside.

Olivia swept past him. As she did she gathered her skirts tightly about her, as if determined not to touch him in any way. It was an unconscious gesture, a wish to hurt him.

It was too much to hope that her mother would remain silent on the subject of marriage. All Olivia could do was prepare herself to defend her decision once more. The gentle onslaught came after they had eaten their midday meal and the pair of them were alone.

'Captain Gilbert had a long chat with your Papa and me last evening,' began Charlotte. 'He was most frank about his income and his prospects.'

'Was he indeed, Mama?' Olivia tried to sound discouraging.

But her mother was not to be deterred so easily. 'Yes, he was, and I must say I had no idea the dear man was so eligible. Did you know he already has a good estate of his own, which came to him through his grandmother, and that he will inherit another, far larger one in due time?'

'Then why does he choose to go to sea?' demanded Olivia.

'No doubt he has his reasons. Some men feel the need for adventure when they are young. It is really quite unimportant. The vital thing is that he is not dependent solely on his captain's pay. And, although he did not say so openly, I gained the impression that he is from a very good family, and is well connected.'

'He must find that very gratifying, Mama.'

'Yes, he must,' said Charlotte, failing to recognise her daughter's sarcasm. 'And it makes it all the more splendid that he has actually made you an offer. I am sure that once you really give it some thought you will overcome your objections to him—though, in truth, I cannot imagine what they can be. Your Papa approves of him most heartily, and so do I. He is truly a delightful man, even discounting his excellent expectations. Of course marriage to him would involve some financial difficulty at first, until this wretched war with America is done, but I am convinced that will be for only a short time. Why do you not say yes to him, and make us all happy? Half the young women of Dartmouth would be green with envy if they knew what has befallen.'

'I don't propose contemplating matrimony simply to make the females of Dartmouth jealous, Mama. As it is, I know that Captain Gilbert asked for my hand because he felt it was his duty. I'll go to no man under those conditions.'

'You are too nice on the subject! I have known many marriages come about for far flimsier reasons.'

'And were they happy afterwards? How could any woman look her husband in the eye, day after day, knowing that he'd wed her because he felt he must.'

'At least she would have a husband!'

'I'd sooner do without, in those circumstances!'

'I do not understand you!' wailed Mrs Kingston. 'You would be set up for life, you would have a place in society, and in addition, you would have the most charming husband anyone could imagine. Why are you being so obstinate?'

'I have given my reason, Mama,' answered Olivia quietly. 'And now I suggest we end this discussion. I hear Captain Gilbert coming.'

But Charlotte Kingston refused to let the matter rest.

'I have been trying to convince my wretched daughter of the advantages of marrying you, sir, but she will not listen,' she cried.

Miles looked awkward, as though not sure how to react.

'I, too, have tried again to persuade Miss Kingston to have me, without success,' he said.

'I cannot think why! Truly I cannot!' exclaimed Charlotte.

'There I have the advantage of you, ma'am,' said Miles. 'Your daughter doesn't like me, and never has. That is so, is it not, Miss Kingston?'

Unwilling to tell a lie, Olivia sought refuge in ambiguity.

'I think I've demonstrated my true opinion of you clearly enough,' she replied, keeping her voice steady with a tremendous effort. As she had expected he misinterpreted her meaning.

'You've certainly never disguised your disapproval of having me in the house, and no one can deny that relations between us have grown increasingly uncomfortable over the last day or two. In my efforts to put things right I seem only to have made them far worse. Therefore, sooner than aggravate your distress, Miss Kingston, I propose applying to Mr Brooking for a change of lodgings.'

'Oh no!' cried Charlotte. 'Dear, dear Captain Gilbert, do not let Olivia drive you away with her foolishness. She will come about eventually, I assure you. Please do not leave us. We enjoy your company so much.'

Olivia's heart seemed to have become immobile. She had always known that Miles would be leaving eventually, she had not expected him to go so soon.

'You don't need to leave,' she said, adding before she could stop herself, 'Having endured you so far I can tolerate you a little longer.'

'Is that any way to persuade him to stay?' cried her mother.

'I think it far better that I go somewhere else. Before I do though, I must ask you one more time. Will you marry me?' His eyes searched her face too intently for her comfort.

'I don't recollect having been asked before!' she cried. 'I recollect being told by you and by my parents that I should and that I must! I recollect being told the many advantages of marrying you! But I have no recollection of ever having been asked!'

He took a step towards her.

'Is that what is preventing you from saying yes? The fact that I failed to make a proper proposal?' he demanded.

The surge of emotion in her faded suddenly, leaving her limp and despondent. The only way she would ever be at peace was for Miles Gilbert to go out of her life.

'No,' she said quietly. 'I have other, far more important reasons, so you see, you've no need to go down on your bended knees. My answer is still the same, so perhaps it would be better if you found lodgings elsewhere.'

'As you wish, Miss Kingston.' He spoke in a clipped, abrupt voice. 'I will attend to it at once, this very afternoon. Though I know it is the right thing to do I shall, nevertheless, be very sorry to leave. I have been shown many kindnesses in this household, and I'm very grateful.'

'Olivia did not show you any kindness!' protested Charlotte, who was weeping loudly. 'She was cruel, spurning your offer like that. And now you feel you must go, dear Captain Gilbert. Oh, what am I going to tell my darling Kingston when he awakes? He will be heartbroken!'

She dashed out of the room, her sobs clearly audible as she ran across the landing to her sleeping husband.

'Miss Kingston— Olivia—' Miles began.

But Olivia did not let him finish. She knew she could stand no more hurt. 'If you please, Captain Gilbert,' she interrupted, her voice little more than a whisper, 'There is nothing else to be said.'

She went out of the room, leaving him gazing after her, his face white and grim.

Although he was more subdued about it than his wife, Edward Kingston was greatly upset by the news that Miles was to leave. He kept querying why the change was necessary, and trying to find ways of persuading the American to stay. Olivia felt guilt tugging at her, especially when she considered what a difference the Captain's company had made to her father. But then she thought about the difference his company had made to her, and she knew that there was no going back.

Of course she would probably still meet him from time to time, walking about Dartmouth. How she would cope with these inevitable encounters, and how she would tolerate not seeing him frequently occupied her mind more often than she cared to admit.

As each day dawned she dreaded hearing that he had found new lodgings, yet she longed for it too. Only when Miles was out of their house and out of her life would the gnawing pain inside her ease.

She awoke, one bright morning in mid-April, to the sound of church bells, which was puzzling for she knew it was not a Sunday. As she listened she realised that the bells were ringing in a happy discord quite unlike their usual rhythmical Sabbath peals. Sleep having deserted her, she rose and washed and dressed. In the drawing-room she found her parents already up, and looking out of the window eagerly.

'What's happened?' she asked. 'Why are the bells ringing?'

'That's what we would like to know,' said her father. 'The Captain has gone into town to see what he can find out for us. It will be a great victory or some major happening in the war, you mark my words. Oh! Here comes Admiral Ranscombe along the street! He's seen me! He's waving! Ah, he's coming in! Now we'll find out what's afoot. If anyone knows it will be the Admiral.'

True enough, a few minutes later, Admiral Ranscombe burst into the room, his face wreathed with smiles.

'What a day, my dear friends!' he cried. 'What a day!'

'Tell us what's happened before we die of curiosity,' demanded Edward Kingston.

'Die? You'll not die when you hear what I've got to tell. It's enough to put heart into a corpse! Boney's been taken!'

'No!' The faces of the Kingston family showed incredulity.

'It is so, I promise you,' the Admiral assured them. 'It's hard to believe, isn't it? The Scourge of Europe under lock and key! What's more he's abdicated, so, to all intents and purposes the war is at an end. Now it's up to the diplomats and politicians to dot the i's and cross the t's.'

'Splendid! Oh what a splendid thing to happen!' In his excitement Mr Kingston threw a cushion into the air, not caring that when it landed it knocked over his carafe of cordial.

'Oh, that's wonderful indeed!' cried Olivia, delighted to have something to rejoice about. 'It means we'll have Charlie home again. I'm so thankful.'

'So are we all.' Mrs Kingston dabbed at her eyes. 'My darling boy back once more! I can hardly believe it!'

'And Napoleon? What's to be done with him?' Olivia asked.

'Yes, what's to become of the rogue?' added her father.

'The news we've received so far is sketchy, so I have no details,' said Admiral Ranscombe. 'But in my opinion, to have him imprisoned somewhere would only invite trouble from his supporters, and he has many. My guess is that there'll be an honourable settlement to the problem, perhaps he'll be forced to retire to some isolated place, where he can be watched, and where his followers can't reach him.'

'So Lieutenant La Fontaine's Emperor will have no further need of his services,' said Olivia thoughtfully. 'Which means he'll go home to his wife and baby.'

'I am glad. We owe him a debt of gratitude for what he did to help you and the dear Captain,' put in Charlotte.

'And the end to the war with France means that Joseph Dunsford did his scheming and plotting to no purpose,' Olivia continued.

'So he did! Well there's great satisfaction to be had from that!' declared Edward Kingston gleefully.

She thought of the unpleasantness she had suffered at the hands of Dunsford, and its painful aftermath. It had all been to no purpose, and for a moment she was unable to share her father's jubilation. But only for a moment. Thoughts of peace and the return of her brother swept away all gloom. This was a day for rejoicing.

'I must be gone, friends.' The Admiral was growing restless. 'As you may imagine I've a thousand and one things to attend to, but I had to come and make sure you heard the great news.'

'Our thanks to you, sir. I can't think of better tidings, nor a more welcome messenger,' cried Mr Kingston. 'When we get our breath back, and we've stopped being addlepated with joy we'll have a proper celebration, eh?'

'You've my word on it!' declared the Admiral, making for the door. Then he stopped and clapped his hand to his head. 'Addlepated is a more appropriate description of me at the moment. I quite forgot the other news I'd got for you. The *Jenny* has been taken by the revenue men!'

'She has? I can't believe it! Even more good tidings!' exclaimed Mr Kingston. 'I suppose there was no sign of the rascally Dunsford aboard?'

'I fear he was long gone, and the Lieutenant with him.'

'A pity, though perhaps it is for the best. I'd dearly love to have given him a hiding, but I know I am no longer capable of it, so I'd only have been more frustrated.'

'Don't worry, my friend, I'm sure he'll get his just deserts,' grinned the Admiral. 'As we expected, the crew swore that they'd never heard of escaping French prisoners or spies and the like, but then they also swore that the vast cargo of brandy on board was for their own use.'

'So that's the end of the affair?' asked Olivia.

'Almost. You'll be pleased to note that your name was never mentioned, Miss Kingston, nor any hint that there had ever been a woman on board. Oh, except that one of the revenue men reported discovering a number of bent hairpins in an empty sail-locker. Either the crew are abnormally chivalrous or else someone has put the fear of God into them.'

Olivia though of Lieutenant La Fontaine, and gave a little shiver. She hoped Lucille never discovered the cold, ruthless side of her husband's character.

'We've made progress in other areas, too,' the Admiral continued. 'We've been much puzzled as to why there should have been so much sabotage and spying activity in this area, when the war against France was in its dying throes. Now information has come to us that it was the work of a group of Frenchmen, fanatically loyal to Bonaparte, who were determined to have one last attempt at invading England. Their idea was to land here, at Dartmouth, so gaining them an excellent port. Then they proposed nipping over the hill, and attacking our fleet in Torbay... Well, all that is history now, and I really must bid you farewell.' With a cheery wave of his hand he was gone.

'I must go too,' said Olivia. 'I'm going to be late for my lesson at the Vicarage.'

'You don't think your pupils will want a holiday today, with all this excitement?' asked her father.

'Perhaps, but at least I must look willing,' she smiled. 'To be honest, I would quite like a holiday myself.'

Although it was still early in the day a mood of celebration had already swept through the town. A group of townspeople had begun to string bunting from one side of their narrow street to the other, shopkeepers were redecorating their windows in red, white and blue, while pictures of Britannia, the Duke of Wellington, and King George were miraculously appearing to adorn windows, walls, and doors. Olivia was stopped half a dozen times on her way to her pupils' house by people eager to tell her the news, and to question her in case she had some detail they had missed. By the time she knocked on the Vicarage door she was considerably late, but no one seemed to mind.

'Goodness, Miss Kingston!' exclaimed the Vicar's wife. 'We did not look to see you this morning, of all mornings. You've heard the news, I presume? Is it not the most wonderful thing? I declare the children are quite beside themselves with excitement. I'm afraid there's little chance of you getting them to sit still at the piano, or of them learning anything if you did. Would you mind if we cancelled the lesson today?'

Olivia did not mind. It was what she had been hoping for. There was so much bustle and excited chatter on the streets that she did not go home immediately; she wanted to join in the fun. Decorations were on every building in record time, giving the town a very festive air, while on the Dart every ship and boat, from an elegant naval frigate to the most battered wherry, was dressed overall. Music was beginning to sound on the air. In the market-square the hastily summoned town band were playing patriotic melodies, and on the New Ground a fiddler had struck up with country airs. The flat expanse of reclaimed land bordering the river was ideal for dancing, and so it was crowded with happy couples jigging and capering.

Never in her life had Olivia seen such happy activity on the streets of Dartmouth. She stood watching the dancing with enjoyment, her foot tapping to the rhythm of the fiddle.

'I might have known you would be where there was music,' said a voice,

She turned to find Miles Gilbert by her side.

'I couldn't keep away,' she said, with animation. 'Everyone is so happy! We've such a lot to celebrate!'

'The day's news certainly affects us all,' he answered diplomatically.

'Oh, I'm sorry.' She was annoyed at her own tactlessness. 'I forgot that you would have no cause to celebrate.'

'Don't worry. I'm not as cast down as my fellow prisoners, the French,' he said with a slight smile. 'To a man they are submerged in gloom.'

'You are remarkably cheerful, under the circumstances.'

'What point is there in being miserable? Boney wasn't my Emperor, as far as I know my country hasn't been defeated, so I may as well enjoy the festivities in moderation. Would you care to join in the dance?'

Olivia was sorely tempted to say yes, for she dearly loved dancing. Then she remembered what having Miles Gilbert as a partner would entail . . . being close to him . . . touching him . . . 'Thank you, but I think I'd best be returning home,' she said, then fearing that her refusal was too brusque she added, 'My parents will be mad to know all that is going on, it would be cruel to keep them waiting any longer.'

'Then have you any objections if I accompany you? I, too, promised to return and tell them what is happening, but what with one thing and another I have been sadly delayed.'

'I am sure my mother and father will enjoy having two accounts of the celebrations instead of just one.'

They fought their way out of the crush, then began to walk home at a leisurely pace. The holiday atmosphere seemed to affect them both, and they chatted with extraordinary ease as they went along. For a brief spell it seemed that the awkwardness and animosity between them was banished. Olivia found herself wishing that it could have always been like this, that Dunsford and the repercussions afterwards had never happened.

Similar thoughts must have been going through Miles's brain, for he said, 'You know, Miss Kingston, I can't help thinking that, given a better chance, you and I might have dealt very well together.'

'What makes you think that?'

'We've much in common, we like the same things, particularly music. We've even been known to share the same jokes. If only things had been different... But they were not!' He gave a regretful smile. 'I know I've handled things very ill— No, don't look so alarmed, I'm not about to propose to you again, I promise! If only I'd shown a bit more sense, and gone about things a different way, instead of blurting out my offer in that crass manner. As you pointed out I didn't even ask you properly. What a foolish mistake to make!'

'It's in the past now, it doesn't matter,' said Olivia faintly, surprised and disturbed that he should choose to discuss such matters there on the open road. The last thing she wanted was to go over the subject again, yet she could not bring herself to end the conversation. There was a softness in his voice, and a sadness that she found so touching she could not prevent herself from listening.

'So it is! A great pity. My parents would have liked you exceedingly, you know, Miss Kingston, I'm sorry that now you'll never become acquainted. I fancy that you'd have liked them too, particularly my mother. It's her lot in life to keep both my father and myself in order; no easy task, as I'm sure you appreciate. You've shown your will capable of withstanding the famous Gilbert charm. Yes, she'd have approved of you most heartily.'

Olivia drew in her breath sharply, not knowing what to say. She had never expected him to speak to her in such a way again. His manner was gentle, almost tender.

'They'll be glad to have you home soon,' she said at last.

'Not so very soon. It's only the war between England and France that's over. An end to the conflict involving my country will follow before long, no doubt, but, unfortunately, when wars are formally ended the repatriation of prisoners tends to be a long way down the list of priorities. I shall tread English soil for quite a while yet.'

He paused for a minute to look at the river crammed with vessels, their flags and bunting fluttering triumphantly in the stiff breeze. Olivia stopped too, and they leaned on the wall together, suddenly reluctant to return home.

Miles gave a sigh. 'There's a lot that I'll miss,' he said. 'Particularly the music. I've enjoyed our playing and singing together very much, and our concerts too. I'd never have imagined that being a prisoner of war could be so delightful.'

In spite of herself Olivia had been dreading the day when he would leave their house for his new quarters. Now, though, she felt quite cheered to learn he would be staying in Dartmouth for a long time. At least while he was still in the town she stood a good chance of seeing him again. Once he returned to America he would be gone for ever. Her head told her that this was the ideal solution to her problems, but her heart refused to agree.

'Perhaps the people at your new lodgings will be musical, too,' she said.

'Perhaps. I hope so, but I shall miss all this also.'

'All what?' asked Olivia.

'This!' He flung out an arm to encompass the town, which still echoed with music and laughter, and the river mouth guarded by its twin castles. 'I have grown exceeding fond of this place.'

'Are you to be lodged outside Dartmouth?' she asked in surprise.

'Aye, way outside. I'm bound for Ashburton. I thought you knew!'

'Ashburton?' Her voice cracked in her dismay. It had never occurred to her that he would be going so far away. 'That's miles distant!'

'At the time, when I made up my mind to remove myself from your household, I decided that the greater the distance the better. Now that my day of departure draws near I'm not so sure.' His voice, as well as his words, showed how much he was regretting his decision.

'You go soon?' she said faintly, dreading the answer.

'In two weeks. I've only just heard. The billeting officer informed me this morning that a military patrol will be going up to Dartmoor Prison, and that they will escort me to Ashburton on their way.'

'I—I've never been to Ashburton. I believe it is quite a way from here.'

'Some twenty miles or so, I've been told.'

Twenty miles! He might as well be across the Atlantic Ocean! She would never see him again! The dull ache in her heart, that had been her companion for so many weeks, became a stabbing pain.

'An arduous journey for you,' she managed to utter.

'Not too bad. I understand we go to Totnes by boat, and Ashburton is but an easy march from there. There are many Americans billeted in the town; it will be good to be among my compatriots again.' His attempt to sound cheerful faded as he added with quiet intensity, 'I regret that matters finished so badly between us. If only we could have been friends. Is it impossible to hope that you don't think too badly of me? That you don't hate me?'

'Of course I don't hate you!' she cried, thankful to be able to speak honestly.

By way of reply he lifted her hands to his lips and kissed them.

Her eyes filled with tears.

'Sir,' she said unsteadily. 'We are in the public gaze.'

'So we are,' he said, sounding uncomfortably like the loving, caring Miles she had known so briefly on the beach. 'Maybe it is just as well, even though there is no one about to see us. Everyone is in town celebrating.' He paused, then said urgently, 'Miss Kingston . . . Olivia . . .'

'Yes?' She waited for him to continue, her breath held in sudden expectancy.

'We had better continue home, had we not? Your poor parents will be growing demented with impatience.' He spoke with a forced heartiness.

He had been going to say something else, she was certain. Whatever it was, he had clearly thought better of it, and she was left with a feeling of dejection.

Without another word they continued on their way home.

'Can I ask a favour of you?' she said, when they reached the house.

'Certainly, I'm yours to command.'

'Would you delay telling my parents of your departure until tomorrow? Today is such a happy day I'd not have anything spoil it for them.'

'Is that all? Of course I'll not say a word,' he replied. She thought he sounded a little disappointed, as though he had hoped she wanted something more of him.

Once indoors her parents were so full of questions that Olivia had little chance for brooding. Not until they were resting, and she had a few moments to herself, did she have time to go over the events of the morning. There had been so much more in Miles's words than regret that he was leaving them, there had been an underlying emotion that both encouraged and stirred her. He had spoken about his relationship with her with such feeling, almost as though he had some genuine affection for her, even that he— No, she balked at the thought of love. Yet he had spoken as though he really regretted her refusal of his proposal.

Too late! It was all too late. In a fortnight he would be out of her life for ever.

Two whole weeks. It's a long time, said a persistent inner voice. You could still change your mind. You could still marry him . . .

But he didn't mean it, cried Olivia's practical self. His offer was made wholly from a sense of duty. Nothing has changed!

'Nothing has changed!' she repeated sadly.

CHAPTER TWELVE

THE curfew had been temporarily lifted so that evening, Miles, with the help of a sturdy neighbour, carried Mr Kingston and his chair downstairs. Together, they all went into town, excited by the rarity of being out so late. The celebrations continued well after dark, with music and dancing and fireworks. Olivia was careful never to dance with Miles, or to be too close to him, otherwise she threw herself into the festivities with enthusiasm. She was grateful for anything that kept her mind occupied, and stopped her from thinking! At least she tried!

Ever since he had told her of his impending departure there had been a new gentleness, a new concern in Miles's behaviour towards her. What it meant she could not tell. She only knew that, in spite of all her efforts to keep it at bay, a tiny ray of hope was beginning to glow in her heart.

Weariness kept Edward Kingston in bed throughout the next day. Charlotte spent most of her time with him, so Olivia found herself alone in the company of Miles. She strove to remain indifferent, but it was impossible. She found herself noting and cherishing his every soft word, his slightest kindly gesture. And all the time the hope in her grew a little more.

For yet one more day he delayed telling Mr and Mrs Kingston that the date of his departure had been fixed, for they had both been exhausted by the excitement and the celebrations. Olivia decided that few men would have behaved so thoughtfully.

The moment had to come, however, and she watched as her father's face went pale and her mother dissolved into floods of tears.

'Twelve days! Is that all the time we have left with you, dear, dear Captain?' wept Charlotte.

'It is, ma'am. You've no idea how much I regret having to leave you.' Miles spoke with sorrow.

'You needn't go. Even now your removal can be over-turned!' declared Edward Kingston. 'Just let me have a word with my friend, Admiral Ranscombe.'

'I fancy matters may have gone too far for that, sir, though I thank you for the thought,' said Miles.

Was it Olivia's imagination or did he hesitate for a moment before he gave his refusal? Hope flickered again within her. Might he stay after all? Twelve days was ample time in which to cancel his arrangements, no matter what he had said.

They were interrupted by the entrance of Abbie.

'That there 'eavy-fisted maid be yer for 'er lesson, just in case you'm interested,' she said.

'Maria! I'd forgotten all about her!' exclaimed Olivia. 'I'll come directly.'

She hurried down to the music-room fully expecting to find Mrs Rowden indignant at being kept waiting. However, the bootmaker's plump wife was sitting down, fanning her perspiring face with a sheet of music. Maria, too, looked hot and out of breath.

'There, Miss Kingston, what will you think of us for being late,' puffed Mrs Rowden. 'You must have thought we weren't coming.'

'You look quite exhausted, ma'am. I hope you haven't been hurrying on my account,' said Olivia.

'I confess we did come along South Town at a great rate. Well, Maria was that concerned in case she missed her music lesson, weren't you, my lamb? Usually I manage things better, but not more than an hour ago we got a message from the Mansion House—Miss Lizzie and Miss Sarah wanted measuring for new boots most urgent, so off I had to go.' Mrs Rowden gave a significant look in Maria's direction and lowered her voice. 'Mr Rowden is a stickler in matters of propriety. Where measuring young ladies for boots or shoes is concerned he always insists that I do it. He wouldn't risk getting a glimpse of any young lady's . . .' And here her voice dropped to a whisper '. . . of any young lady's ankles!'

'Very commendable of him,' said Olivia, keeping her face straight with difficulty.

'Yes, isn't it,' said Mrs Rowden, in her normal tone. 'As it happened both Miss Lizzie and Miss Sarah wanted a pair of boots and a pair of shoes apiece, so it proved to be a nice bit of business. But you know what young ladies are, Miss Kingston;

could they make their minds up about what leather they wanted or what colour? By the time they'd decided I was sorely behind for bringing Maria here.'

'Don't worry about it,' said Olivia. 'You couldn't turn away good customers, and besides I've not been at all inconvenienced.'

'There, I knew you'd understand!' Mrs Rowden beamed. 'Mind you, my poor Rowden's going to have to burn some midnight oil, I reckon, to get this order done as well as the other work he's got in hand.'

'He's such a good craftsman, no wonder he's in demand,' murmured Olivia politely.

'That's exactly what Mrs Hunt said. "My girls are going to need good stout waterproof boots if they're going to walk on the moors, and I'd trust only Mr Rowden to do the job!".'

'The moors? So Miss Lizzie and Miss Sarah are going away?'

'Yes, well, Miss Lizzie is, Miss Sarah's just going along for the look of things. I think you can guess where they're going and why?' Mrs Rowden gave a sly smile.

'I'm afraid I can't.'

'Didn't you know that Mrs Hunt has a sister who lives in Ashburton? There, I can see I've surprised you! But neither of us is surprised at the reason, eh? She's after the Captain! Mind you, not that I blame Mrs Hunt. With four daughters to marry off it's only natural that she should do everything in her power to find husbands for them. Fortunately that's not a problem that will ever bother us. When the time comes, with her accomplishments and a profitable little business to back her up, our Maria will be able to pick any young man she likes.'

'Oh Ma!' Maria went crimson, and squirmed with embarrassment on the piano-stool.

Olivia did not notice her pupil's bashfulness, she was too electrified by what she had heard.

'Lizzie Hunt is going up to Ashburton to be with Captain Gilbert?' she said in disbelief.

'Well, the official story is that the two girls are going to visit their aunt, but if that's the case then why the urgency, says I? Very particular they were to have their boots within the sennight—I suppose it does look better if Miss Lizzie is already there when the Captain arrives. Less as though she was chasing him, as it were. The Captain's worked things out very nicely for himself. I doubt he had much trouble persuading Miss

Lizzie to visit her aunt, or her mother to allow her to go. A fine couple they'll make, too. I believe Captain Gilbert's well-to-do in his own land, so now these dreadful wars are finishing that makes him very eligible, and anyone can see that he's Quality. Yes, Miss Lizzie Hunt's doing very well for herself.'

Olivia's stunned astonishment was giving way to a smouldering fury. That Miles Gilbert should have spoken so softly and so charmingly to her, as though he truly regretted the way things had turned out, when all the time he was intending to continue his courtship of Lizzie in Ashburton... It was more than she could credit. Worse still, she had come perilously close to being taken in by his soft words and—yes, she admitted it—by his charm! She could feel herself begin to shake with a rage she dared not reveal.

'As we are so late I suggest we begin the lesson without delay, if you're quite recovered, Maria,' she said through gritted teeth.

'Ooh, yes, I've quite got my strength back, thank you, Miss Kingston,' the child assured her. 'I'll be able to play ever so loud, really I will.'

'The clever little love,' beamed Mrs Rowden.

For once the thunderous noise that to Maria was music did not penetrate Olivia's senses. She must have said the right things at the right times, for mother and daughter eventually went away quite happily, but she had no real recollection of the lesson. All she could concentrate on was the duplicity of Miles Gilbert, and her own stupidity in nearly falling for it.

After she had closed the door on the Rowdens she stamped grimly up the stairs. Miles was alone, reading in the drawing-room. He looked up as she entered.

'My one consolation in leaving this house is that Maria's playing will no longer inflict punishment on my ears,' he grinned.

It was his most charming smile, lighting his eyes and making them dance with humour. A smile intended to melt a heart of stone. No doubt it was the smile he also used on Lizzie Hunt.

'I dare say you'll have plenty of other consolations when you get to Ashburton. From what I hear they'll be lining up in wait for you!' snapped Olivia angrily. 'Well, they're welcome.'

'Now what have I done?' demanded Miles in dismay.

'Done? Why should you have done anything?' She set about tidying the room, noisily slamming cupboard doors and snatching books from under the American's arm.

'Something must have happened to put you in a temper, and I seem to be the obvious culprit,' he said, moving his feet so that she could pick up the newspaper which lay there.

'Why should your conduct put me in a temper? I love clearing up after you. Having nothing better to do, I simply live for the moment when I can pick up the things you drop in your wake. How I shall manage when you get to Ashburton I do not know. But a word of warning. You'd best start training Lizzie Hunt immediately. Ashburton is not a large town, and you are capable of submerging it under a deluge of books and papers all by yourself!'

'Lizzie Hunt? What has she to do with my going to Ashburton?'

'Oh bravo, sir! A creditable performance! I could almost believe you,' jeered Olivia.

'Olivia, do give me a sensible answer. What are you on about?'

'Why, nothing that isn't common knowledge. How nice for you to have a pretty companion waiting for you when you get there. You won't have a single moment's loneliness. It's quite touching!'

Miles rose to his feet.

'Are you saying that Lizzie Hunt is going to Ashburton too?' he demanded.

'Full marks! Give the gentleman a prize!'

'Olivia! Just calm down for a minute. I don't know where you got the story from, but if Lizzie Hunt is going to Ashburton it has naught to do with me.'

'A likely tale! So it's just coincidence she should be going to that particular town, and at that particular time? I have to give you full credit for organising things with incredible speed and efficiency. What did you do? Go running to the Mansion House the moment you knew you were to be sent to Ashburton? Or did you work the other way round? "Tell me, Miss Lizzie, in which towns do you have amenable relations, so that I may arrange my imprisonment accordingly!".'

'I did neither of those things!' retorted Miles. 'I've no idea how Miss Hunt got to know of my removal to Ashburton—if indeed she does know about it. I certainly didn't tell her.'

'Then how did she find out? Is she another Dunsford? Adept at spying?'

'Oh come! Be sensible! You've lived in Dartmouth all your life, so you must know that if there is one thing at which the townspeople excel it is the gathering and spreading of news. Why, if I wished to know what Napoleon had for breakfast this morning or what colour coat King George has decided to wear today, I dare say someone in this place could tell me. It would be the easiest thing in the world for Lizzie Hunt to discover that I was being transferred. I'm surprised that the town crier has not announced it in the market-place!'

Olivia's anger did not abate.

'Very well,' she cried. 'So it is now common knowledge that you are leaving—though I confess I have yet to hear many people speak of it! Answer me this, then! Whose idea was it for Lizzie to follow you? Yours or hers? Or did you hatch the idea between you?'

'It must have been Miss Hunt's, for I had no hand in it.'

'Ha!' retorted Olivia disbelievingly.

'I didn't, I tell you! For all I know her visit was arranged months ago.'

'Then why is Jack Rowden having to sit up till all hours to finish her boots within the week?'

'I beg your pardon? How did boots get into this conversation?' Miles looked bewildered

'Oh nothing! It is not important. Let us say that it is most unlikely that Lizzie's visit is of long standing, and that it was most probably arranged hurriedly in these last two days.'

'What does that prove?' he cried in exasperation. 'Why shouldn't she visit her aunt if the fancy takes her?'

'No reason at all. It is not Lizzie's actions I'm objecting to, it is yours!'

'Mine? I haven't done anything!'

Their voices were rising steadily, angrily.

'Haven't you?' Olivia cried. 'Haven't you said more than once, how much you regret having to leave us? How much you wish things had been different? How nice it would have been if we could have been friends? When all the time you couldn't wait to get to Ashburton to carry on your dalliance with Lizzie Hunt.'

'But we never did become friends, did we?' yelled Miles furiously. 'Because you are the most difficult, odd-tempered fe-

male on this earth. And I don't need to go to Ashburton to
carry on a dalliance with Lizzie Hunt! I can quite easily do so
here!'

'Ha! Now the truth's coming out!' snorted Olivia with decision. 'So that's—' She stopped abruptly, interrupted by a
knock at the door.

It opened, and to her acute embarrassment the cheery face
of Admiral Ranscombe peered round.

'It's only me,' he said, smiling. 'I should have blown my
horn, for I'm playing post-boy today.'

'Why, Admiral, do come in,' said Olivia, all too well aware
that her face was crimson and that Miles's eyes still glittered
angrily.

The Admiral could not have helped hearing their angry exchanges, they had been shouting loudly enough. However, he
seemed oblivious to the fraught atmosphere. He simply took a
letter from his pocket and handed it to Miles.

'This is for you, Captain. It is from America.'

'From home?' Miles grasped it eagerly, his anger forgotten
in his surprise and delight. 'I saw no notice at the agent's this
morning about there being any letters.'

'Shall we say that this one arrived by an unorthodox route,'
said the Admiral, his eyes twinkling. 'Boney isn't the only one
who can be devious. We have our ferrets in his rabbit-warren,
too, you know. I offer you my congratulations, sir.' Then seeing the puzzled look on Miles's face, he explained. 'Regretta-
bly, I had to be informed of the letter's contents before handing
it to you. A distasteful business, but then that's war. On this
occasion it's pleasing to be able to deliver good news to someone. Read it, sir. We'll excuse you, won't we, Miss Kingston?'

The American needed no second invitation.

'It's from my family,' he explained, his face lighting up. 'My
father has sent me a banker's draft. Didn't I say he was a man
of great resourcefulness?'

'A trait he passed on to his son,' said the Admiral. 'It seems
your undoubted talents are to be put to good use.'

'I beg your pardon?' Miles looked puzzled.

'No, I beg yours. I'm very glad my doubts proved ground-
less. If you knew the anxiety you've caused me, sir. Why, I even
took the trouble to find you lodgings with my dear friends, the
Kingstons. I wanted you somewhere where I could keep an eye
on you. I didn't get it quite right, did I? Never mind. Our two

countries will soon be at peace. Whatever you were up to, it i
academic now.'

'Sir, I don't understand you,' protested Miles. 'What do yo
mean?'

The Admiral was on his way downstairs. He looked up a
them as they gazed down over the bannister.

'Let us say that I wouldn't fancy setting foot on any ship tha
was under your command,' he grinned, and left.

'The Admiral was in his cups,' said Miles, 'He must hav
been. He made no sense.'

'He was perfectly sober, as well you know,' said Olivia flatly
'No wonder he wouldn't set foot on any ship under your co.
mand. Nor would anyone with an ounce of sense. It's as pl:
as day that you are no sailor.'

'How can you say such a thing?' demanded Miles.

'Because of the evidence of my own eyes. You're like r
sailor I've ever met. Your walk is too straight, you're too u
tidy, your knowledge of the sea and ships is limited, oh, and :
dozen other things. Why you should have chosen to masquer
ade as a sea captain beats me. Everyone realised you weren'
what you claimed. Dunsford, Lieutenant La Fontaine, th
Admiral, even me, we all knew you were playing a part. Yo
should have picked a role for which you were more fitted.'

Miles was standing very still.

'You saw through my disguise, you say?' he said, quietly
'How long ago?'

'When did I realise you weren't a sailor?' Olivia considere
carefully. 'I think I had my doubts about you from the begin
ning, and I became more and more certain as time went on
After all, I doubt if even in America there are many ordinary
sea captains who speak fluent French and are invited to recep
tions by Bonaparte. I expect most American sea captains car
tell a ketch from a brig, too.'

'And having decided I wasn't a sea captain, in what role hac
you cast me?' he asked.

'I—I don't know,' she said, suddenly hesitant. 'What does
it matter anyway? You'll be gone soon.'

'You tried to persuade me not to go,' he said.

'I did not!' protested Olivia indignantly.

'Your pardon, but you did! You said that having endured me
so far you could tolerate me a little longer. Those were your
very words, as far as I recall!'

'And what if I did?' she said, awkwardly.

'If you truly disliked me, you'd want rid of me as quickly as
possible.'

'I do!' she cried.

'Then why are you so annoyed at me going to Lizzie Hunt?'

'I'm not! She's welcome to you.'

'That's all right then. I can dally with pretty Lizzie as much
as I please. I can gaze into those lovely blue eyes of hers, utter-
ing the most heartfelt of sighs. I can clasp her little hand to my
bosom and compare it to a tender flower—'

'What foolishness are you up to now?' she demanded.

'Not foolishness. I think I'm regaining my sense at last.
Come, some honest answers, for a change.'

'Are you accusing me of being untruthful?'

'Yes,' he said. 'What I must find out is are you telling these
lies just to me, or are you deceiving yourself too?'

'You're being idiotic!'

'Very well, humour me.'

'Oh, get your silly joking over, and have done!'

'I'm not joking. Since you are so convinced I am not a seaman, what do you think I am?'

'A fool!'

'Apart from that!'

'I don't know.'

'What did you suspect I was, then?'

Olivia did not answer. It seemed ludicrous to say a French
spy!

In the end Miles said it for her. 'Did you share Dunsford's
view? Did you think I was spying for France?'

She did not reply.

'Did you?' he persisted.

'Yes', she admitted, at last.

'Of all the foolishness— And you've harboured this idiotic idea...' He shook his head, half amazed, half amused. 'I
suppose I'd better tell you the truth. It'll do no harm now—
Goodness knows, I'd no idea what fantastic theories you were
hatching in that brain or yours— You're right, I'm not a naval captain. But nor can I admit to be anything as exciting as a
spy. I suppose all I can claim is the role of courier. I was, however, on a mission of some secrecy, taking documents from my
country to France. Circumstances dictated that I travel on a
French ship, so I was hastily given an honorary naval commis-

sion to protect me in case we were captured by a British vessel
as indeed did happen. I confess I've been uncomfortable a
deceiving you and your parents, but it couldn't be helped. If I'
been in civilian clothes I would have been treated as a spy an
probably shot.'

She blenched at the idea.

'Mind you, it is seemingly just as well I wasn't a proper spy,
he went on. 'Clearly, I have no aptitude for it, else half o
Dartmouth, including you, wouldn't have marked me out as
suspicious character. The important question is—why did you
tell no one of your doubts?'

She did not answer.

'Admiral Ranscombe's a reasonable fellow. Surely you could
have gone to him with your fears?' he persisted.

'I could have done, but I didn't.'

'And I would know why not. You say you dislike me, you
suspected I was a French spy, and yet you didn't denounce me.
His tone was getting more and more insistent. 'You must have
had a very strong motive.'

'And what if I had?'

He reached out and grasped her wrists. 'Tell me what it was!

'Let me go!' she protested, trying to pull away. 'Why must
you hold me so tightly?'

'Because then you can't evade me.'

'Release me at once!'

'Not until I get the right answers from you.'

'And what if I give the wrong ones?' she retorted defiantly.

'Then I'll keep you like this until you get them right.'

'How dare you—'

'I dare because I'm determined to get at the truth. Tell me
your reason for not informing on me. That's all I ask.'

'Then you ask too much.'

'Why? Your motive must have been important for you to
have considered harbouring a French spy. It can't have been
money, so I can think of only two forces strong enough to have
influenced you—hate and love. Which was it?'

'Let me go this minute!' she cried, struggling against him.

'Hate doesn't seem a likely motive. Hate would have been
reason to denounce me. So there is only one alternative. It must
have been love. Am I right?'

'Of course not! This is nonsense!' Frantically she fought to
free herself.

'Answer me! Was your motive love?'

His voice was becoming more determined as the grip on her wrists grew tighter.

'Don't be so ludicrous— You are hurting me!'

'Answer me! Do you love me?' He was shaking her gently now. Suddenly she could stand it no longer.

'Yes!' she cried. 'Yes! Yes! Yes! Now are you satisfied?'

His hold on her lessened, but he did not release her. He took a long look at her.

'Then why did you never admit it?' he roared. 'You've had me in a torment, do you know that? And I would know why?'

'Because... because...'

Olivia searched in her heart for the true reason.

'Because I was afraid to love you,' she said. 'I fought against it very hard... You are so charming, you please people so easily... I loved a man like that once—Richard Hayter. Seeing him now it is hard to believe it, but in his youth he had a golden tongue, too. He could flatter, and charm, and delight—and hurt. It was the pain that stayed with me long after all else had faded. I was reluctant to risk being hurt like that again.'

'Surely you could see I was not like that wretch? Was that why you refused so steadfastly to marry me?'

'Only partly.'

'So what was your other reason?'

'You don't love me.'

'Of all the— How can you say such a thing?' he cried.

'Because it is true.'

'No, it is not! I love you to distraction! I fear I'm bound for Bedlam because of you. Yet you say I don't love you!'

'Then why did you flirt with Lizzie Hunt?' she demanded.

'Lizzie Hunt! Lizzie Hunt! I'm beginning to rue the day I ever clapped eyes on that young woman! She had a pretty face, and I have a weakness for pretty faces. Surely you know that by now? But she does not mean anything to me, and never has, because behind that exceedingly lovely countenance there is an excessively empty head! Now does that dismiss the question of Lizzie Hunt once and for all?'

He looked so angry and indignant that Olivia did not know whether to laugh or cry.

'You still don't believe me, do you?' he said more gently.

'I want to,' she admitted.

'Then what is stopping you? Surely you don't still hold that stupid challenge against me? I know I swore I would make you like me, but—'

'No, not even the challenge.'

'Then what? That night we were together on the beach, for a brief time I thought you cared for me, but you changed and became all cold.'

'I changed!' cried Olivia indignantly. 'All the change was with you! Calling me Miss Kingston again, and looking as though you regretted being there with me. Can you blame me for thinking that your kisses and sweet words meant nothing?'

'They meant everything,' said Miles quietly. 'That was why I may have seemed somewhat distant. Loving you so much, I realised how easily my feelings could overwhelm me, and I was forced to draw myself back from you. I wanted things between us to be perfect, not some hurried love-making on a stoney beach!'

'I didn't know... I didn't understand...'

'And so you became the cool disapproving Miss Kingston again, eh? At least that was how you seemed to me.' Miles gave a wry laugh. 'What a wretched tangle we seem to have woven between us. So many stupid mistakes and misunderstandings. Do you know, you have caused me the greatest anguish of any female I have ever met? I like the company of women, a fact of which you are well aware, and I'm not averse to flirting with them, but you are the only woman I have ever loved. You say you love me, too, and yet we are still growling and snarling like a pair of angry terriers. If I had known love was so painful I would have stayed in Mill Prison. At least, there I would not have been jealous of a block of wood like Dunsford.'

She stared at him in astonishment.

'You? Jealous of Joseph Dunsford? Surely you know he could never hold a candle to you!'

A slow smile spread across his features.

'I must put modesty aside, and say that in the normal way of things I'd agree with you. But things were far from normal. As a prisoner of war, what had I to offer you? And Dunsford was prosperous and successful. I suffered agonies in case he proposed to you before I was in a position to make my feelings known. And besides, you'd told me time and time again that you weren't like other women, and that you disliked me. You told me so often, and with such conviction that I thought it was true.'

'Then you should have had more sense than to have believed me!' she said suddenly. 'I did not want to love you. You are exactly the sort of man I swore I would never choose to love. Yet I couldn't help myself.'

He started to laugh, hugging her to him.

'I am so glad,' he said. 'So very glad.'

Quite when she reached out to return his embrace she did not know. It was only when she became aware of an aching in her arms that she realised how tightly she was holding him. Miles loved her! Miles truly loved her!

'Do you still doubt that I love you?' he asked.

'No,' she replied, 'But perhaps you could prove it, just to make sure.'

'Hussy!' he laughed. 'Maybe this will convince you!'

His mouth claimed hers with a tender authority leaving her bereft of breath, bereft of any thought save him. The wonder of his closeness, the delight of his heart matching hers beat for beat, the joy of loving him—these were the only things she knew. Her acceptance of his love for her came much more slowly, a gentle pulse beating within her, faint and regular at first, then gradually swelling to a joyous crescendo. He loved her! Miles loved her! Her doubts were finally swept away, leaving a supreme happiness in their wake.

It was a long, long time before they could bear to break away from one another.

Reluctantly, Miles loosed his hold on her—but only so that he could gaze at her the better.

'Is it too much to hope that, at last, you might consent to be my wife?' he asked softly.

'Having surrendered my principles about loving you so completely, I can hardly say no, can I?'

She decided she had been apart from him quite long enough, and nestled her head once more against his chest.

'I hope that housekeeping in Rhode Island isn't too different from here.'

'London,' said Miles.

'I beg your pardon?'

'London. That is where you will be doing your housekeeping at first. I hope you aren't too disappointed.'

'Certainly not, so long as I'm with you . . . But I don't understand. Have you no wish to go home?'

'I'll go home in good time. Correction, we'll go home in good time. Although I am not really in the United States Navy, nevertheless, I have my orders to obey. The letter I received from my father included more than money and family news. There was a message from President Madison. I fancy that was why Admiral Ranscombe offered his congratulations.'

Olivia looked up in astonishment.

'First you attend a reception held by Emperor Napoleon, and now you receive messages from the President of the United States. Seeing that I've confessed to loving you, and have agreed to marry you this may appear an odd question, but, my darling, who are you?'

He laughed. 'I am Miles Gilbert, never fear. I haven't deceived you there. Nor am I a person of any great importance. My family has, however, been in the service of my country for nigh on a hundred years. A long time, in a land as young as ours. My uncle is Governor of Rhode Island, for example. When a job needs doing it is not unusual for a member of our family to be chosen, as I have been now.'

'And what is this job, that requires an Admiral to play postman?'

'The war between America and Britain will be at an end before long. Once it is, diplomatic relations will begin to be established again. My task is to go to London as soon as is possible and make the preparations. On the practical side a house must be found, servants taken on. There's work to be done in diplomatic circles too. Making an acquaintance here, a contact there. Anything what will help to smooth national sensibilities that have become ruffled during these last few years.'

'I think you're considerably more important than you're admitting,' she said, regarding him intently.

He smiled. 'Not really. I'm as much a servant as . . . as Abbie. Talking of Abbie, shall we take her with us? She'd cause a sensation in diplomatic circles.'

Olivia considered. 'Abbie would certainly cause a sensation,' she said. 'She'd probably also cause an outbreak of hostilities again, you know what she's like. I think she'd better stay here and take care of my parents.'

'Anything you say, my love, though we'd best get her some help. Some good robust help who enjoys a battle of words. She'd like that! All that is in the future, however. Before we discuss our life together in London I'd first better go to your father and ask him if I can have the hand of his daughter after all. Also, I must plead with him to intercede with Admiral Ranscombe, on my behalf, to let me stay here.'

'Oh, much pleading that will need! And what of poor Lizzie Hunt, hastening to Ashburton, but not finding you there?'

'She'll find lots of other nice Americans; she can have one of those!'

'So she can. How very satisfactory. Now, before you seek out my father I would like an answer to one vital question. You were very insistent about me answering your questions a while back, now you must answer one of mine,' she said severely.

'Oh, and what is that?'

'You said that if I gave you the wrong answers to your questions you would hold onto me until I gave the right answers.'

'So I did.'

'And have I given the right answers?'

'You have, my darling. To my questions, do you love me, and will you marry me, you've answered most satisfactorily.'

'So, having given the right answers, what happens to me now?'

'That's easy. I'll hold you so tightly to me you'll never want to be free ever again.'

'Oh good,' said Olivia, sliding her arms about him with a sigh of utter contentment. 'That's exactly what I hoped you would say!'

PENNY JORDAN

Sins and infidelities . . .
Dreams and obsessions . . .
Shattering secrets
unfold in . . .

THE HIDDEN YEARS

SAGE — stunning, sensual and vibrant, she spent a lifetime distancing herself from a past too painful to confront . . . the mother who seemed to hold her at bay, the father who resented her and the heartache of unfulfilled love. To the world, Sage was independent and invulnerable— but it was a mask she cultivated to hide a desperation she herself couldn't quite understand . . . until an unforeseen turn of events drew her into the discovery of the hidden years, finally allowing Sage to open her heart to a passion denied for so long.

The Hidden Years—a compelling novel of truth and passion that will unlock the heart and soul of every woman.

AVAILABLE IN OCTOBER!
Watch for your opportunity to complete your Penny Jordan set.
POWER PLAY and SILVER will also be available in October.

HIDDEN-RR

MILLION DOLLAR JACKPOT
SWEEPSTAKES RULES & REGULATIONS
NO PURCHASE NECESSARY TO ENTER OR RECEIVE A PRIZE

1. Alternate means of entry: Print your name and address on a 3″ ×5″ piece of plain paper and send to the appropriate address below.

In the U.S.	In Canada
MILLION DOLLAR JACKPOT	MILLION DOLLAR JACKPOT
P.O. Box 1867	P.O. Box 609
3010 Walden Avenue	Fort Erie, Ontario
Buffalo, NY 14269-1867	L2A 5X3

2. To enter the Sweepstakes and join the Reader Service, check off the "YES" box on your Sweepstakes Entry Form and return. If you do not wish to join the Reader Service but wish to enter the Sweepstakes only, check off the "NO" box on your Sweepstakes Entry Form. To qualify for the Extra Bonus prize, scratch off the silver on your Lucky Keys. If the registration numbers match, you are eligible for the Extra Bonus Prize offering. Incomplete entries are ineligible. Torstar Corp. and its affiliates are not responsible for mutilated or unreadable entries or inadvertent printing errors. Mechanically reproduced entries are null and void.

3. Whether you take advantage of this offer or not, on or about April 30, 1992, at the offices of D.L. Blair, Inc., Blair, NE, your sweepstakes numbers will be compared against the list of winning numbers generated at random by the computer. However, prizes will only be awarded to individuals who have entered the Sweepstakes. In the event that all prizes are not claimed, a random drawing will be held from all qualified entries received from March 30, 1990 to March 31, 1992, to award all unclaimed prizes. All cash prizes (Grand to Sixth) will be mailed to winners and are payable by check in U.S. funds. Seventh Prize will be shipped to winners via third-class mail. These prizes are in addition to any free, surprise or mystery gifts that might be offered. Versions of this Sweepstakes with different prizes of approximate equal value may appear at retail outlets or in other mailings by Torstar Corp. and its affiliates.

4. PRIZES: (1) *Grand Prize $1,000,000.00 Annuity; (1) First Prize $25,000.00; (1) Second Prize $10,000.00; (5) Third Prize $5,000.00; (10) Fourth Prize $1,000.00; (100) Fifth Prize $250.00; (2,500) Sixth Prize $10.00; (6,000) **Seventh Prize $12.95 ARV.

   *This presentation offers a Grand Prize of a $1,000,000.00 annuity. Winner will receive $33,333.33 a year for 30 years without interest totalling $1,000,000.00.

   **Seventh Prize: A fully illustrated hardcover book, published by Torstar Corp. Approximate Retail Value of the book is $12.95.

   Entrants may cancel the Reader Service at any time without cost or obligation (see details in Center Insert Card).

5. Extra Bonus! This presentation offers an Extra Bonus Prize valued at $33,000.00 to be awarded in a random drawing from all qualified entries received by March 31, 1992. No purchase necessary to enter or receive a prize. To qualify, see instructions in Center Insert Card. Winner will have the choice of any of the merchandise offered or a $33,000.00 check payable in U.S. funds. All other published rules and regulations apply.

6. This Sweepstakes is being conducted under the supervision of D.L. Blair, Inc. By entering the Sweepstakes, each entrant accepts and agrees to be bound by these rules and the decisions of the judges, which shall be final and binding. Odds of winning the random drawing are dependent upon the number of entries received. Taxes, if any, are the sole responsibility of the winners. Prizes are nontransferable. All entries must be received at the address on the detachable Business Reply Card and must be postmarked no later than 12:00 MIDNIGHT on March 31, 1992. The drawing for all unclaimed Sweepstakes prizes and for the Extra Bonus Prize will take place on May 30, 1992, at 12:00 NOON at the offices of D.L. Blair, Inc., Blair, NE.

7. This offer is open to residents of the U.S., United Kingdom, France and Canada, 18 years or older, except employees and immediate family members of Torstar Corp., its affiliates, subsidiaries and all other agencies, entities and persons connected with the use, marketing or conduct of this Sweepstakes. All Federal, State, Provincial, Municipal and local laws apply. Void wherever prohibited or restricted by law. Any litigation within the Province of Quebec respecting the conduct and awarding of a prize in this publicity contest must be submitted to the Régie des Loteries et Courses du Québec.

8. Winners will be notified by mail and may be required to execute an affidavit of eligibility and release, which must be returned within 14 days after notification or an alternate winner may be selected. Canadian winners will be required to correctly answer an arithmetical, skill-testing question administered by mail, which must be returned within a limited time. Winners consent to the use of their name, photograph and/or likeness for advertising and publicity in conjunction with this and similar promotions without additional compensation.

9. For a list of our major prize winners, send a stamped, self-addressed envelope to: MILLION DOLLAR WINNERS LIST, P.O. Box 4510, Blair, NE 68009. Winners Lists will be supplied after the May 30, 1992 drawing date.

Offer limited to one per household.

LTY-H891

Coming Soon

Fashion A Whole New You
in classic romantic style
with a trip for two to Paris,
a brand-new Mercury
Sable LS and a $2,000
Fashion Allowance.

Plus, romantic free gifts* are yours to
Fashion A Whole New You.

From September through November, you can take part in
this exciting opportunity from Harlequin.

Watch for details in September.

* with proofs-of-purchase, plus postage and handling

 **Harlequin Books**